BIG EASY ESCAPADE

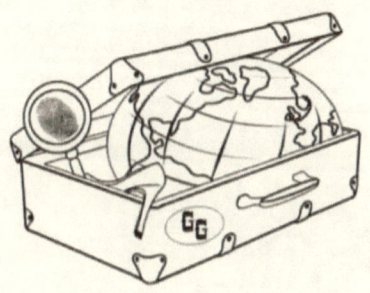

Joan Rylen

Also by Joan Rylen

Named one of "20 recent releases, worthy of attention…"

— Maggie Galehouse, *Houston Chronicle*

"The book is SASSY and FUN. All women can identify with the escapades of the characters. Couldn't put it down!"

— Rebecca Lopez, senior reporter, WFAA-TV (Dallas)

To Mom, if I can be even half the mother you are, my daughter will turn out amazing. Thank you for being a great Mom, teacher and friend.

Love, Robbyn

To Gran, Your sassy Southern ways have guided me well and filled my heart with love. Thank you.

Love, Johnell

P.S. You're not allowed to read this book.

Prologue

Detective Leffall pointed a latex-clad finger toward the built-in dressing table. "Be sure to get the vase, flowers and the card." White lilies, lavender roses and pink calla lilies lay strewn across the table and floor. A water-logged card read, "As always, I'll be watching. Love, H."

Heat radiated from the bulbs outlining the mirror, spotlighting a disarray of cosmetics, body paint, glitter and hair products, several of which had fallen to the floor. Leffall pushed aside a few of the costumes that hung from a rack on the wall, then knelt and inspected those on the floor. Using his pen, he lifted a feathered bustier, revealing a broken hanger and a hot-pink, fake fingernail tip.

"Record all the clothes and rack, and especially this hanger and what looks like her fingernail." He let the bustier fall back into place, next to a jungle outfit. He stood and glanced around the room while the crime scene videographer recorded the mess. His eyes stopped on the strappy, metallic, five-inch heel in the doorway.

"Looks like our girl pulled a Cinderella. You see the other one anywhere, Bud?"

Bud turned the camera to the lone shoe, then scanned across the floor. "Negative."

Leffall paused in the doorway, looking into the dressing room. "This one feels different."

Bud kept filming. "They all feel different."

"Dammit," Leffall said and sighed as he continued looking around the room. "When you're done here, meet me by the back door." He walked toward the rear exit and knelt to get a better look at an abandoned phone, the green message indicator light flashing, waiting for its owner. Bud's Nikes squeaked coming down the hall.

"The screen is cracked. Get a close-up of that."

Bud zoomed the camera to the hot-pink phone, then down the hallway in both directions.

Leffall shouldered open the back door. The stench from the dumpster across the alley reminded him of another crime scene that hadn't turned out so well. He walked down three steps and over to a uniform. "Dumpster's been checked, right?"

The young officer nodded. "Yes, sir. We did an initial search, didn't see her."

"I want someone to go through it again. I'm missing a stripper shoe. The match is in the doorway of the dressing room."

Leffall clicked his pen as he walked back toward the club. A Plexiglas dome covered a security camera, angled down at the entrance.

To no one in particular, he said, "Hope that thing works."

1

Vivian stepped off the escalator, into baggage claim, just as the buzzer sounded on carousel two. The belt jerked to life and bags pushed through the plastic dividers. Her UT burnt-orange, grandiose suitcase was in the middle of the pack. She went to check the monitors for Wendy, Kate and Lucy's flights, but before she could pinpoint the Denver arrival, she heard, "Hey, sexy momma!"

She turned toward Lucy's cheery voice but didn't see the familiar face she'd known since sixth grade. Lucy's normally auburn, curly hair was now almost black, and straight. Dark eyeliner around her sparking green eyes was a new touch, too.

Lucy met her at the monitor and wrapped Vivian in a big hug. "You look great!"

"So do you," Vivian replied, "and I like your hair, but it's just so different. When did you do it?"

Lucy tugged on a strand and shrugged. "Yesterday. I don't know why. I guess I needed a change. Do you hate it? Be honest."

Vivian touched it. "No, I've just never seen you with straight hair. It's a good change."

"Where are the other girls?" Lucy asked, referring to their childhood friends, Wendy Schreiber and Kate Jameson.

Vivian had known Wendy since kindergarten and Kate since ninth grade. They'd all grown up in a working-class suburb southeast of Houston, Pasa-"Get-Down"-dena. Nobody knows where the "Get-Down" came from, though they joke it's either to shield yourself from the high winds of a hurricane or the occasional refinery explosion, both of which the four girls had been through. Just another day in the Get-Down.

"Monitor shows they just landed. Should be here any minute," Vivian said.

"Good, because I'm ready to boogie on Bourbon."

"Yeeehawww! Now that's the Lucy I'm looking for!"

Yeehaws echoed from the escalator and they looked up to see Wendy and Kate waving and shouting, wearing matching green T-shirts. As they got closer, Vivian could make out the details of the shirts. The top said "Wendy's last hurrah" in emerald green letters and had the four of them portrayed as caricatures. Vivian standing under a Bourbon Street sign, slinging a boa around a guy's neck, Lucy and Kate, doused in beads, hurricane glasses held high cheersing, and Wendy, also holding a hurricane but wearing a veil and sash that said "bachelorette."

"Hey there, soon-to-be-married lady!" Vivian gave Wendy a big hug, then Kate. "I love the shirts!"

"Yeah, they look great," Lucy said, reaching out and touching Kate's. "Love the soft cotton and the V-neck."

Kate squeezed her back. "Thanks, I made them online. Thought we needed something to commemorate the trip." She whipped two more out of her carry-on. "You gotta change into your getaway gear!" She tossed them to Vivian and Lucy.

"Yes, go change!" Wendy clapped.

"Okay, we will, but first I have something for you," Vivian said to Wendy, reaching into the outside pocket of her suitcase. She pulled out a gold sash decorated with purple, sparkly letters that spelled out Bachelorette. Condoms were glued here and there, along with little mini-penises and shamrocks. "I made it and you gotta wear this the whole time we're here."

Wendy shook her head and made no move to grab it. "Oh no, no way. I'll wear it tonight on Bourbon, but that's it."

Kate delicately placed it over Wendy's head. "We knew you'd say that, but we're here to celebrate you getting hitched, so you're wearing it! Plus, it's decorated for St. Patty's day!"

"Yes," Vivian said. "It's a multipurpose penis Patty sash!"

Wendy threw her head back in defeat and laughed. "You guys are too much." She straightened it out and grabbed her suitcase. "Y'all go put on your shirts. Let's go!"

Vivian and Lucy hustled off to the restroom to don their new duds, while Wendy and Kate hung out with the bags. New shirts on, the girls headed outside to the taxi stand. An Astro van made in the previous century pulled up. The cab driver opened the back and assisted with their luggage, his underarms and back wet with sweat. Lucy gave everyone the look, then climbed inside, inspecting her seat before sitting down.

Once everything was loaded and the van was in gear, the driver asked, "Where to?"

"Hotel De Lis on Canal Street," Kate instructed, then she turned to the girls. "Have y'all been watching that 'Swamp People' show?"

"Uh, no," Lucy said.

"I've seen the commercials, it looks awesome," Vivian said. "I just don't have time to watch trash TV."

"It's not trash TV," Kate, the brainiac, said.

Wendy dropped her sash, which she was inspecting. "If it hasn't been mentioned on Ellen Degeneres, I haven't heard of it. What the hell are Swamp People?"

"Choot 'em! Choot 'em!" Kate yelled.

"Choot dat alligata!" the driver shouted, making a gun with his fingers.

Wendy laughed and said, "What?"

"It's a show about people who live in the Louisiana swamp and hunt alligators," Kate said. "But with their accent it sounds like 'choot' instead of 'shoot.' "

Lucy shook her head. "I can't believe you watch that."

"I've been studying up for the trip. It's actually pretty interesting. One of the guys uses a hook to snatch them off the bottom."

The driver nodded his head in agreement.

"What you're watching there is not what we're about to experience here," Wendy said. "Gator huntin' is not in my plans."

"Hell, only gator I wanna see is one that's fried and on my plate," Vivian said.

Wendy gave her a high-five. "Acme Oyster House, here we come."

"You know I'm not really going to eat that right," Vivian said, reaching up to the vent above her head. Not much air was flowing, and what was, wasn't cold. "Can you crank up the A/C, please?" she asked the driver. "I'm suffocating back here."

Lucy fanned herself. "It's probably all the humidity."

The driver turned the knob, but not much happened. Definitely no increase in airflow.

Lucy raised her meticulously shaped eyebrows and said under her breath, "Now we know why he has the perspiration problem, don't we?"

"Yeah, your hair's starting to do a little frizz fest already." Wendy smiled and nudged her with an elbow.

Vivian rolled down the window and they chatted as the buildings in the business district grew closer.

They turned off the interstate onto Poydras.

"There's the Superdome," Wendy said, pointing out the window. "The Saints are my second-favorite team behind the Texans. That Drew Brees is a cutie."

They went a few more blocks and Vivian pointed to a line coming out of a restaurant in the warehouse district. "There's the Motha-lode, right there!

Mother's Restaurant. We're so going."

"I brought my expandy pants!" Kate lifted her T-shirt to reveal black pants with an elastic waistband. "I'm already wearin' 'em!"

"Even with all the walkin' we're about to do, we'll put on a few," Wendy said. "But it'll be worth it."

The driver pulled to a stop under the porte cochere of Hotel De Lis. Valets helped the girls out of the van, and the bellman loaded their luggage. Giant planters of lush hibiscus with bougainvillea vines pouring over the sides lined the brick ledge around a fountain.

The glass doors slid open and the cool air rushed forward, blowing Vivian's blonde curls away from her face. "I love this place already," she said, fanning herself with her shirt. "I'll go check us in since I have the trust fund credit card!"

The girls cheered.

On their last trip to the Rocky Mountains, the girls helped to capture a fugitive. Since then, Vivian received a $50,000 reward check from the Thai government and a letter thanking her and the others for helping capture the criminal who had stolen millions in jewelry from one of their diplomats. The girls split some of the money, then put $20,000 into an account they called the Getaway Girlz Traveling Trust Fund.

"Screw checking in. I'm wearing this freakin' sash and I need a drink," Wendy said. "We're goin' to the bar first!"

"Tru dat!" Vivian said, following Wendy through the French doors leading to the Sazarac Lounge.

"I love this place!" Kate said, running her hand along the back of the cowhide and chrome barstools. "And I love that!" She pointed to the backlit onyx bar, admiring the translucent panels within mahogany liquor shelves.

The bartender tossed four beverage napkins onto the bar. "Welcome to the Sazarac, ladies. I'm Dabney, what can I get you?"

"What's a Sazarac?" Kate asked.

"It's a French Quarter concoction of whiskey, bitters, Herbsaint and a twist of lemon," she answered. "It's one of our signature drinks."

"I've had one." Wendy shivered. "Go for it, Lucy."

"Oh what the hell, okay."

"I'll have a Dos Equis for now," Vivian said, hopping onto a barstool. "Saving myself for drinking debauchery in the Quarter."

Kate looked over the specialty drink menu. "I'll have one of the De Lis Delight martinis."

"That sounds naughty! Maybe I need one of those," Vivian said.

"Says here it's coconut vodka, blue curacao and a splash of pineapple."

"Nah, too sweet for me, I'll stick with my cerveza."

Wendy looked at all the bottles behind the bar. "I'll have a Grand Marnier 150."

"Coming up," the bartender said and grabbed a hand-painted bottle off the shelf and poured it into a brandy snifter.

"That looks fancy," Kate said, whipping out her phone for a picture.

"It is." She held her glass up high. "And get a good look 'cuz this is the classiest I'm gonna be on this trip. It's all downhill from here!"

2

The girls relaxed in the lounge enjoying their first cocktails of the trip before Vivian checked them in. She mentioned to the front-desk clerk that they were there for a bachelorette party so he upgraded the girls to a room with a balcony overlooking Canal Street.

A bellman helped the girls to their room and made sure they had everything they needed before opening the French doors to the balcony and pointing out various attractions. "Harrah's is across the street. You can take Decatur to Café Du Monde and the French Market. Bourbon is a few blocks down. If you want to go to the Garden District I recommend the St. Charles streetcar, which you can catch at Carondelet. It's a great way to see the city."

Lucy slipped him a tip and closed the door after him. She turned around and started dancing in the room. "Woo-hoo! Let's get this party started!"

"Let's unpack real quick, then go find some Cajun cooking," Kate said, unzipping her suitcase.

Vivian lugged her suitcase onto the bed. "So is your soon-to-be hubby in Vegas yet?"

"He's probably landing right about now," Wendy said, checking her phone for the time. "I imagine he'll text me when he and the guys get settled."

"So what's the story there?" Kate asked. "I thought y'all were going to have 'the talk.' "

Wendy folded a shirt and put it in a drawer. "We did and we hashed out all of the miscommunications we'd had before the Rocky Mountain trip. We love each other and want to make it work, so we figured it out."

"So figuring it out equals getting married?" Vivian asked.

"Yep," Wendy answered. "And he's moving back to Houston. Turns out he was offered a great opportunity with his company, so it was kinda meant to be."

"We're happy for you!" Kate said.

"Thanks. The hardest decision was where to get married. With his family

14

in North Carolina and mine in Houston, I suggested a destination wedding, but he thought a big wedding in Houston would be best. I'm looking forward to celebrating with everyone, so giving up my idea of a beach wedding wasn't too hard."

Lucy placed the last neatly folded shirt into her drawer and shut it. "So what happened to Mr. FBI guy?"

"Yes," Vivian said. "Whatever happened to Waaaaaaaaaade?"

"Nothing ever really happened with Wade. And it never would, not with his job. We talked a couple times after I got home, and he was in Houston one weekend. We met for cocktails, but it was after the engagement."

"How'd he take it?" Vivian asked.

"He said he was happy for me, but I think he was a little disappointed. I also think he was kind of relieved."

"On to serious business — where we goin' for lunch?" Lucy asked.

"I have a few places I absolutely want to hit while we're here," Wendy said. "Johnny's Po-Boys is one of my favorites. It's off Decatur, walking distance. Let's start there, then see what other kinda trouble we can get into!"

"Sounds like a plan," Vivian said, shoving the last of her stuff into a drawer and forcing it to close.

"Hold your horses, I need to freshen up a bit," Lucy said, walking to the bathroom.

"Give it up with the hair, sister," Wendy said. "In this humidity, it's either going to get frizzier, wilt or melt."

Lucy adjusted her girl's trip shirt, then she sleeked her hair into a high ponytail and exhaled, frustrated. "That's about all I can do with it."

"It looks cute," Kate said, then looked at her own reflection. "Maybe I should do mine too."

"Nah, yours isn't spazzing out as much as mine is," Lucy said, running her fingers through Kate's shoulder-length, brown hair. "You sure you want to wear white shorts today? Green beer will match our shirts, but won't look good on your pants."

Kate brushed her hair. "I'll watch out for the yahoos sloshing their beer."

"There's bound to be a lot of yahoos," Vivian said, standing next to her but wearing black capri pants with her matching shirt.

Wendy joined the girls at the mirror in jean capris and her green shirt and stared at her bachelorette sash. "I look like a big dork."

Vivian straightened a tiny penis on the sash and pushed it up more on her shoulder. "I think it looks fantastic!"

Wendy twisted her mouth to the side. "Uh huh. Let's get outta here."

They left the hotel and took Canal to Decatur. They passed a T-shirt shop with a display of feather boas draped across an alligator that was standing upright, in the window, mouth open wide.

"We need a picture!" Kate said, pulling out her phone. "Choot 'em!"

They went inside and asked a twenty-something girl to take a picture for them. Wendy draped the boas over their shoulders and they kicked up their legs like showgirls, gator in the middle.

"Everybody say jambalaya!" the girl said.

"Jambalaya!"

"That's goin' on Facebook," Kate said, thanking the girl. "The caption will be 'Lock up your gators, these Texas girlz are loose in the French Quarter!' "

Feeling guilty for using the gator, Vivian bought a variety of magnets for her hospital co-workers: alligators, fleur-de-lis, hurricanes, Mardi Gras masks.

As they left the shop Vivian spotted a court jester doll dressed in satiny purple and green, wearing a goofy bell hat. "Wendy, didn't you used to have one of these in your room?" She couldn't help herself, picked it up and jingled it.

"Man, what a memory!" Wendy said. "I stopped here in sixth grade with my dad on our way back from Florida and he bought it for me. I still have it."

"Only reason I remember it is 'cuz it kinda freaked me out. Me and clowns. No." Vivian set it down. "Lauren's the same way. Only 4 1/2, she already knows the evil of the clown."

Lucy rolled her eyes as they left the shop. "It's just a doll. I remember it and it wasn't creepy."

"Thank you," Wendy said as she pointed out an uneven brick in the sidewalk.

"Kate had a creep-ola doll, too," Vivian said. "I spent the night with her when we were sophomores and didn't get a wink of sleep. It stared at me all night."

"What? I don't remember that."

"Yes, it was on your dresser. It reminded me of Chuckie."

Kate laughed. "My grandpa sent me that doll from Taiwan when I was 4."

Kate's mom was Taiwanese, her dad an American sailor. The two got together when he was on tour and the rest is history. The combination created a beautiful Kate, long, smooth, brown hair, almond-shaped brown eyes, trim figure and long legs. More than one man had stumbled craning his neck to look at her.

"I don't care where it was from, it was scary." Vivian maneuvered around a public trash can.

"No scarier than that guy." Lucy pointed to a man painted head to toe in silver. The milk crate he was standing on top of was painted silver, too.

They stood for a while, watching intently, waiting for him to make any movement. There was none.

"He's probably at least blinking behind those sunglasses," Wendy said, snapping his picture.

Vivian took a step back. "I don't like him. Let's go."

Kate pulled two bucks out of her purse and dropped them into a silver hat propped up in front of the crate. "I liked my doll and I like him, too."

They turned the corner onto St. Louis and walked into Johnny's.

"Mmmmmmmm, smells good," Wendy said, stepping into line just inside the door.

"This place is packed," Kate said.

"Yes, but look at that sign there." Vivian pointed up behind the counter. "Says there's dining in the rear." She snickered. Lucy did, too.

"What grade are y'all in?" Wendy asked.

Kate laughed. "I'm thinking oyster po-boy dressed and eating at a table out here, not in the rear."

"You rhymed!" Vivian laughed.

They were in a narrow pathway between several tables covered with red and white checked tablecloths, all occupied. The menu was on a board above and behind the counter. The po-boy combinations were endless, but the place also served traditional options like jambalaya and gumbo.

"Red beans and rice and a big-ass piece of sausage for me." Vivian rubbed her hands together in anticipation. "Lucy, whatcha havin'?"

"Seafood muffaletta for me."

"Muffa-whata?" Kate asked.

"Super yummy sandwich smothered with olive paste on French bread. You should try it."

"I'm sticking with my old standby, half shrimp po-boy and a cup of gumbo," Wendy said. "Extra tartar."

Their turn came up, the girls ordered, paid, got drinks and nabbed a table. Not in the rear.

Vivian picked up the food when their number was called, then dug into her red beans and rice. "This is the perfect level of heat. Delicious."

"The French bread is just the right combination of crunchy on the outside and soft on the inside," Wendy said after her first bite. "And the gumbo, mmm!"

Kate held half her oyster po-boy in one hand and adjusted her expandy pants with the other. "These are fillin' up already. Lucy, how's your lots-a-muffin?"

Lucy's mouth was full of muffaletta, so she gave a thumbs up.

The table got quiet, but the good kind of quiet. Finally, stuffed to the brim, the girls sat reveling in the bliss that was their lunch.

"Wake me up outta this food coma," Wendy said.

"You're right," Lucy said, slamming her hand on the table. "Time to get walking."

They headed back out into the Quarter, eventually ambling up Decatur to Jackson Square. The large, old oak trees lining the Square had new buds and inside the iron fence of the park, flowers were in full bloom. Tourist and locals alike lounged on the benches. A toddler splashed her hands in the fountain in front of St. Louis Cathedral , and just beyond, the statue of Andrew Jackson reared up on horseback. Sketch artists, painters, fortune-tellers and potters selling ceramics had set up shop on the sidewalks around the Square. Horse-drawn carriages lined Decatur, waiting for the next vacationer to hop aboard for a tour. Across the street, on the river side, an acrobatic troupe performed death-defying stunts off the concrete stairs in the Moonwalk plaza, near Café Du Monde.

After watching for a few minutes, Wendy said, "I'm wearin' this sash and it's official — it's time for an adult beverage."

Lucy clapped. "Let's get this girl some sash benefits. Where to?"

"Let's get a to-go in the French Market," Vivian said, doing a little sashay to the music flowing out of a nearby bar. "God, I love New Orleans!"

3

The high roller slowly lifted the corner of his cards. Seven, king, both diamonds. He raised the $1,000 bet, casually tossing in a gray $5,000 chip, then ran his thumb over the initials on his starched cuff. *SBS.*

The move prompted all but one at the table to fold. The sly redhead to High Roller's left had fooled him more than once during the tournament, but he didn't mind; her demeanor was pleasant, she stayed quiet and her form was subtle, not overdone. He breathed in her nice, clean scent. The other remaining challenger sat to the left of the dealer and was dressed in a white T-shirt, loose jeans, several gold chains, a baseball hat and dark sunglasses.

I'd like to take a baseball bat to that hat and what little lay beneath it.

The dealer, Margie from Detroit, swiped the chips into neat stacks, then picked up the deck. She burned the top card, then laid out the next three — ace of hearts, jack of diamonds, eight of diamonds.

Hoodlum's eyes flashed, but he checked.

"Bet's to you, sir," Margie said.

High Roller nodded, then checked as well.

Red bet $2,000.

Hoodlum squirmed in his seat, looked at his cards, then tossed four $500 chips into the pot. "Let's see what you bitches got."

Yes, let's see, High Roller thought, shuffling his large stack of chips, enjoying the click they made as they came together. *One hundred seventy five million is a tremendous amount for that decrepit refinery. Twelve hundred a barrel for the 100,000 capacity and processes is generous. They will have to come to more reasonable terms if they expect me to sign off on this deal.*

Hoodlum picked at the fingernails on his left hand, then switched to his right. Red kept her hands folded on the table and patiently waited out his stalling.

And this deal will work. The profits will make this look like loose change.

High Roller slid two $1,000 chips onto the table. "Call."

19

Margie burned another card and placed one face up on the table. Nine of diamonds.

Interesting.

"I'm goin' all in." Hoodlum shoved the rest of his chips forward, knocking over the stacks.

Margie took the time to count his chips. "That's $8,450 to you, sir."

"Call," High Roller said without looking at his hand or his chips, and pushed $9,000 out. Margie made change.

Red tapped her French-manicured fingernails on her cards. "I'm in, but I think I'm short." She pushed her chips toward the dealer.

Margie counted them. "We can make it a side bet — $7,900. That's the most you can win."

"Okay," Red said and sat back in her chair. She picked up her clear beverage, swirled the ice with a red sword, two olives speared on the end, and took a sip.

All bets were in, no more could be made, but they had one card to go. Margie looked at the players. "Show 'em."

Hoodlum flipped over his cards.

"Trip aces," Margie said, straightening Hoodlum's cards.

He stood and pointed. "Whatcha have to say 'bout that, muthafuckas?"

High Roller smiled on the inside and gently turned over his cards, showing his seven and king of diamonds.

"King-high flush," Margie said and put his cards in order. Seven, eight, nine, jack and king of diamonds.

Red put her drink down and nodded, then turned over her cards. Ten and queen of diamonds.

"Straight flush," the dealer said and neatly arranged Red's cards.

"What? This is bullshit!" Hoodlum slammed his hand on the table.

"Sir, the hand is not over yet. Please take your seat."

"What a load," Hoodlum said and sat down, obviously agitated.

High Roller knew nothing could save his hand from Red. Only an ace would save Hoodlum's.

Margie burned one last card before playing fifth street. Seven of spades.

Hoodlum stood again. "Total fucking bullshit." He stormed off, his pants hanging below his ass, showing plaid boxer shorts.

Because Red's bet had been less, Margie divided out the portion of Hoodlum's and High Roller's bet that was owed and gave the change to High Roller.

Red tipped Margie generously and stood up. Her chips went into a carrier. "I think I'll call it a night." Her eyes flashed and she looked at him. "Would you like to join me for one quick drink at the bar?"

High Roller's penis pulsed at the request, but he knew he could not. *She's not the one.* "No, thank you." He could see her surprise at his response. She picked up her small, black clutch, took her chips and left.

The man next to him lit a cigarette and took a drag. "You're a fucking idiot."

***

The girls moseyed up Decatur to the market and found a place that sold all kinds of things on a stick. It also sold alcoholic things in large, plastic cups, each with a few strands of Mardi Gras beads.

"Whatcha want?" Vivian asked Wendy.

"Surprise me, I'm gonna go look in the hat shop next door."

Kate asked for a water, Lucy wanted a hurricane. Vivian ordered one for herself and Wendy as well.

Vivian paid with their special account card and passed out drinks to Kate and Lucy. They put the beads around their necks.

"I'll go get Wendy," Kate said.

"Oh, hold on!" Vivian said, digging into her purse. "I brought something special to corral us or alert us when there's a woman down." She pulled out a plastic, two-inch penis whistle, complete with little balls. "Totally bachelorette-party appropriate." She handed it to Kate. "Give it a blow!"

Kate looked at it, shrugged, then put her lips on the head. A piercing toot rang out and she started to laugh, embarrassed.

"Give it to me!" Vivian snatched it away. "You gotta really give it a blow!"* (see appendix)

Shrieeeeeeeeeeeeeeeeek!

Wendy came around the corner carrying boas in purple, hot pink and blue. "Holy guacamole, what the hell is that awful noise?" she asked, tossing each of them a boa. "If I have to wear this sash, y'all've gotta wear these."

Vivian smiled, threw the hot pink one around her neck and gave Wendy some beads. "See, the penis whistle works!"

Wendy laughed. "I guess it did. Keep that handy."

Vivian blew the whistle as she walked to a small, public seating area surrounding a fountain. She plopped down on a bench and put the whistle back in her purse. "Best three bucks I ever spent!" She swirled her hurricane with the straw and turned to Lucy. "Now that you and Steve are back together, how are things going?"

Lucy slumped on the bench, then took a long sip of her hurricane. "Not the greatest. I've tried so hard to get that flame blazing, and frankly, my lighter's about out of fluid."

Kate sat down, scooting close to her. "What's going on? Is counseling not helping?"

"Counseling has helped, but it hasn't fixed our problem. It's like we're roommates, not like the married couple I want to be. You know, the kind that has passion. And sex."

Wendy tossed a coin into the fountain and closed her eyes, then said, "What are you going to do?"

"I don't know yet. Boulder is freakin' expensive! I need to make sure I can support myself before I seriously consider…" She didn't finish.

Wendy fiddled with her engagement ring. "Better stock up on your Jimmy Choos now. 'Cuz god knows you've got expensive taste."

Lucy got a little defensive. "I can reel in my spending if I need to."

Wendy tossed another coin into the fountain and closed her eyes again. "It's tough being single and on a budget."

"I think you only get one wish a day, Wendy," Vivian said.

"Today, I need two."

Lucy stared at her expensive shoes. "I've not made any decisions yet. I do love him, and his fiscal attributes are attractive. We'll see." Then she turned the tables. "What about you, Viv? Met anyone we need to look out for on this trip?"

"Ha ha." Vivian flipped her hair. "I'm not *dating* anyone. I am, however, having sex with someone. Maybe more than one someone on occasion — not at the same time in case you're wondering. I'm just playin' the field."

"You hooker!" Kate exclaimed. "What kind of field, soccer? That game has lots of players on the field."

"I do like soccer," Vivian joked. "But not to worry, I have not become an official hooker. There're no monetary transactions involved. We're just consenting adults meeting one another's needs."

Lucy shook her head.

Vivian shrugged her off. "You're too monogamous."

"Hello, I'm married."

"And when I was married, I was faithful, too. Now I've opened myself up to new possibilities."

"What the hell kinda possibilities are you opening yourself up to?" Wendy asked.

"Viv, do we need to get you some shots?" Kate asked.

"Juggling two is about all I can handle, but don't you worry. I'm a responsible sexoholic. I'm disease free and I plan to stay that way. Me and Mr. Trojan, we're buds. But you *can* buy me a tequila shot later."

Kate laughed. "I'm so glad I'm married to Shaun. He's amazing. My true soul mate. "

Vivian made gagging noises. Lucy joined her.

Wendy sucked the last of her hurricane through the straw. "I need some music and another drink. Let's wander up to Frenchmen Street."

The girls continued on Decatur to Esplanade and passed a building being renovated. Construction debris littered the sidewalk, including an old toilet.

Kate, Lucy and Wendy kept walking, but Vivian stopped. "Hey, wait! Get my picture!"

She went down on one knee in front of the toilet — close, but not too close — and pretended to throw up. "Bleeeehhhh! Oops, my feathers!" She scooped up her boa before it hit the rim.*

"You're a sicko," Wendy said, but she snapped the picture anyway as a car drove past, honking.

"Anyone else want a turn?" Vivian asked, brushing dirt from her knee.

Lucy coughed. "I feel like I'm getting infected with germs just walking by it, no way I'm getting any closer."

"Think I'll pass on that Kodak moment," Kate said, "but you looked fantastic. That car thought so, too!"

Wendy zipped up her purse. "We're in New Orleans, that lovely display could happen for real. No need to pretend!"

4

The girls crossed Esplanade and continued onto Frenchmen Street where they passed several bars with bands playing. As they approached the Three Muses, Vivian said, "Things are kickin' in there."

A woman's voice crooned onto the sidewalk. The back of a five-piece band was in a window beside the entrance to the bar. A guy on a stool by the door waved them in.

"Ladies get in free, $2 drafts, $3 wells."

"That's good enough for me," Vivian said, and they walked in. She looked over her left shoulder at the band. The woman wore a red vintage dress with a scoop neck. Her light brown hair fell just below her shoulders, with gentle curls at the bottom. She had the sides swept up with a mother-of-pearl clip, and her bangs had a perfect curl. Ruby red nails matched her dress to a T. A trumpet sat on a stand next to her and she sang into an old-school microphone, her soulful voice sultry and deep. Vivian was captivated.

The rest of the band consisted of a guy on banjo, a clarinet player who could really jam, a drummer, a sax player and a tuba. They put out a lot of sound in the small bar.

Several people sang along and others danced. It was not the same crowd as down on Bourbon Street. No beads, no boas, no bachelorette sashes. In fact, Vivian felt a little self-conscious wearing all of her merriment among the locals. But oh well, tourists they were, no sense trying to hide it. Not like they could at this point.

Vivian passed the crowded tables and found a vacant spot at the 30-foot wooden bar. A woman with several tattoos tossed four napkins out. "What can I get ya?"

The girls ordered a round of frosty beverages and turned their attention to the band.

The song ended and the crowd clapped. "Thanks so much, we're the Shotgun Jazz Band." The singer introduced the members individually by first

24

name. "Next we're going to play 'Algiers Strut,' an old favorite." She picked up the trumpet, placing it gently to her lips, and blew the first notes of the New Orleans jazz staple.

The girls hung at the Three Muses for about 45 minutes, or two drinks each. Kate gathered them around. "I could use a snack."

Tab paid and sun down, they ventured out onto Frenchmen and happened across a large patio draped with white lights. Local artisans selling their wares were sitting here and there, and in the middle of it all was a bright, white, light-up couch. Kate couldn't resist.

"What is this made of?" she asked no one in particular, walking up to the couch. "I love it!" There were also a loveseat and an armchair, but the couch glowed the brightest among them.

A man in his late 20s approached her. "It's made of recycled television parts."

Kate traced her fingers across the back of the couch. "I've never seen anything like it."

He smiled at her. "I'm a little far out with my designs." He handed her a business card.

"You win first prize on this patio," Lucy said. "No doubt."

They chatted with him a bit, Kate and Lucy mostly, then moved on to the other vendors. Kate tried on hats and ended up buying a black, wide-brimmed number that made her look like a movie star, especially when she pulled a Corey Hart and wore her sunglasses at night.

They walked toward Esplanade and Kate pointed out a place called Mojito's.

Vivian heard the strum of a guitar coming from the patio. "Sure, let's do it."

They walked inside and Vivian was immediately drawn to a life-sized cutout of The Most Interesting Man In The World.

"Oh my god, it's a sign," Lucy said, nudging Vivian. "This place is gonna be great!"

Vivian threw an arm around the distinguished, bearded gentleman who was the spokesperson for Dos Equis. "Take our picture together!"

"You're aware he's not real, right?" Kate asked.

"Shhh!" Vivian covered his cardboard ears. "You'll hurt his feelings."

"Goofy girls," Wendy said. "I'll see you on the patio."

The three took turns taking pictures with Mr. Dos Equis as Wendy headed outside. Vivian picked him up and tucked him under her arm. "Think I could sneak him out?"

"Uh, no. I think they'd notice a 6-foot fake man protruding from your armpit," Lucy said. "It may be every day for you, but around here...actually, wait a second."

Vivian carefully propped him back up and kissed her pointer finger and placed it on his lips. The girls laughed as Kate pushed open the door leading to the patio. Wendy was relaxed underneath a dark green umbrella, feet kicked up into a chair. The courtyard had a three-tiered fountain centerpiece and a small elevated stage offset to the right where a three-piece band played "The Girl from Ipanema."

Kate tugged on Wendy's foot chair. "Excuse me ma'am, is this seat taken?"

Wendy put her feet on the ground. "Y'all are gonna love these guys. They're from Brazil and they're really good."

"Let's make a request!" Vivian said, sitting in the wrought-iron chair next to Wendy. She pulled out a pen and grabbed the napkin that was on the table. "What do we want to hear?"

"Something jazzy, don't you think?" Kate asked.

Lucy snapped. "Let's request 'Damn Right I've Got the Blues.' "

"Never heard of it." Vivian asked.

"It's a Buddy Guy classic. You've got to branch out!"

Wendy gave Lucy a sad puppy-dog face. "Do you have the blues?"

Lucy snatched the pen and beverage napkin from Vivian. "I'm requesting it."

"I'll take it to the band," Wendy said. "I've gotta hit *el baño* anyway."

Lucy finished writing and handed Wendy the napkin. "Let's see if these Brazilians can sing the blues!"

Wendy handed the singer the request and a five and he gave her a wink. She joined the girls back at the table after using the facilities and picked up a menu. "What looks good? I have a feeling this is gonna be a late night and we need sustenance."

Kate put her menu down. "And alcohol absorbers. Mmmm, lobster mac-n-cheese."

"Oh, I need some of that. Wanna share?" Vivian asked. "And I need some gumbo."

"I second all of that," Lucy said.

"I'm in!" Wendy said, tucking her menu between the umbrella post and the condiments.

While waiting for their food, the band broke into their request. The girls clapped and Lucy sang along, saying she, too, had the blues from her head down to her shoes. The adjacent table gave her a standing ovation and the singer blew her a kiss. Dinner was served, and by the end they were sopping up the last of the gumbo with French bread.

"I do believe that was the best macaroni and cheese I've ever had," Vivian said, leaning back in her chair, strumming her fingertips on her belly.

"I don't know," Wendy said. "Morton's makes damn good mac."

"True, I forgot. In any case, I need to walk or I'm gonna take a happy nappy right here."

Kate signaled for the check, and Lucy sang and danced along with the band.

They walked out onto Esplanade, across from the Old U.S. Mint, which was lit up like a gas station in a bad neighborhood.

Kate stood on the sidewalk in front of it and took a picture. "I love the columns."

"That's where they have Satchmo Summer Fest every August," Wendy said. "I saw the Rebirth Brass Band a couple of years ago. They were awesome, but I have to admit, I must be getting old because they were loud. My ears rang for two days, but it was worth it."

"Let's Satchmosey on down to Bourbon," Vivian said. "We need to get this party started. I'm ready for some action!"

5

The walk down Bourbon Street from Esplanade was mainly residential and quiet at first, then the girls started passing a few bars.

Lucy pointed at one. "Ouu, ou, look at him. This looks like a good place."

A guy in nothing but a G-string danced on top of a bar. The mostly male customers surrounding him held clear plastic cups of green beer and pulsed to the music.

Kate pointed to the rainbow flag out front. "He may be hot, but he's not hot for what you got."

"The hot ones are always gay!" Vivian said.

The density of bars increased, as did the tourists on the street and sidewalks. Bad karaoke blasted from the open windows of Cat's Meow, and Wendy bowed her head. "There's a video floating around of me, Ali and Samantha singing 'Respect' during Mardi Gras many moons ago. It's awful."

Kate pulled on Wendy's elbow. "Want to go recreate that experience?"

Wendy laughed. "No, thanks. Once was enough. Trust me!"

Vivian stopped a couple of girls walking past them drinking something out of neon-green skinny cups, the bottom shaped like hand grenades. "What is that and where did you get it?" she asked them, pointing to their foot-long beverages.

The girls giggled and pointed to the neon orange, blue and green glow of the Tropical Isle sign. "I love blue balls!" one of them yelled and stumbled off.

"Uh-oh," Vivian said. "I'm not sure if I need to drink one of those after all." As she turned to continue down the street, a kid about 13 bumped into her. "Excuse you!" she called after him as he sprinted away.

A moment later she stopped and checked the front pocket of her capris. "Dammit!"

"What?" Kate asked.

"That little shit pickpocketed me. All he got is my driver's license, but

28

I'm gonna need that!" She looked around for the kid, but he was long gone.

A policeman on a Segway and wearing a helmet rolled up the street toward them. Wendy flagged him down. "Help! Robocop!"

He glided over and Vivian told him what happened, then described the pickpocketer. "A skinny kid with an Afro, looked about 13, maybe 5-foot-3, wearing a navy shirt and torn-to-shit jeans. Oh, and he had really bad acne."

Robocop expertly maneuvered around the tourists and zoomed about a block in the direction the kid had gone. The girls ran after him and watched as Robo slowed to talk to a policeman on horseback, then speed off again. The mounted patrol looked around for a moment, then spurred the horse into a gallop at a cross street.

Robocop turned the corner moments later, with the girls still trying to catch up. When they finally did, the mounted patrol was off his horse and holding the squirming pickpocket by the shirt. "This him?" he asked Vivian.

"Yes, he's the one," she answered.

The kid had a defiant look. "I didn't do nothin'."

Vivian's maternal instincts kicked in and she wanted to dish out some discipline. "Shame on you. You look like you're in middle school, for goodness sakes. You don't need to be down here in this kind of environment. What would your Momma say if she knew what you were doing?"

The kid rolled his eyes.

Robocop got off his horse on wheels and approached the kid. "Is there anything in your pockets that will stab me?" He snapped on a pair of blue latex gloves. "Got any weapons on you?"

The kid cut his eyes to him and stuck out his bottom lip. "No."

Robocop went through every pocket and turned them out. He found three smart phones, a watch, a man's wallet, a stack of credit cards and driver's licenses, Vivian's among them.

"You're violating my rights," the kid said after the search was over. "I'm a juvi and I want an attorney."

"Shut up," the policeman said and flipped through the credit cards. "Looks like you've had a busy night." He gave Vivian back her driver's license and took her information, then he looked at the other girls. "Nice shirts."

They laughed and Kate said thanks as a squad car pulled up. The mounted patrol handed over a piece of paper to the new officers and Robo handed over the stolen goods, then put the kid in the back seat.

He walked back over to the girls. "Y'all have a good time, but know that there are many more where this kid came from. If you're going to keep items in your pockets, be sure to spread it out."

"Okay, thank you!" Vivian said and stuck her ID into her small purse.

"Can we get a picture with you, you know, to commemorate my first, and hopefully last, pickpocketing?"

He grinned. "Sure." They asked a passer-by to snap the shot of them surrounding Robo on his Segway, then they said goodbye.

As they walked back to Bourbon, Lucy said, "That must have been some St. Patty's Day luck of the Irish right there, Viv. It's damn amazing you got your ID back."

"No kidding," Wendy said and waved to a guy on a balcony, who threw down a strand of gold beads. "That probably almost never happens here. I think to celebrate, it's time for beverages. Green ones!"

"What about one of those Hand Grenades?" Lucy suggested. "They're green!"

Wendy caught a second strand of beads. "Never had one, I hear they'll do you in."

"Not sure about green drinks," Kate said. "I know it's St. Patty's day and all, but I'd like to find out more about those blue balls." She steered the girls toward Tropical Isle where Jimmy Buffett's "Fins" blasted out of the open doors.

"Holy hair gel, Weird Al's on the stage!" Lucy yelled as they walked in. "But it's all messed up with Jimmy Buffett!"

A three-piece band, all wearing tropical gear, played on an elevated stage behind the bar. The lead singer looked just like Weird Al Yankovich. Dark, curly, greased-up hair hung around his face, and his upper lip sported a porn star mustache. His smirk accentuated strong cheekbones, just like Weird Al.

"What's with the blue balls?" Vivian called to the bartender.

The fit, short, bearded bartender hit a switch, and a sign on the wall began to blink on and off. It read, "15-minute special. Blue Balls. Shooters $2 each when flashing."

Kate crossed her arms and stood defiant. "I'm not flashing my boobs for a $2 shot!"

6

The bartender at Tropical Isle tossed beverage napkins in front of the girls. "So what's it gonna be? Shots or Grenades?" He pointed to Kate and winked, "Feel free to flash if you like."

Kate blushed and uncrossed her arms. "I knew the sign meant when *it* was flashing. Not me."

"What did you score on your SAT?" Vivian joked.

"Yeah, yeah. I was just testing y'all."

Wendy ordered a round of Blue Balls, and the Weird Al look-alike started up with "Cheeseburger in Paradise."

The turquoise test-tube shots were delivered and Vivian held hers high.* "Here's to the balls, the balls of blue. Here's to our friendship, always so true. Let's suck 'em down, let's suck 'em good, but listen up, ladies, we can never spew."

"Wooooooo!!!!" the girls yelled and cheersed, then sucked down their shots.

A nose-pierced, tattooed bald guy in jeans and a white T-shirt yelled to the bartender, "Get them four more! Actually, make it six!" He wrapped his muscular arms around the red-headed, trim girl next to him, dipped her back and kissed her.

After their kiss, the redhead flipped Wendy's bachelorette sash. "Congrats! When's the big day?" She was the bald guy's height, compliments of her high-heeled shoes, with fiery-red hair swept into an up-do reminiscent of the '60s. A white satin ribbon crowned her hairline and wrapped back to the deep undertones. Her pale, unblemished skin was completely free of makeup, yet she looked beautiful in her cut-off shorts and T-shirt.

"In a month, and thanks." Wendy held out her hand. She introduced herself, then said, "These are my friends, Vivian, Lucy and Kate."

The girls said hello and waved as the new Blue Balls were handed out. Tattoo guy offered a toast: "To hot women suckin' blue balls!"

31

The girls laughed and turned 'em up.

"Thanks for the shot," Lucy said and toasted the bald guy. She turned to Red. "I'm totally diggin' the hair. Love the color!"

"Thanks, it's called Jamaican Spice. My hairdresser had to talk me into it, but it's kinda been my shtick ever since."

The guy set down his empty test tube and held out his hand to Lucy. "I'm Jason, by the way, and this is my fiancé, Daisy."

"Fiancé? When are y'all gettin' married?" Wendy asked. "And congrats!"

Daisy gave Jason a squeeze. "Next week. We're road-tripping to Vegas."

"Oooooh, I love Vegas," Vivian said, eyes wide. "Are you doin' the drive-through or something more romantic?"

"We'll see when we get there." Jason pulled Daisy close and gave her another kiss, no dipping this time. When they pulled apart he said, "Anyone need a Hand Grenade? I hear they kick ass."

"No way, not after those two shots," Lucy waved him off, "but I would love to have one of the cups they come in."

Jason ordered two Hand Grenades and tipped his way to two more cups. He handed a drink to Daisy, then handed Vivian the empties. "Waste of a couple good cups, if you ask me." He winked.

Vivian tossed one of the cups to Lucy, then turned to Jason and Daisy and their full, neon Hand Grenades. "Be careful with those, they can cause you to blow up, if you know what I mean."

The band started playing "Let's Get Drunk and Screw," another Buffett favorite, and Lucy headed out into the street, singing along and using the bottom of the Hand Grenade cup as a mic. Vivian joined her, and the six took the party onto busy Bourbon.

Vehicle traffic was blocked off, and people, many with drinks in hand, ambled from bar to bar. People on balconies beckoned to women on the street, offering beads for boobs and had several takers.

Vivian stepped around a puddle and pointed her makeshift mic to it. "That stinks! It's the one thing about Bourbon I could do without."

Daisy sidestepped the puddle. "Just watch where you step. I already messed up one pair of heels and just bought these."

"I love those, by the way," Lucy said, admiring her three-inch wooden platforms with dark silver, crisscrossed leather straps, adorned with silver studs. "Those are hot! I might need some."

"I got them at the coolest boutique. Shoe-Be-Do on Chartres."

"How were the prices?" Vivian asked.

"For handmade shoes, not bad, and they're having a great sale. I got these for 40 bucks!"

"We're so hitting that tomorrow," Lucy said. "But for now, I need karaoke." She pointed to a place called Voodoo Vibes and crossed the street, cutting off a group of guys, one of whom spilled his beer. "Sorry," she called, but he didn't seem to notice.

One of the guys, wearing a giant green and yellow foam cowboy hat, scooped Wendy up and swung her around. Before she could react, he dipped her back and laid one on her.

Wendy tapped the guy's shoulder, but he didn't let up. Kate snapped a picture* while everybody around whooped and egged him on. He finished the kiss and spun her about. She looked dazed but shook her head and yelled, "Woo!"

"Happy bachelorette party," he said, then gave her a strand of his Happy St. Patrick's Day beads and kissed her once more on the cheek before continuing down the street with his buddies.

Jason, Daisy and the girls grabbed a table in Voodoo Vibes, and a shot girl approached with test tubes in a variety of colors.

"Would anyone like some Voodoo Vexes?" She pointed to the purple tubes, then to the green. "Or here we have our Voodoo Viagra."

Daisy held up her Hand Grenade. "I'm set, thanks."

"What else do you have?" Kate asked.

"Three-for-one wells and domestics."

"I'm up for a beer," Vivian said. "Anybody else?"

Wendy and Kate raised their hands, but Lucy said, "I'll take a vodka tonic." Lucy grabbed a songbook from the table next to them. "Who's singing with me?"

"We all need to go up there!" Vivian said. "Even you, Daisy!"

"I'm more of a dancer than a singer, but sure!"

"I'll stay here and rock the air drums, pretend I'm on stage," Jason said.

"Are you in a band?" Kate asked.

"I'm the drummer for 12 Stones."

"You are?" Lucy asked. "I saw y'all in Denver with Panic of the Disco. I loved that song 'Anthem for the Underdog.' It totally rocked!"

He nodded. "Cool."

"Is that the concert where the concrete chunk fell on your head?" Vivian asked.

"That's the one."

"You could have been killed!" Kate said.

"Don't I know it!" Lucy said, rubbing her head. Then she went back to flipping the pages of the karaoke book with frenzy. "We need some rock! Oh, I know, Rush! Can you kick it to 'Dreamline'?"

"Hell, yeah," Jason said.

Lucy turned in the request and their drinks were delivered. Lucy's came in a giant plastic cup that had the Voodoo Vibes logo surrounded by musical notes.

"Now that's what I call a drink!" Lucy said and took a long sip.

"Jason, are y'all on tour right now? Is that why you're here in New Orleans?"

"Actually, 12 Stones is from NOLA. Right now, Daisy's the one on tour."

"Are you in a band, too?" Kate asked her.

Daisy smiled and shook her head. "I have a different talent. I'm a burlesque dancer."

"What's that?" Wendy asked.

"It's basically a stripper, but I don't get all the way naked. Plus, I'm in a lot of competitions."

Jason squeezed her knee. "She's up for newcomer of the year in the Exotic Dancer National Championships. She's amazing."

She smiled at him and placed her hand on his.

He picked it up and kissed it. "We're on a cross-country exhibition ending in Las Vegas where I know she'll win. Nobody can compete with her. She's fantastic, a true athlete on the pole."

"That's amazing, congratulations!" Vivian said, then raised her beer. "To Daisy! Our new friend and soon-to-be grand champion dancer!"

The DJ announced their song, so the girls got up and boogied their way to the stage. Vivian looked down and couldn't believe who she saw.

7

Sitting front and center at a table beyond the stage at Voodoo Vibes was Adrienne Russo. Her tan hadn't faded a bit since Vivian and the girls met her and Al, her boisterous husband, in Playa del Carmen a year and a half ago. They owned a restaurant in Chicago's Little Italy neighborhood that Al inherited from his father who had inherited it from his father. Al and Adrienne had been a huge help in getting unjust murder accusations cleared up, and they and the girls became friends for life.

Despite the humidity, Adrienne's hair was styled to its usual perfection and her bling was still blinding. Earrings, necklace, bracelet and a ring of silver and blue sapphires sparkled, and then there was the wedding ring — kaboom!

"Hey!" Vivian called and waved to her just as the guitar licks of "Dreamline" began, so the girls got into position in front of the microphones.

Lucy belted out the song, with Vivian and Daisy singing the lines off the prompter best they could. Kate and Wendy mostly danced in the back. Jason, true to his word, played stellar air drums at their table.

Song over, Daisy went back to the table while Vivian hopped off the stage and hugged Adrienne's neck. "I can't believe it! What are you doing here?"

"Came in to see family. I saw on Facebook you girls were here, too. I had a feeling I'd run into you!"

Lucy hugged her, too. "Where's Al?"

"He's with his cousin, Gino. This is his wife, Michelle."

"Come sit with us!" Kate said.

They pulled up two more chairs, and Vivian introduced Jason and Daisy. "We met Adrienne in Playa del Carmen on our first girls trip."

"Look out for these girls," Adrienne joked. "They've got killer instincts."

"Ha ha ha," Vivian said. "He's spoken for, so in no danger of any of us. Daisy's his fiancé."

"Congratulations! Are you getting married here in New Orleans?" Adrienne asked.

Lucy picked up her giant three-for-one vodka. "Actually they're here for Daisy's big show. They're on their way to Vegas."

"What kind of show?"

Daisy answered. "It's a burlesque exhibition."

Adrienne and Michelle looked at each other and smiled.

"My husband owns the French House," Michelle said.

"What a small world," Kate said.

"I met Gino," Daisy said. "He's really nice. It's an awesome club, one of the nicer ones I've danced in."

Adrienne tugged on Wendy's sash. "So who's the lucky guy?"

"Same guy I was dating in Mexico — Jake. He's from North Carolina."

"Yeah, I remember you talking about him. That's great, I'm happy for you. When's the big day?"

"Only a month away!"

Michelle looked at her watch. "I hate to meet and run, but the guys are expecting us to be home by 2 a.m."

Adrienne nodded her head. "Okay, okay. I'm on a short leash tonight. Are y'all coming to the show tomorrow?"

Vivian shrugged. "We didn't know about it."

"You've got to come. We'll reserve you girls and Jason a table down front. What do you say?"

"Sure, why not!" Lucy said.

The other girls nodded.

"We'll be there!" Vivian said, then they said their goodbyes to Adrienne and Michelle.

After some bad karaoke, everyone decided it was time to hang up their beads and boas for the night. They all walked down Bourbon toward Canal together since Jason and Daisy's hotel was only a few blocks from the Hotel De Lis.

The streets had started to clear out and trash was strewn about. As they walked, Daisy told them more about the show and her competition.

Vivian noticed a dim light coming from a small alcove of a building and got an eerie feeling. "What's that?"

As they got closer, she saw a petite lady with long, black hair sitting on a milk crate at a makeshift table that held a small candle. "Would you like to know more about your future?"

Vivian shuddered, immediately recognizing the woman. "Let's go." She grabbed Kate's elbow and pulled her along.

"I want to know more about my future," Lucy said as she sat down across from the woman.

The rest of the group stopped in the street, close by.

Kate turned to Vivian. "What's wrong?"

"I swear that's the lady who read my aura when I was here in college. She totally freaked me out. She told me Rick would hurt me very badly and I should leave him. She knew his name. I hadn't said a word. I ran away, upset, and a few hours later she popped out of nowhere and asked if I was okay, which of course I wasn't."

"Oh my gosh, I'm totally talking to this lady," Wendy said. "I have so many questions. I want to hear what she says."

"I'll see what Lucy thinks," Kate said. "I might do it."

After a while, Lucy stood up and walked over.

"How was it?" Kate asked.

"She's better than my shrink."

"I'm goin' next," Wendy said, then walked over to her.

"What'd she say?" Kate asked Lucy.

"You aren't supposed to talk about it. But I will tell you there are big changes coming in my life."

Vivian rolled her eyes and groaned. Kate clapped.

"How much was it?" Daisy asked.

"Only 15 bucks and soooo worth it."

"For that, I'll probably do it, too."

After several minutes, Wendy finished up and Kate went next.

"Anything you'd like to share?" Lucy asked Wendy.

"She sees a lot of travel in my future, and I'm livin' to the ripe ol' age of 92."

"It's all that good, clean living," Vivian laughed.

"Right," Lucy smirked.

Vivian turned to Daisy. "So where are y'all from?"

"We started out from Trenton last week, had a stop in DC, Charlotte, then Atlanta, but originally I'm from Minneapolis. Jason's a Jersey boy."

"Man, that's a lot of stops," Lucy said.

"We've got five more on our way to Vegas."

Kate finished up and Daisy sat down on the milk crate. Vivian watched as the fortune-teller took Daisy's hand and began her reading. Daisy was there for almost 10 minutes when her expression turned from amusement to questioning. Jason saw it and took a few steps closer. Shortly thereafter, the reading was over and she joined the group.

"What'd she say that pissed you off?" Jason asked.

Daisy waved her hand. "Oh, my job puts me in danger, blah blah blah."

Jason pulled her close and nuzzled her neck. "I'll keep you safe, baby."

"Oh Bam Bam, not in front of the children," she joked but turned into his embrace.

Vivian was about to start walking toward their hotel again when the fortune-teller came her way.

"I want to read you again. No charge."

Vivian waved her off and took two steps back. "No, no, no. I'm not ever doing that again."

The woman looked into Vivian's eyes. "I was right before. No?"

8

Day 2

Vivian woke to the sound of water running and shuffling around in the bathroom. Light peeked through the corner of the drapes, and though she couldn't see the clock, she figured it was close to 10 a.m. Another couple hours of sleep would be good, along with some ibuprofen. Wendy, always prepared, had left the whole bottle on the nightstand. She reached for it and a cup of water.

Lucy came out of the bathroom, looking freshly scrubbed and ready to start the day. "Oh, good. You're up. I'm starving!"

Vivian swallowed three pills and fell back onto the pillows. "This is not up. This waking is for medicinal purposes only."

Kate threw back her covers. "I'll go next. I need to wash the Bourbon funk off me."

"Yuck," Wendy said and rolled over. "I washed off the funk last night. Now you've contaminated the bed. Thanks."

"Not everybody showers at 3 o'clock in the morning," Vivian said.

Wendy burrowed further under the covers. "I couldn't sleep until I washed off. There's just no telling what all kind of filth we had on us."

Vivian threw the covers back but made no attempt to get up. "Bourbon definitely isn't the cleanest street I've ever walked down."

"Speaking of walking," Wendy said.

"Nobody was talking about walking," Vivian said.

"Oh, come on," Wendy said. "The Friends of the Cabildo have a walking tour this afternoon and I'd like to go. Please?"

Lucy tied the laces on her tennis shoes. "I'm in!"

Vivian tossed a pillow at her. "You and your exercise."

Lucy caught the pillow and then flexed her right bicep. "Look at that. All that exercise is paying off."

Vivian was impressed, but she still didn't want to go on a walking tour. She looked at Wendy. "We're on vacation, can't we just relax?"

Wendy sat up and clicked on the bedside light. "There's more to the Quarter than the booze and bimbos on Bourbon. The tour gets into the history and we'll learn new stuff." She threw a pillow at Vivian.

Lucy threw Vivian's pillow back at her. "We're here to celebrate Wendy's last few days of bachelorette-hood and she wants to do this, so we *have* to do it. Rally up!"

Kate poked her head out of the bathroom. "What are we rallying about?"

Wendy got her up to date and then said, "But we need breakfast first, and I know just the place."

"Now that I can do!" Vivian said and finally sat up in bed. She took a hot shower, then threw on a yellow and green blouse and khaki capris. She went to grab her flip-flops from the closet and noticed Kate's shoes were all in a row with one shoe face up, one face down.

"Did you do this on purpose?" Vivian asked Kate, pointing to her shoes.

"I've always done that. You've just never noticed."

Lucy peeked in the closet. "What's that about?"

"It's a Taiwanese thing. I think it's something to do with ghosts taking their place in your body."

"Uhhh, you don't know for sure?" Wendy asked.

"I get all these superstitions mixed up. Mom does it, so I do, too."

"Hmmm," Vivian said, then flipped over one of each of her shoes. "Better safe than sorry."

"In Taiwan, they have a whole month where you're not supposed to go swimming because of their fear of ghosts. I think it's even called 'Ghost Month.' "

"What month is it?" Lucy asked.

"Don't quote me, but I think it's August."

Wendy pulled the comforter off the bed and threw it over her head. "Oooooooooooooooo!"

They got a good laugh out of that, then finished up and left the hotel at the crack of 11 a.m. Wendy directed them across Canal and down a block to Poydras where the line to Mother's was already out the door.

"It moves pretty fast, I promise," Wendy said. "And it's totally worth it."

True to her word, the line did move fast, and once at the front, Vivian ordered sweet tea and a Turkey Ferdi with a side of grits and debris. Her stomach rumbled thinking about the creamy grits smothered in roast beef drippings.

They took a seat at a table that had a small bit of water on it. Vivian looked up as a drop fell from the air conditioner overhead. Lucy got stuck next to the splashage but quit complaining about it the second her shrimp Creole was put in front of her. Kate dug into her Jerry's Jambalaya and side of red beans and rice while Wendy scarfed down her crawfish étouffée.

Vivian wrapped a paper napkin around half of her sandwich and stuck it in her purse. "Savin' that bad boy for later."

Wendy threw in her napkin. "Good thing we aren't here in the middle of August. That thing would be rancid after 10 minutes outside." She looked down at her watch. "Are y'all ready for the walking tour? We've got 20 minutes to get to Jackson Square."

Kate groaned. "Not sure I can walk around half of New Orleans after eating all that."

Lucy pushed in her chair as the other girls stood slowly to leave. "You'll be fine, come on. My tummy is happy and I'm feelin' rejuvenated. Let's do this!"

Vivian dug in her purse. "Don't we need to leave a tip for the waitress?"

Wendy pointed to a large sign that hung between the dining areas. "No tipping allowed. They pay their folks well, so we don't have to."

"All right, movin' on then!"

Lucy held the door open and they trudged along Tchoupitoulas toward Canal where it turned into North Peters, eventually merging onto Decatur.

"There's Jax Brewery," Lucy pointed out. "There's a Rocky Mountain Chocolate Factory up there, on the third story."

"I can't really think about chocolate right now," Wendy said, "but there's a great view of the river up there. We should try to make it up there at some point."

They continued a couple more blocks to Jackson Square, then to the 1850 House, where the Friends of the Cabildo tour started.

"What's a Cabildo?" Vivian asked, then snickered and leaned over to Lucy. "Cabildo rhymes with…"

"We know what it rhymes with, trashy." Lucy shook her head. "One-track mind with you!"

"I can't help it, that stuff just pops in there!"

Wendy pointed to the three-story building topped with a golden dome. "The Cabildo was the Spanish government building way back when."

"Spanish?" Vivian asked. "I thought we bought Louisiana from the French."

Kate laughed. "I have a feeling you're about to learn a lot on this tour, which is good because it knocks out my required educational portion of our trip."

The guide met them out front, and the girls did indeed get educated. They learned the difference between a balcony and a gallery, could accurately spot a carriage entry, notice the numerous differences in Spanish and French architecture, learned all about the subterranean termites that can run rampant in season, and heard about the importance of the giant bolts that run through the buildings.

Vivian thanked the guide and slipped him a 20 from their group. "I never even noticed those bolts before, or the little termite plates on the sidewalk. Guess I need to start looking up. And down."

He wished them a pleasant visit. "Come back any time. We have other tours available."

They wandered around the Square, checking out paintings and talking to vendors.

"Let's go find that shoe store Daisy told us about," Lucy said.

"Who?" Vivian asked.

"Daisy, from last night! Geez, you drink too much!"

"Oh, her. I just forgot her name." Vivian bumped butts with Lucy. "You're the one who drank that massive vodka! Speaking of, I need a drink."

"I can't believe I'm about to say this, but I'm actually a little hungry." Kate tugged on the waistband of her capris. "My expandy pants have some expansion left in them."

"Ooooh, the Gumbo Shop is on the way to the shoe place," Wendy said. "Let's go there."

"Yeah, I can get my gumbo on," Kate said, and she did a little jive.

"They got a liquor license?" Vivian asked.

"Of course," Wendy said. "That's a silly question."

"I'm in. Aaaaaiiiiyyyyyeeeeeeeeeeeeee!"

9

The cool air of the Gumbo Shop was a relief after walking the French Quarter for the last two hours, and the cold Dos Equis made Vivian happy. And it felt good to sit down.

Wendy had a cup of seafood okra gumbo and Kate had the chicken andouille. Lucy followed Vivian's lead and just had a liquid snack of a bloody mary.

Wendy had a bite, then tore off a couple of pieces of her French bread, dipped them into her gumbo and handed them to Vivian and Lucy. "I know y'all aren't hungry, but you have to at least try this. It might be the best I've ever had. I don't even need to add Crystal's or Tabasco."

Vivian slowly chewed her bite, then nodded in agreement. "It's pretty damn good."

Lucy reached for more bread. "I think I need another taste before I can truly decide." She winked.

Wendy pushed her plate closer. "Go for it."

Kate offered hers, too.

They took turns using the tiny one-holer located off the courtyard before paying the tab and starting out again. They ambled down Chartres toward the Shoe-Be-Do, Vivian pointing out every silver termite plate they passed.

After pointing out yet another, she looked up and saw a sleek, black Lincoln Town Car pull in front of Hotél Versailles. The driver stopped and two stocky guys got out of each back door and looked around. One held the door open for a tall, olive-toned, dark-haired man. A tailored navy suit fit his athletic frame perfectly, and he had an aristocratic air. His chiseled face and sunglasses completed the I-just-stepped-out-of-GQ look.

One word popped into Vivian's mind to describe him. *Powerful.* Then another word. *Yummm.*

Two more guys stepped out of the car, and the first two walked ahead of GQ into the hotel as the doorman greeted him personally.

Vivian couldn't make out the name, but she wanted to find out. "Holy

Versace Versailles. Who the hell was that? I need to meet him."

Lucy grabbed her elbow and tried to steer her across the street. "I think he might be out of your league. The man has four bodyguards, for god's sake."

Vivian pulled her arm away. "I could just go introduce myself. You never know, and it doesn't hurt to flirt."

Kate wrapped her arm around Vivian's shoulders. "I'm with ya, sista. Let's go in!"

Wendy laughed and said, "I've heard they have a neat bar in here. We should probably check it out."

The doorman politely said hello and held the door for the girls. They made a pass through the ornate lobby, then a quick run through the bar, Galerie des Glaces.

Kate lagged behind, obviously impressed with what she saw. "This place is beautiful. I wouldn't mind sitting down for a glass of vino."

"I doubt we can afford to drink here," Wendy said. "They won't have three-for-one, and we don't want to blow the trust fund on a glass of wine!"

"I'm on a mission, let's get going." Vivian looked around but didn't see GQ anywhere.

They went back outside to the doorman.

"Who was that guy?" Vivian asked.

"Just a guest. Can't tell you more."

"Come on! Spill it. I know you know."

The doorman smiled and leaned close. "He's some bigwig from a sandy, oil-laden country. I don't know which one exactly, but you know what I mean."

"All right, all right," Vivian said and raised her eyebrows.

"Black gold," Lucy said.

"Texas Tea," Wendy added.

The doorman laughed and said, "Y'all come back now, y'hear?"

The girls cracked up and kept on going down the street. The Shoe-Be-Do wasn't much farther and Lucy happily skipped in.

She took a deep breath through her nose. "Y'all smell that? It's the smell of fine, Italian shoes."

"That has a distinct scent?" Vivian asked.

Lucy picked up a strappy leather sandal from a display and sniffed it. "It does to me." She said to the sales clerk, "I'd like to try this in a size 8."

Wendy took the shoe from Lucy and turned it over. "Oh my god. Did you see the price on this?"

Lucy shrugged. "You're the one who told me to stock up. These aren't Jimmy Choos, but they're handmade Italian. I don't discriminate."

"True that. Let me help ya look."

Vivian pointed to the back of the store. "I see the sales rack. I'll be back yonder where the single-moms shop."

Kate picked up a shoe, looked at the price, and set it down. "I'll be with Viv."

Wendy helped Lucy compare several pair before they agreed that the first was it. Vivian had found four pair on the sales rack, and the total price, $100, was still a fraction of Lucy's one. Kate also picked out a pair on the sales rack, and Wendy chose one of the same pair as Vivian. The wooden-soled sandals were more comfortable than they looked, and the jean and leather strip across the toes would go well with lots of outfits.

Vivian put hers on. "We match!"

Wendy strutted around in hers. "I've never had handmade shoes before. I might've started an addiction like Lucy. Oh no!"

Lucy approved of their choices. "Welcome to the club, my friends."

Vivian picked up her bags and kept on the new shoes. "Time to break 'em in. Hotel's close. Pay up, ladies. We've got places to go, people to see and presents to give."

Wendy handed the clerk her credit card. "Presents?"

Vivian clicked her wooden heels together. "You'll see!"

They finished up at the Shoe-Be-Do and slowly made their way down Chartres, stopping at a few art galleries along the way. Their favorite painting was of a Chihuahua looking in a mirror and seeing a German shepherd as his reflection. The one beside it was of a cat doing the same but seeing a lion.

They stopped at a walk-up bar and got a round of hurricanes to go, then went straight to the hotel. They took turns getting freshened up and trying on Vivian's shoes while working on their drinks.

Wendy held up two tops. "Which one of these should I wear tonight?"

"Whichever one looks best with your bachelorette sash," Lucy said. "But I think the red one."

Wendy slipped on a black tank top, then pulled on the red, semi-sheer cotton blouse with red and black swirly designs and beaded cuffs.

"Looks cute with your black capris and new Italian shoes!" Lucy said. "This is what I'm wearing." She held up a solid emerald green V-neck sundress. "It hits right above my knee, compliments of my fabulous seamstress."

"Love that color," Vivian said. "I'd steal it but I think it'd be too short. Would look great with my eyes!"

Kate poked her head out of the bathroom. "What are you wearing, Viv?"

Vivian dug into the disorganized drawer and pulled out a flowy poncho-style top, turquoise, green and pale yellow with beads sprinkled around the neckline.

"Ooooh, like that," Wendy said, touching it. "Which pair of new shoes are you going to wear?"

"Probably the Yoyo-wanna-be wooden ones with the jean and brown on top. We can match!"

Kate, hair and makeup done but still wrapped in a towel, broke out the iron and ironing board. She then set to de-wrinkling her purple, button-down top and white skirt.

Once everyone was ready, they sat Wendy on the edge of the bed. Vivian pulled out a hot pink bag with velvet kisses all over it and handed it to her. "What's in here rhymes with Cabildo. And it's rechargeable."

Wendy took the bag, which was quite heavy, glanced inside and gasped. Kate snapped a picture.

Vivian just smiled. "You'll thank me. Trust me."

Kate handed Wendy a pure white box with a white satin ribbon. "Mine's not nearly as trashy, but I think Jake will like it nonetheless."

Wendy pulled the ribbon, which fell to the floor, and opened the box. She held up a white, lacy negligee.

"There's a garter in there, too," Kate said.

Wendy blushed. "Thanks, Kate. It's beautiful."

"One left!" Lucy handed her a red bag with silver metallic strands pouring over the sides.

Wendy threw the confetti all over the girls and the room. "I like this stuff! Reminds me of Christmas tinsel."

She dug into the bag and pulled out some massage oils and a heart-shaped candle. She popped the lid on the candle. "Mmmm, smells good. Thanks, Lucy."

"It's not just any candle. It's special. Once you light it you can pour the wax on Jake."

"Won't that hurt? And get stuck in his chest hair?"

"That's where the special comes in! It burns to body temperature and soaks into the skin like massage oil. Don't tell him, just freak him out with it!"

Wendy laughed. "Y'all are a mess. Thank you for the gifts. I can't wait to shock him, delight him and scare the hell out of him."

They woo-hooed to that and finished off their hurricanes.

"Let's book it, ladies," Kate said. "We've got a reservation."

Wendy clapped. "Reservations? Where?"

"A fancy Creole place. We'll have to pretend to be civilized." Lucy laughed.

"Whatever. This is New Orleans," Vivian said. "Anything goes!"

10

The maître d' of Broussard's greeted the girls warmly and showed them to their table. Vivian peeked into the bar as they walked by. A baby grand sat in one corner, and the windows were open to the courtyard. *We'll have to stop in there later!*

Their table in the main dining room was covered in a white tablecloth and fully set. A flower in a crystal vase and a candle completed the scene.

Vivian fiddled with her napkin. "I hope I don't spill anything. I tend to do that, you know."

"You'll be fine, quit playing with your napkin," Lucy said.

"It's in the shape of a swan or something." Vivian giggled. "I can't get it undone."

Lucy took it, unfolded it and put it in her lap. "Here, now calm down."

Wendy looked pleased. "I've always wanted to come here. I've walked by it so many times and thought it looked fabulous."

Kate sat up in her chair. "I asked around and everyone said this was the place to go. Did you know this is a historic building? Part of it was a prep school in the 1800s. And the courtyard used to be the carriage house."

"So horses used to run through here?" Vivian asked.

"No, silly," Kate said.

The waiter approached. "Actually, she's right, but they were usually walking by the time they made it back here."

Lucy smiled and lifted her menu. "Y'all have done a great job cleaning up."

The waiter asked if they had decided on a bottle of wine or wanted something else from the bar.

Wendy held the wine list. "I think we'll have the Caymus Special Selection Cabernet, please."

"Nice choice. Off menu tonight is our stuffed mirliton with wild Louisiana shrimp and lump crabmeat."

"I do like wild stuff," Vivian smirked.

"What's mirliton?" Kate asked.

"It's also known as a mango squash or vegetable pear. It's a southern Louisiana favorite."

"You lost me at squash," Vivian said. "I'm more of a meat eater."

"The filet mignon is excellent, and the redfish Broussard is one of our most popular items. It's a filet dusted in cornmeal, topped with shrimp, crabmeat and crawfish, and served with an oyster mushroom étouffée."

"Sold!" Wendy said and put down her menu.

Vivian went with the filet mignon, Lucy ordered the swordfish Vera Cruz and Kate the mirliton special.

Dinner was superb and as they shared the Crepes Broussard for dessert, an elegant woman in her '50s approached.

"Good evening, ladies, I'm Evelyn. What are you celebrating?"

Wendy held up her tacky sash. "Bachelorette party. I'm getting married in a few weeks."

"Congratulations. Thank you for celebrating with us. I'd like to offer you a bottle of champagne." She signaled the waiter, who arrived with a bottle of bubbly and four flutes.

The girls cheered as he popped the cork and poured.

"Would you like to join us?" Kate asked.

"Oh no, thank you. I have a lot to do around here. You ladies have a fun night. I hope to see you again sometime."

"Thank you!" Wendy said, holding up her champagne flute. "We will most definitely be back!"

Evelyn walked off and Lucy said to Wendy, "So how are the wedding plans coming along? Your invitations were beautiful, by the way."

Wendy smiled. "Thanks, and yes, everything is planned and pretty well wrapped up."

"Who's your maid of honor?" Vivian asked.

Lucy looked perplexed. "It isn't you?"

Vivian waved her hand. "Nah, I opted out. I'm 300 miles away and busy with four kids."

"All of you live out of town and I didn't want to burden y'all with trekking to Houston to help me plan and pick stuff out," Wendy explained. "Ali's my maid of honor. She and I have saved each other from annoying men, supported each other with good ones, and laughed at the dumb ones. And she's lots of fun. My cousin, soon-to-be sister in-law and old friend, Silly Sally, are my other bridesmaids."

Kate held up her glass in a toast. "It's going to be a beautiful wedding and I'm so excited for you!"

The girls cheersed, then Vivian said, "Let's take this party to the bar!"

She snagged the champagne bottle and danced her way through the dining room, directly to the baby grand. A gentleman in his '60s played Fats Domino's "Blueberry Hill."

Toward the bottom of the champagne bottle Vivian pulled out the penis whistle. "I think we need to jazz this song up."

She started blowin' and goin', the accompaniment to "Tutti Frutti."

Kate pulled out her camera and took some video. "She's going to regret this someday, but for now it's fantastic!"

They sang and blew along for several songs, joining other patrons for a spin on a makeshift dance floor in front of the piano. Evelyn sang along with Tom, the piano player, to "What a Wonderful World," and Vivian took a break on the whistle.

They clapped when the song was over, then Wendy said, "Let's hit Razzoo's before we go to Daisy's show!"

"Woo-hoo!" the rest of the girls chimed.

They said goodbye to Evelyn and Tom and wandered out to Bourbon. The crowd had grown in the last couple of hours, and the girls just jumped right in. They went with the flow up Bourbon a few blocks until the crowd almost stopped where guys were throwing beads from a balcony.

Vivian blew on the penis whistle to get their attention, but they didn't throw any her way. "Here," she said and shoved the whistle at Wendy. "You try, and get up there with your sash!"

Wendy took the whistle and wiped off Vivian's lipstick before putting it in her mouth. She gave it a shrill blow and got closer to the balcony. One of the guys threw down a long strand of pearly beads and she caught them. She waved and tooted on the whistle before joining the girls. "These are great! Quite the throw!"

Kate admired the beads, then said, "You know, that whistle could come in really handy if one of us gets lost in this crowd."

Lucy picked up her new Shoe-Be-Do high heels. "Or if one of us goes down."

"Woman down! Woman down!" Vivian shouted.

Wendy blew the whistle and led the way through the crowd. A block later, another group of people on a balcony threw beads into the crowd. Vivian looked up to catch a strand and stumbled on the uneven cobblestones. She couldn't get her footing and went down, smack, on her hands and knees, right in the middle of Bourbon Street.

Lucy and Kate shouted, "Woman down!" several times and Wendy blew the whistle.

Beads showered them from every angle, especially hitting Vivian, who was laughing and unable to get up because of it. A strand of Jamaican bobsled beads hit her on the side of the face and neck. A guy next to her picked up the beads and grabbed her by the elbow, helping her to her feet.

"You deserve these," he said, draping them around her neck.

Wendy checked Vivian over for blood or serious damage, but Vivian waved her off. "I'm fine, hardly even scratched my knees. I'd like to wash my hands, though!"

Wendy pulled a packet of hand wipes out of her purse and waved it in front of her. "Who's your girl?"

"You are!" She grabbed the wipe and cleaned up.

They made it to Razzoo's without further incident and bellied up to the bar, ordering a round of drinks. The bartender set down nine Bud Lights and a large cup of Lucy's vodka and tonic. "Three-for-one," he said when the girls looked at him like he was hard of hearing because they'd ordered three beers total.

"Can you keep these on ice for us?" Wendy asked, slapping down a 20.

"You can." He pulled out a bucket and filled it full of ice.

Wendy expertly maneuvered the extra beers into the bucket, then it set on a table near the railing. They watched some crappy dancing on stage and listened to some bad karaoke. After a few minutes they went outside to the courtyard. The guy from the night before, in the giant foam cowboy hat, was out there with his friends. He saw the girls through his sunglasses and made a beeline for Wendy. Before she could escape, he leaned her back and planted another one on her.

She laughed and shoved him off, so he reached for Lucy and leaned her back for his version of a gallant kiss. Lucy went with it for quite a while, until he finally set her upright. Foam Hat looked over the top of his sunglasses at her and wiggled his eyebrows before returning to his buddies.

Vivian cheersed Lucy. "Enjoyed that, did ya?"

Lucy grinned. "He is the funniest guy, wearing that hat and sunglasses at night. Not to mention, he's a damn good kisser."

"Uh huh," Kate said and Wendy laughed. Karaoke hour over, they made their way to the dance floor for a few songs and finished off their bucket before hitting the street again. They weaved through the crowd, making their way toward Canal.

Kate hailed a cab and Vivian jumped in the front as the other girls piled into the back.

"Where are you girls headed tonight?" the cabbie asked.

"French House Cabaret, please!"

11

The cabbie drove through the warehouse district and dropped the girls off under the porte cochere at the French House. They gave the doorman their names and said they were guests of Al's. He motioned for a bouncer, who whisked them to a table front and center of the stage.

Al, Adrienne and Jason were already there and watching the pre-show entertainment. The girls sat down after a round of hellos and hugs, then Al did his usual — ordered a bottle of bubbly, from a waitress wearing a black, strapless spandex bodysuit that stopped just below her ass.

"That looks more like something you'd wear in the bedroom than in public," Kate said.

"I own something like that!" Vivian laughed. She soaked in the scene, which was different from what she'd expected. It was an upscale club and had several stages with poles. The tables were draped in black with small brass lamps in the center. Almost every table was occupied, some with couples, and the bar area was packed full of men, many of them watching one of the numerous big screens broadcasting March Madness.

Lucy turned to Jason. "Is Daisy nervous?"

He shook his head. "Nahhh, she's a pro. She's ready to rock it. You'll be impressed."

"Gino told me she's fantastic," Adrienne said, then took a sip of her freshly poured champagne.

"This is so exciting!" Kate said. "This is my first time in a strip club, you know."

Al leaned over. "They're not all like this, honey. This one's in a class of its own."

Vivian scanned the crowd and was shocked to see a face she recognized — GQ. She knocked Wendy in the arm. "Oh my god! Oh my god!"

"What? Is everything okay?"

"Better than okay! Look who's here!" She discreetly pointed a few tables over.

"Wow, he looks even better up close. Go talk to him!"

Kate saw who they were talking about. "Yeah, go talk to him!"

Lucy waved her hand to stop. "We don't want you causing an international incident."

"I won't. I just want to say hi." Vivian got up and walked over to the table where GQ sat with two other men.

He looked up at her with bored, hazel eyes.

"Hey there! I'm Vivian. I saw you earlier today at Hotél Versailles. We almost booked there but switched at the last minute. How is it?"

He shrugged. "It is fine."

"I think we may go back tomorrow for happy hour. I heard they have a cool drink they light on fire at your table. Have you had it?"

"No, I do not drink."

Vivian glanced at his bottle of Perrier.

"Well, I hope you enjoy the show. My friend, Daisy, is performing. I think she's last."

"You as well."

Vivian turned and rolled her eyes as she approached the girls. "He's a dud. Such a waste of beautiful features."

"What'd he say?" Kate asked.

"Not much. A man of few words. It's pretty obvious he's not interested in what I've got goin' on."

"Stupid boys," Lucy said. "His loss."

"Don't sweat it, honey," Al said, checking his phone, then putting it away. "I saw that schmuck in here yesterday. Never tipped any of the dancers. That's a sign."

The music stopped and a rotund middle-aged man walked onto the main stage with a microphone.

Adrienne pointed. "There's Gino. I think the show's about to start!"

Gino welcomed the crowd and thanked them for coming out. He explained that the dancers being showcased were finalists for the Newcomer of the Year award being given out in Las Vegas.

"So without further ado, let's get this show started. First up tonight is Trikki Vikki, who comes to us from Miami, Florida."

Gino moved off stage and the lights dimmed. ZZ Top's "Legs" started up and a single light shone backstage. A petite woman with freckled skin and jet-black hair pulled into a bun, glossy red lips, wearing reading glasses and a single strand of pearls strutted into the spotlight. Her boobs spilled out of the plunging neckline of her white top, which was tied just below them. Her silver metallic pencil-skirt reflected the sparkles from the disco ball.

She danced in her clear, seven-inch platform heels to the pole in the middle of the stage, where she slithered around it once before throwing her glasses off. The song changed to "Pearl Necklace" and Trikki Vikki pulled her bun loose. Her straight black hair fell across her shoulders as she rolled around on the floor. Her top conveniently came loose and was next to go, but she was still partially covered by a tiny white bikini. As the song changed to "La Grange," she ripped her skirt off, revealing a white G-string. She was officially ready to hit the pole.

"Dear lord, I didn't know a body could bend that way," Vivian said, watching as Trikki Vikki moved from an unnatural position to having her legs clamped around the pole, hanging upside down.

Vikki's routine varied from the floor to the pole, lots of twirling and swirling. She closed out her performance with ZZ Top's "I'm Bad and I'm Nationwide," and boy, was she wide. Her splits went beyond horizontal.

"Ouch!" Lucy said, squirming in her chair. Trikki Vikki ended with an impressive final pose on the pole.

Gino came back on stage and announced the next dancer, Lala Lollipop. Her routine started out as little-miss-innocent to a sexed-up version of "The Good Ship Lollipop." Her cocoa skin set off her lacy white bikini top that did not have a lining, and playful short skirt with a tulle underlining. She pulled a few lollipops from her imitation doily and handed them to guys in the crowd, including Al.

He took it and laughed. "I wonder how many licks it takes to get to the center of her lollipop?"

Adrienne smacked him on the arm. "Al!"

He grinned.

Lala flopped into the splits in front of them.

"I wonder if she's going to shoot them out of her cooch like I saw in Thailand once," Jason said.

The table erupted in laughter, and Lala gave them a dirty look.

The Good Ship Lollipop set sail and Lala's head-banger music was a bit much for Vivian, who was relieved when the next dancer took the stage. They watched a few other dancers perform until finally it was Daisy's turn.

Jason sat on the edge of his seat, focused on her. A drumbeat started and she crawled onto the middle of the stage, graceful as a jungle cat. She was dressed in a tribal outfit that tied on the side, and she had animal-print body paint on her arms and legs. Her hair was tousled and wild, and her eyes were painted in a glittery gold.

"She looks amazing!" Kate squealed.

Daisy brushed against the pole like a cat wanting attention, but unlike a cat, she reached out and spun sideways, one leg up by her head, the other gripping the pole. She did a few more tricks, showing her sleek yet muscular form, then a vine lowered, and she pulled herself halfway up to the ceiling. The rest of her time on stage consisted of acrobatic stunts using the vine and the pole. She looked more like a gymnast than a burlesque dancer.

Halfway through the routine Vivian noticed a balding, paunch-bellied man standing behind their table, eyes focused on Daisy. A trickle of sweat ran down his face. The French House might have been a nicer club, but it was still a strip joint, and creepy men were free to roam.

As Daisy finished up, she swung from the vine to the pole, then to the floor, landing in the splits. The crowd went wild, cheering more for her than for anyone else.

Jason beamed. "She's got this competition in the bag."

Daisy took her bows, then walked offstage, smiling and waving.

Lucy, still clapping, asked Jason if he'd recorded the music.

"Yes, and I'm working on some new stuff for her, too."

"It was fantastic," Wendy said. "And Daisy inspires me to get in better shape! Those push-up thingies she did with her legs wrapped over her shoulders were amazing."

"She's impressive," Jason said. "She works hard."

Al ordered two more bottles of champagne, and everyone chatted and watched the other performers as they waited for Daisy to join them.

The showcase was over and one of the regular entertainers came out in a tight, white, shimmery mini-dress and wore big angel wings. "She Talks to Angels" by the Black Crowes rang out through the club.

"I love love love this song!" Vivian said and reached into her purse. "This girl gets my money." She stood up and waved a few ones around. The stripper slowly made her way over, taking her time to unzip the front of her dress as she did. Vivian stuffed the money down her dress as Kate snapped two pictures.

The bouncer started to walk over but Al waved him off. He leaned over to Kate. "No more pictures, sweetheart. And make sure that one doesn't end up online anywhere."

Kate put her phone away. "Sorry. I didn't know the rules."

Commotion erupted in the bar as one guy cracked a beer bottle over the head of another guy, who then punched that guy in the face. They went to the floor yelling and grunting. After a few moments, two bouncers appeared, pulled them apart and carted them toward the exit.

"Amateurs." Al smirked and shook his head.

Jason checked the time on his phone. "Takes Daisy a while to get all that paint off, but she ought to be out soon."

They finished up both bottles of champagne, during which time Jason tried to call Daisy twice.

"She's probably back there talking to the other dancers," Adrienne said.

Twenty more minutes passed. Vivian could see the worry on Jason's face as he tried calling again.

He stood, slipping his phone into his pocket. "Something's not right, she should be here by now. I'm going backstage."

12

Daisy toweled dry after scrubbing off body paint in the shower. She threw on a black, satin robe and flip-flops and walked to her dressing room. She sat at the lighted mirror countertop, brushed out her hair, applied some light makeup and turned the curling iron on before changing into a white miniskirt and turquoise blouse studded with silver sequins. She slipped on her new, favorite heels from Shoe-Be-Do and reassessed in the mirror.

Stacey, one of the French House dancers, knocked, then popped her head in. "You were amazing tonight. You're gonna win it in Vegas. Good luck, babe!"

"Thanks," Daisy called after Stacey's echoing heels. She heard the back door slam.

Daisy applied dark red lipstick and picked up the hair dryer. She blew her hair dry in about three minutes, flipping her head over and using a large, round brush to smooth out her locks. She flipped the switch to cool and blew it into her face.

She looked at her red hair in the mirror. *Lovin' this megawatt color.*

She picked up the curling iron and twirled a strand of hair around it. She was hurrying, knowing Bam-Bam was waiting for her, but she wanted to look good. The look in his eyes when he first saw her was always worth the effort.

A knock sounded at the door, and before she could respond a stocky, dark-haired guy walked in followed by a leaner, but definitely fit, dark-complected man.

She didn't turn around, just smiled at them in the mirror. "I'm sorry, I'm not — "

The stocky guy presented her with a pink martini. "You earned this, that's for sure. We just wanted to stop by on our way out to tell you how great your performance was tonight. We are with Desert Glitter in Las Vegas

56

and would like you to perform at our club next week, if you can squeeze it into your schedule."

Daisy smiled and took the drink. "Nice place. I'd love to do a show at your club." She took a refreshing sip and picked up her phone, clicking on the calendar. "I'll be in town for four days and I think maybe Thursday night would work. I'll have to check with the promotions people at the awards, to make sure they don't have anything they need me to attend."

The leaner guy looked at her drink, then at her. "We understand completely and will do whatever is necessary to accommodate your schedule."

Daisy chatted with them about the competition in Vegas while she worked on the martini and her hair. Just as she perfected the last curl, she felt a little woozy.

Did I eat today? she thought and started to say something but couldn't. She slumped against the countertop and heard a crash right before everything went black.

***

Jason walked toward the backstage door of the French House, a look of concern on his face.

Al pushed back his chair. "I'll get him past the bouncer."

Kate jumped up. "I want to see what the back of a strip club looks like!"

"Come on, girls," Adrienne said. "Let's go see what the heck's going on."

As they approached, the bouncer was shaking his head and waving Jason away. Al stepped between them, and soon the bouncer nodded and allowed them back.

Adrienne walked by the bouncer and touched his arm. "We appreciate you taking such good care of us, Bruno."

The back of the club still looked like the warehouse it had once been, only the small offices had been converted to dressing rooms.

Jason hustled down the hall, calling Daisy's name. He poked his head through a room with multiple dressing stations. "Have you seen Daisy?" he asked a sailorette and a nurse.

"Who?"

"No."

He kept moving and looked into the few dressing rooms they passed, which were empty.

They came to a bathroom, and Vivian walked in calling for Daisy. The toilet stalls were empty, as were the two showers, one still wet. She exited and shook her head. "No one's in there, but someone has taken a shower recently."

Jason turned the knob on the next closed door they came to just as Trikki Vikki opened it.

"Shit! You scared me," she said.

"Have you seen Daisy?"

"No," she said, curtly. "It's not like we're friends. She does her thing, I do mine." Vikki tried to get by him but he blocked the door.

"When's the last time you saw her?"

"I don't know. Get the fuck outta my way." She pushed him and moved past. "I've got a private show to get to." She looked the girls up and down like they were trash, then flung open the back door.

Jason dialed Daisy's number again. Lionel Richie's "Hello" echoed from down the hall. He followed it and bent down to pick up a phone. "It's hers," he said, then turned the phone toward them.

The screen was shattered but Vivian could still make out Jason's smiling face and the words "Bam Bam." She walked to the door of the dressing room closest to the exit. A strappy, silver, studded shoe lay on its side in the middle of the floor. She glanced up at the lighted mirror above the dressing table where a vase of flowers had been knocked over. The purple ribbon around the vase had bled into the water, staining the white laminate countertop and still slowly dripped onto the floor. The burning scent of hair and chemicals reached her.

"This is dangerous," Vivian said, unplugging a curling iron from the multi-plug outlet on the wall. The lavender puddle was inches from a short circuit, or worse. The live feed from the stage showed on a small monitor in the corner. The naughty nurse was already down to her skivvies and in full swing on the pole.

"Isn't that her Shoe-Be-Do shoe?" Wendy asked, pointing to the high heel.

Lucy gasped. "She'd never leave that behind."

Jason bent down to pick it up but Al stopped him. "Hold up there, chief. I wouldn't touch anything. Adrienne, call your brother. I'll get Gino."

Adrienne pulled out her phone and began dialing.

"Who's your brother?" Jason asked.

"Cop."

Jason leaned against the wall and sank slowly to the floor. He put his head in his hands.

Kate went to him and rubbed his back. "I'm sure she's fine."

"No, something really bad has happened. I can feel it."

13

After talking to her brother, Adrienne shuffled the girls and Jason into a large, empty dressing room down the hall. "The police are on their way. Won't take them long to get here."

Vivian flipped through the outfits that hung on a portable costume rack. "Holy cow, check this out." She held up a sliver of black lace material with elastic ties falling here and there. "How does this work?"

Kate walked over and picked up two of the ties. "You put your legs through these, and these two tie around the back." She held up two straps that were connected to a silver ring at the top of the material. "These go around your neck."

Lucy slapped at Kate's hand. "Don't touch that!"

"You are a sneaky kinky, aren't you," Vivian said, putting the hanger back.

"Shaun doesn't complain." Kate flashed her sneaky smile.

They heard commotion down the hall and Jason headed for the door, but before he reached it, Al appeared with Gino and two uniformed officers.

"Cops are here searching the warehouse and surrounding area," Al said. "They want to talk to you guys."

One of the policemen pulled out a small steno notebook. "I'm Officer Perez, let's start from the beginning. What's going on here?"

Jason approached him. "My fiancé is missing."

"When's the last time you saw her?"

"When she came out on stage about an hour and a half ago."

"Why do you think she's missing?"

"She was supposed to come back to the table after the show. When she didn't, I called and called, but she never answered."

"We found her phone. The screen was shattered." Kate pointed to the phone, which was still in Jason's hand.

"Where did you find the phone?" Perez asked.

"Right by the back door," Kate said.

Joan Rylen

The other policeman pulled an evidence bag from his pocket and held it out. Jason hesitated before dropping the phone in. "I'll need you to show me exactly where you found it."

Jason took him down the hall.

"Her dressing room is messed up," Vivian said to Perez. "The flowers are knocked over."

"And there's only one shoe," Lucy added.

"The clothing rack was tumped over, too." Wendy said.

Jason walked back into the room. "I know something's wrong. She would never just leave."

"Okay, let me go take a look," Perez said.

Gino escorted the officers to Daisy's dressing room, not allowing Jason or the girls to follow.

Jason paced the room. "I know who did this. That fuckin' guy Harry. I told Daisy he was bad news but she insisted he was harmless."

"Who's Harry?" Adrienne asked.

"He's a fucking stalker, that's who he is. He follows her around the country, goes to every show."

"Was he here tonight?"

"Yes. That fat fuck was standing right by our table during her performance."

Vivian snapped. "I saw him! He was super sweaty."

"That's him, and he always sends her flowers. The ones in the room are probably from him."

"Maybe that's why she knocked them over," Vivian said. "She was sending you a sign."

Jason reared back and slammed his fist through the wall. The wallboard crumbled and fell to the floor, leaving a hole twice as big as his fist.

Gino poked his head through the door. "What the hell, man?"

"Sorry, sorry," Jason said and continued his pacing around the room.

"Okay, calm down and let's try to focus," Adrienne said. "Other than being fat and sweaty, what does the guy look like? Gino will have security video that we can check."

"I don't know. Old and hairy. White." Jason started to walk toward the door.

Adrienne reached out a hand to stop him, touching his arm. "Hold on. Is there anyone else you can think of who would want to hurt her? Was anyone mad at her?"

Jason blew out a breath. "No, not really. She and Vikki aren't the best of friends. Vikki talks a lot of shit about her. I think it's pure jealousy."

60

A man with great arms, brown eyes, olive skin and dark, cropped hair came into the room. He hugged Adrienne. "There you are, what's going on?"

"So glad you're here," she said. "This is Jason. It's his fiancé that's missing. She's one of the dancers who performed tonight."

"I'm Detective Antonio Robichaux," he said and motioned toward Jason. "Come with me." He and Jason left the room.

"Uhhh, hello. Was that incredibly hot man your brother?" Vivian asked Adrienne.

"The one and only. And yes, he is pretty cute."

"Single?"

"He's that, too."

A tall black man came into the room and gave Adrienne a one-armed hug. "I should have known you'd be here."

"Eddie, how are you?"

"Can't complain," he said to her, then continued, "I need to get a statement from each of you, then y'all can clear out." His voice was smooth and deep as the ocean.

Adrienne introduced him as Antonio's partner, Detective Edwin "Eddie" Leffall. He sat each girl down at the dressing station and took a statement, making a few notes. During his interview with Lucy she fiddled with the plastic lid on a container of cotton balls, taking it off, setting it back down, over and over. He asked her, "Do you think Jason has anything to do with Daisy's disappearance?"

Lucy dropped the lid and it clattered to the floor. "No! He was with us and he's freaking out. He loves her."

Leffall nodded and closed his notebook. "Thank you. You don't have to stay. I've got your contact info if we need you."

"Can we talk to Jason real quick before we leave?" Vivian asked.

"Sure. I'll be right back."

A few moments later, Jason came in, his face flush and eyes red.

Vivian gave him a hug. "We're here for you. Call us if we can help in any way." She handed him her phone. "Call yourself from my phone. That way you'll have my number, too."

He reached out a shaky hand and dialed, his pocket buzzed a moment later. He handed it back and said, "Thanks," then turned and left the room.

Adrienne whipped out her phone. "Let me call Al, see where he got to and what's going on."

Before she could dial, Al popped out from around the corner. "I'll tell ya what's going on. Something went down here, and it ain't good."

"Jason told us about a stalker," Adrienne said. "We want to see the security video."

Al reached into his sports coat pocket and held up a flash drive, grinning mischievously. "One step ahead of ya, babe."

14

drienne hugged and kissed Al. "I love you. Always thinking ahead."
"Shhh," he said. "Gino doesn't know."
"How can we watch it?" Vivian asked.
"Haven't gotten that far yet."

The group was quiet for a minute before Wendy spoke up. "My laptop is in the room, we're staying at Hotel De Lis. Let's go get it and maybe go to Café Du Monde. I could use some café au lait."

"Yum," Vivian said. "I could use a sugary snack."

"I'll call our driver," Al said.

The group headed toward the back door but Officer Perez stopped them. "Sorry, folks, gotta go out the front. This is a crime scene."

A chill ran up Vivian's spine at the sight of the crime scene tape. An image of the cordoned-off beach in Mexico where Jon Tournay had died popped into her head. She didn't have to be told twice and turned around. They walked through the backstage door, the bodyguard now replaced with a police officer, and made it toward the front. The club was mostly cleared out. Cops in a strip club were a buzz kill.

A black Cadillac limo pulled into the porte cochere. The driver got out and opened the back, left door. Al stepped forward and motioned for Adrienne and the girls to get in. As the driver shut the door for him, Al said, "Hotel De Lis. Thanks, Tony."

"Ooh la la, this is fancy shmancy," Vivian said, rolling down the window partially, then rolling it back up. "I need a better job. Or a rich husband."

Adrienne picked up a crystal decanter that was in a built-in bar. "Anyone like a drink?"

Everyone said yes.

"Let me," Al said, then he began placing cubes from an ice bucket into rocks glasses. "What's everyone want? We have bourbon, rum, vodka, scotch and gin."

"Got any Coke to go with that rum?" Vivian asked.

He opened a small refrigerator. "I do. Anything you'd like."

He poured and mixed to the girls' requests, then handed out glasses.

The driver pulled up to the hotel and Wendy went inside with Kate, buddy system back in effect, and emerged shortly with the computer.

Al buzzed the driver, telling him their next stop would be Café Du Monde. The streets were fairly empty of pedestrians, and the horse-drawn carriages that typically lined Jackson Square were long gone. The driver pulled directly in front of the entrance to the café that never closes and the six got out.

They quickly put a couple of round tables together, and a Vietnamese lady approached wearing black slacks, white button-down dress shirt, white apron, black bow tie and the signature white paper hat with Café Du Monde printed in green letters on each side. Al ordered four plates of beignets, and everyone put in for various drinks ranging from water to milk, hot chocolate to café au lait.

Wendy's laptop finished booting up just as the order was delivered.

"Can I have some beignet with my powdered sugar, please?" Vivian said as she picked up one of the hot, square, perfectly fried French donuts and took a big bite. Powdered sugar stuck to her lips and fell from the pastry, dusting her shirt. "Mmmmmmmmmm."

They all dug in as Wendy pressed play on the front-door security video. She positioned the computer so everyone could see.

"How do we know who Harry is?" Kate asked.

Adrienne finished a big bite, then said, "Jason told me his white hair sticks out everywhere and he's got a big belly."

"Eeewe!" Lucy squealed.

"Doesn't sound like a good look," Kate agreed.

They hit fast forward and watched as man after man entered, paid and moved on.

"Hey! There we are!" Wendy said and pointed with her beignet.

"But we don't pay!" Vivian said.

"Benefits of the guest list," Lucy said.

They watched a few more minutes, then Wendy hit pause. "That's gotta be him. Look at that bad hair."

Lucy coughed from laughing at the frozen image. A puff of powder floated across the table and landed on the computer screen.

"Look at the chest hair busting out of that shirt. It's Hairy Harry!" Vivian pointed to the tremendous tuft of chest hair being held back by the buttons of a hideous, bowling-style shirt. "What the hell is all over it? Stamps?"

Kate gasped. "Oh my gosh, I saw that guy. He was standing right next to me. Those aren't stamps, those are tiny Playboy covers!"

"Oh geez, no," Lucy said.

64

"Yes!" Kate said. "I was going to point it out to y'all, but he disappeared after Daisy danced."

"Look, you can almost make out the little bunny image," Wendy said, pointing to a square.

"Okay, so we know he looks like," Adrienne said. "Let's pull up video from the back door. See if he shows up there."

Wendy closed out of that file and opened another. She sped past images of the back door until a guy appeared carrying a vase of flowers and wearing a Louie's Flowers T-shirt.

"What time was this?" Adrienne asked.

"Says 10:26," Wendy said.

"Almost 30 minutes before she went on stage," Vivian said.

The guy hit a buzzer by the door, then a few moments later Daisy opened it, smiling. She took the flowers, the door falling shut behind her, and the guy turned and left.

Fast forward again. Two guys approached the back door. Wendy slowed the video, and everyone watched as the guys tried to get in. One guy even took a credit card and tried to jimmy the lock. They were unsuccessful and wandered off.

Wendy fast forwarded the video ahead eight minutes until the door opened from the inside and Trikki Vikki emerged, using a nearby brick to prop open the door. She lit a cigarette and waited until a guy walked up from outside the club. She talked to him for a minute.

"Is there any way to get sound on this?" Kate asked.

"Nope, it's only video," Al said.

Vikki looked agitated, pointing with her cigarette inside the club, then outside. After a few more moments, she flicked her cigarette in the man's direction, then waved her hands in the air as she yelled something. She kicked the brick away from the door and slammed it as she went inside.

"Rewind it," Kate said, moving closer to the screen. "Let's see if we can figure out what she's yelling."

Wendy did, but after several attempts, no one could agree.

"I think she's yelling, 'Just fucking do it,' " Lucy said.

"It does kinda look like that," Vivian said. "But it also looks like, 'You're a fucking screw-up.' "

"He did look like a screw-up," Kate said.

"Hard to tell, for sure," Al said, "but it does make you wonder."

Adrienne set down her coffee. "Maybe my brother's team can make more sense of this. Let's keep going."

Wendy fast forwarded 22 more minutes when the door flung open from the inside again.

And then they saw it.

15

The girls, Al and Adrienne cringed at the sight of Daisy being carried out the back of the club, arms draped over the shoulders of two guys. Her head hung forward and her feet dangled between them.

"She looks drugged," Al said.

Adrienne's eyes filled with tears. "That poor girl. I can't believe she's number three."

Vivian looked at her. "What do you mean three?"

"Two other strippers have gone missing in the past month. Both disappeared after work."

Vivian's heart dropped and she couldn't talk.

"Are those Antonio's cases?" Lucy asked.

Adrienne shook her head. "No, different jurisdictions, but I'm sure he knows about them. He's probably already asking the detectives working the other cases to share information."

"Three? So there's a serial stripper snatcher out there?" Wendy said, shaking her head.

"Not necessarily, don't get worked up. Let's do what we can to help," Al said and looked at the laptop.

They backed up the video and played it slowly, second by second, squinting for clues.

Lucy pointed to the screen. "She's only wearing her one Shoe-Be-Do shoe."

"Who are these guys?" Wendy asked. "They don't look like creeps; they look well dressed."

"Well-dressed guys can be crazies, too," Kate said.

"Yes, but how did they get back there, and what do they want with Daisy?"

"I feel like I should text Jason and tell him about this," Vivian said, picking up her phone. "Do you think he knows already?"

Adrienne shook her head. "I doubt it. Most likely the police consider him a suspect. That's generally the way it works in the beginning."

Vivian set her phone back down.

"Yeah, but he was with us," Lucy said. "When the cop asked me that question, I told him absolutely not."

"It's just part of the job," Adrienne said. "I'll call Antonio and ask him if Jason has been cleared as a suspect yet." She got out her phone and stepped away from the table. She came back and said, "They've seen the video and are trying to enhance it to pick up any details."

"I wish I could zoom in and sharpen images on this computer, but I don't have that kind of technology. Not like I need it for the mortgage business," Wendy said, and she paused the video.

"Let's concentrate on what we can see," Kate said. She got a pen out of her purse and dusted sugar off of a napkin. "Two guys, dark hair, wearing dark slacks and jackets, pretty tall from the looks of it."

"That's not much to go on," Wendy said.

"What else do we see?" Kate asked.

"They seem to know to hold their heads down," Vivian said. "We can't see their faces."

Al cleared his throat. "They probably knew there was a camera out there. That's why they're doing that. These guys aren't your run-of-the-mill idiots like those other two shmucks we saw earlier."

"Maybe the police can pull a fingerprint off the door," Lucy asked.

Adrienne frowned. "I wouldn't count on it. They probably just leaned into it to get it open."

Everyone was solemn for a moment. Wendy rewound Daisy's abduction one more time and played it at regular speed. Still, everyone was quiet.

Kate clicked her pen, then started writing again. "We have the flower guy, the two younger guys and the guys who hauled her out."

"What about Vikki and whoever she was yelling at?" Lucy said. "I don't trust that girl."

"They are up for the Newcomer of the Year award," Adrienne said. "It's worth 25 large."

"Wow!" Vivian said. "That ain't no chump change. That's a big deal."

Al tapped the table. "It's a lot of money, but it's all about the prestige for these girls. The winner will make thousands more on the road all year. Big demand for her shows."

"Cha-ching! Sounds like motive to me," Vivian said.

Kate underlined Vikki's name on her napkin. "We need to let Antonio know."

"He's a good detective. I guarantee he already knows all of this and more," Adrienne said.

Kate clicked her pen again. "Shouldn't there be video of the valet area or parking lot? We have video of the back."

Al shook his head. "Two of the monitors were black, which makes me think a coupla cameras are out. It's gotta be the parking lot and the valet."

Everyone groaned.

"I imagine Gino's going to get some shit from the cops for that," Al said.

Lucy snapped. "Oh, wait a second. The gypsy lady."

"What?" Adrienne asked.

"She said Daisy's job would put her at risk, or in danger, or something like that. I can't remember exactly. But we should go find her."

Vivian was doubtful. "I don't know. That's pretty vague."

"She was right about you, wasn't she?" Wendy asked.

Vivian looked down at the ground, then nodded her head.

Al called for the car, and soon Tony pulled up and the group piled in.

"Can we drive by the gypsy lady's corner, see if she's around?" Lucy asked.

"Absolutely," Al said. "Tell Tony where."

Tony drove around the Quarter a bit, going down Royal and Bourbon and back and forth on side streets, but they didn't see the fortune-teller, so Tony dropped the girls at their hotel.

Wendy got out of the limo, then turned back to Adrienne. "Get the scoop from Antonio in the morning and give us a shout. We'd like to help all we can."

Adrienne pointed her blinged-out finger at her. "I'm on it."

" 'Night!" the girls called as Tony shut the door, then they went up to their room.

"I can't believe this happened," Vivian said, sitting on the bed.

Lucy poked her head from around the corner of the bathroom, rubbing makeup remover on her eyes. "I think it was that Trikki bitch. Did you see the way she looked at us?"

Wendy pulled off her shoes. "She could just be a really big bitch."

"I don't know. There's a lot riding on winning," Kate said.

"I'm too tired to think about it anymore," Vivian said, lying back on her pillow. "And yet, I'm wired. I hate this feeling."

Lucy emerged from the bathroom. "Next."

Vivian got up and grabbed her jammies. "I don't care if y'all come in. I'm running a hot bath." She went in and started the water. Kate and Wendy came in together and did their nighttime things. Vivian watched as Wendy removed her contacts. "I don't know how you do that. I could never stick my finger in my eyeball like that."

"Eh, it's no biggie. I'd rather stick my finger in my eye to take out a contact than wear glasses all day."

Vivian shuddered. "Twenty-twenty, baby. At least for now."

"Just you wait. I hear at 40 you'll wake up and need bifocals." Wendy said and shut the door behind her. Then she opened it again. "Enjoy your soak."

Vivian undressed and stepped into the hot, bubbly water. It took her a second to sink down into it, but she eventually acclimated. She squeezed out a washcloth, leaned back and placed it over her face.

I wonder what the kids did today? I hope Rick remembered to give Audrey her allergy medicine. He always forgets shit like that. And it's not like that bitch is going to help with anything like that. She took a deep breath, enjoying the warm humidity of the washcloth. *Thank goodness I know where they are at least and that they're safe. But poor Daisy. I can't even imagine what she's going through. Or Jason, or her family. It's unbelievable.*

Vivian dipped the washcloth back into the steaming water, squeezed and reapplied it to her face. She sunk a little lower in the tub, her blonde curls falling into the water. *We've got to help.*

After a cry and a 20-minute soak, she got out and finished getting ready for sleep. The room was dark as she made her way to the bed where Lucy was snuggly tucked away. Vivian tried to get in without disturbing her. Lucy didn't move.

As she lay there, thoughts of Daisy popped in and out of her mind. She finally reached for her phone and texted Jason.

Any updates? Any news? We're here for you.

She put her phone on vibrate and placed it on the nightstand, feeling a little better. She heard Kate mumbling and then say, "I've missed you."

Vivian couldn't help but smile as she drifted off.

16

Day 3

Vivian stirred at the noise of her phone buzzing, indicating a text message. She started to roll over and ignore it but then thought it might be Jason responding to her message from the night before. Her eyes still closed, she fumbled on the nightstand for the phone. Jason.

> **no ransom, no calls. no word. this is BULLSHIT.
> they r moving n slow motion. pissing me off.**

Vivian:
> **We'll work to get updates from Adrienne. Hang in there!**

Jason:
> **called n da troops. family, friends, fans
> who will get shit done. have to find her.**

Vivian placed the phone on the nightstand and kicked back the covers as Kate emerged from the bathroom holding a coffee cup. "Wasn't expecting to see you up so early."

"I wasn't expecting to be, but I just got a text from Jason. He's ticked off and calling everyone he knows to help."

Wendy removed her sleep mask and sat up. "Maybe we should Google those other two missing girls?"

"Great idea," Kate said as she set her coffee down. "Let me run downstairs and get a paper."

Lucy plumped her pillow behind her, pulled her phone from underneath it and started searching. Wendy got out her laptop and connected to Wi-Fi.

70

Vivian clicked on the TV, found local news and put it on mute. A sports guy was talking Saints, so she clicked around. Nothing. "Y'all found anything yet?"

"Here's a story from a week ago, but it doesn't say much," Lucy said. "Looks like the other two worked at different clubs, one out by the airport and another in the Lower Ninth. The first girl, Lisa Miller, was white, 26, disappeared almost four weeks ago. The other, Simone Hitchens, was black, 31, and went missing a week and a half ago after her shift." Lucy showed the pictures of the girls.

"Any description of a suspect?" Vivian asked.

"Not yet. Says no witnesses."

Kate came back through the door carrying the *Times-Picayune*. They caught her up on the story as she flipped through the paper. "I can't believe this. Daisy's disappearance is buried on page six. Whatever happened to 'if it bleeds it leads'?"

"What's it say?" Vivian asked. "Read it out loud."

"The headline is 'Third dancer missing,' " Kate read, then continued. "Daisy Easley is the third exotic dancer to go missing in less than a month. Easley, in town for a competition, was taken from the French House early this morning. Police believe the kidnapping could be related to the disappearances of two local dancers and are looking for links in the cases."

Groans.

Wendy pulled up a video clip of the early-morning local news. The girls hovered around her computer as it played.

The reporter stood outside the French House giving a brief statement about this being the third dancer missing within a month, but this time from the warehouse district. His white teeth were a stark contrast to the predawn darkness behind him.

"Police are giving out few details at this point, but the tip line is open. Police hope someone knows something that will lead to the perpetrator."

The screen flashed with the phone number.

"We'll share more details as they become available. Back to you, Becky."

"Really? That's it?" Vivian said when the video stopped. "That was 30 seconds."

"And we didn't find much on the other two girls at all," Wendy said and closed her laptop.

Kate said, "I don't want to freak y'all out any more than you're already freaked out, but I had one of my dreams last night."

Lucy got up and stretched. "Which dead relative visited you?"

"Aunt Mimi. She was always an eccentric one."

"Did she tell you where Daisy is?" Wendy asked.

Kate reached for the notepad on the nightstand. "Not exactly, but I wrote it down. Aunt Mimi held my hand and looked me in the eye, then said, 'Don't be tricked. Flower petals will float and fly. You must look through the dense forest to see into the mirrors.' "

"What the hell does that mean?" Wendy asked. "I appreciate your relatives' help and all, but couldn't they be more specific? This ain't a Nancy Drew novel."

Kate shrugged. "I know. They just don't work that way."

Vivian reached for Kate's note and ripped it off the pad. "Let's think about this."

Kate pointed to the paper. "Obviously the tricked is Trikki Vikki. But does it mean that she's tricking us, or to forget her as a suspect?"

"I don't know, but at this point I don't think we can rule her out," Vivian said. "What about the float and fly?"

Wendy cleared her throat. "I hate to be negative, but it sounds like Daisy's going to die. Like maybe her soul flies away?"

"Or she's floating down the river or in the lake," Kate said.

"Let's not think that way," Vivian said, then scratched out the "die" she had just written on the notepad.

Lucy stood up. "I think the dense forest is that freak-show Hairy Harry. I mean, come on. I've never seen that much hair on any mammal, and I used to work at a vet's office!"

"I can't figure out the mirror thing," Kate said. "I've been thinking about it since I got up, and I got nothin'."

They all pondered that for a minute. Lucy spoke up. "Is there a place here that has a lot of mirrors? I haven't noticed anything out of the ordinary, and I pay attention because it's kinda what I do." Lucy was an interior designer in Boulder, Co., where the renovation market was booming.

Everyone was quiet. Vivian slammed the pen down. "We aren't going to figure it out sitting around here. I'm getting dressed. Let's go grab some breakfast and we'll call Adrienne. See if she has any updates from her brother."

"We need to find out more about the other cases, too," Wendy said.

The girls got ready quickly, dressing in capris and skirts, short-sleeve blouses and tank tops, then headed over to Stanley's on Jackson Square for brain food.

They each hopped on a stool at the counter and ordered after perusing the menu. Lucy got the Breaux Bridge Breakfast with boudin, ham, eggs, cheese and Creole hollandaise. Wendy ordered the Bananas Foster French Toast complete with ice cream on top. Vivian played it safe with the Stanley

Classic — scrambled eggs, bacon, Creole potatoes and toast. Kate went out on a limb, rather leg, Eggs Stella — cornmeal-crusted soft-shelled crab with eggs, Canadian bacon and Creole Hollandaise on an English Muffin.

"I'm covering lots of culture with this breakfast."

Vivian couldn't help herself. "Stelllllllaaaaaaaa!!!"

The girls cracked up laughing. A few minutes later, breakfast was served, and everyone was quiet. Vivian finally threw in her napkin and reached for her phone. "Time to call Adrienne."

Adrienne picked up on the first ring. "Hey, V."

"Hey, A. Anything from Antonio? I heard from Jason this morning and he's pissed. Thinks the cops aren't working hard enough."

"I know it's tough for him, but believe me, they're working. Antonio only slept two hours last night. I'm sure they're not able to tell Jason all the details of the investigation." She paused for a moment, then said, "I do have some news, though. Remember the fight at the club? While Bruno was dragging their asses outside, two guys slipped backstage. Antonio thinks it's the same two who took her out the back but he can't be 100 percent sure."

A chill ran down Vivian's spine. "Do the police know who they are or how to find them?"

"Antonio said they reviewed the video from the front door and haven't been able to put anything together."

"Shit," Vivian said. "I hope there's something on the video that connects."

Adrienne sighed. "I know, honey. And you can bet if there's something to find, Antonio will find it. They're doing a recreation of the crime scene today with the club's video system. They use stand-ins, then compare to the original video so they can get a better idea of the height and weight of the kidnappers."

"That's smart." Vivian could hear Al in the background.

"Al wants you to know that he's got his feelers out, too. He's meeting some associates later at Mosca's to get the lowdown. Gino's pretty pissed and these guys are good at getting information."

"Sounds good. I don't know what we're doing today, but we're going to do something to help. We watched a news story this morning about the two kidnappings. Got any news there?"

"Not much, Antonio's being pretty tight-lipped. He did say that the bouncer saw the second girl leaving the club *voluntarily* in a newer, gray Mustang. They're not even convinced she has been kidnapped, but her family is pushing for an investigation. Unfortunately, there are thousands of gray Mustangs in New Orleans and not much else to go on."

"At least it's something, and good for her family for pushing."

"Okay, listen, you girls be safe and try to have some fun while you're at it."

"Always." Click. Vivian turned on her stool to face her friends and relayed the conversation. "So other than keeping our eyes peeled for gray Mustangs, what are we going to do today to help?"

Wendy stood up and rubbed her belly. "I basically had dessert for breakfast, so whatever we're doing, I need to walk. Where are the notes from Kate's dream?"

Vivian pulled them out of her blue-jean-skirt pocket. "Since we don't know whether the cryptic dream told us to trust Vikki or not, I guess we go with not and look into her."

"We need to see if she's dancing at Gino's again or anywhere else," Wendy said.

Kate whipped out her phone. "I bet she has a Facebook page. I'll look her up."

While Kate worked on that, Vivian asked, "Y'all have any thoughts on the float and fly thing?"

Wendy and Lucy looked at each other. Lucy answered, "I'm afraid nothing that doesn't involve Daisy floating down the Mississippi."

"Eeew. Okay, moving on. What about flower petals?"

"Well, her name is Daisy. And she did get flowers," Kate said. "I think we find out who delivered them."

Lucy snapped her fingers. "I saw on the envelope it said 'Louie's' and there was a flower that looked like a trumpet. I thought it was pretty clever."

"Good memory," Vivian said.

"Let me look them up."

Kate hopped off her stool. "I found Trikki Vikki's page. She'll be swinging around a pole tonight at Kitty City on Bourbon. I think we go!"

"Definitely!" Vivian said.

Wendy looked up at the ceiling. "Oh my god, that sounds trashy."

"Come on, we gotta do it for Daisy!" Vivian said.

Wendy picked up her coffee cup and offered a toast. "To Kitty City we'll go. For Daisy!"

17

Louie's Flowers opened at 10, and since it was a quarter 'til, the girls decided to take the streetcar to Uptown. They caught the Riverfront car to Canal, then walked the few blocks to the St. Charles line.

Kate snapped pictures as they passed the historic homes, most built in the mid-1800s and survivors of many a hurricane. The oak trees along the esplanade were draped with Mardi Gras beads, and the yards were immaculately landscaped.

"Doesn't Anne Rice live around here?" Lucy asked.

Wendy shook her head. "She doesn't anymore. I was here 10 years ago for Mardi Gras and passed her house on the way to a parade, though it was more like a mansion."

"I wonder if Harry Connick, Jr. lives close-by?" Kate said as she took another picture. "He is one very talented guy."

"Wouldn't surprise me," Wendy said. "He's on my list of people I'd like to meet."

"Mine, too," Lucy said. "He's cute."

Vivian agreed and laughed and tagged them all on Facebook as they passed Tulane University. "Getting edumacated."

Wendy pulled the signal cord on the streetcar. The driver stopped and they hopped out on Hillary Street, then walked a few blocks to Maple and found Louie's Flowers.

Vivian opened the door and walked in and stopped, breathing in the fresh blossoms.

A petite brunette met them near the front of the store. Her name tag read Sonya. "Can I help you with something in particular?"

They looked back and forth at each other until Kate spoke up. "A friend of ours received a flower delivery from your shop last night, and we just wanted to inquire as to who sent it."

Sonya glanced at the balding man behind the counter perfecting an arrangement of tulips, calla lilies and baby blue hydrangeas.

He looked up. "The delivery to the French House?"

"That's the one."

He walked out from behind the counter and put his arm around Sonya's shoulders. "We've already talked to the cops about this."

"We just want to know who sent it," Wendy said.

Vivian put her hands together in front of her chest, begging. "We won't share it with anyone. We're just trying to find our friend."

"Please," Lucy and Wendy pleaded simultaneously.

Sonya shrugged and looked at her beau. "Aw, go ahead, Larry."

He sighed. "Oh, all right. The guy's name was Harry Houghton. He had a very specific order, and he wanted it delivered at a very specific time. Kinda weird, but he paid in cash so I didn't ask any questions."

"What was his request?" Kate asked.

Larry went back behind the counter and got on the computer. He pulled up the order and read it to the girls. "Petite pink calla lilies, white Oriental lilies and 20-inch stem, lavender roses." He looked up from the screen and shook his head. "He insisted on the 20-inch roses. It was weird."

"Is there anything else you can tell us about the order?" Vivian asked.

Larry glanced back at the screen. "He wanted it delivered at 10:30 on the dot."

"He instructed us to double the driver's tip if it was delivered within three minutes of that," Sonya added, joining Larry behind the counter.

"Our delivery guy is in high school and was downright excited to be delivering to the French House. He was on time," Larry said and grinned.

Sonya bumped him with her hip and tsked him.

"What? He's going to find out about these things one way or another."

"Not on our time. I'm friends with his mother, for god's sake! If Pat found out she'd be madder 'n a mudbug in a pot."

"We appreciate you talking to us," Vivian said and took a step toward the door. "We're going to do our best to help find her."

Sonya handed her a card. "If y'all need anything, call us."

"We'll do what we can," Larry said with a warm smile.

***

Daisy could hear a television coming from another room and faint music on the street. She lay in bed with her eyes closed, slowly waking up, trying to place the day and where she was. Her head felt like 20 pounds of sludge.

French House last night, night off tonight, Houston tomorrow. She felt for Jason in the bed beside her, not finding him, and opened her eyes. The floor-length, beige curtains were closed but light crept in around the edges.

76

An oversized armoire held a television and a desk with a bottle of water and bowl of fruit sat in a corner. She turned her head. A blue-and-tan-striped chair was in another corner, and the clock on the nightstand read 12:08. The closet and bathroom doors were closed, as was the door to the room. *Where the fuck am I? Where's Bam-Bam?*

"Jason!" she called but got no response. "Jason!" She yelled louder.

She thought back to last night. *I danced, showered, got ready and ... think! What happened after that? Did we go out?* She looked under the covers and was relieved to see she still wore the clothes from last night. She turned over on the bed and her hair fell around her face. *What the?* She pulled her hair in front of her eyes, running it through her fingers. What was supposed to be fiery red was now pitch black. *What the fuck is going on?*

The door opened and a tall, muscular, olive-skinned man wearing black slacks and a crisp, white shirt closed the door and walked into the room.

Daisy flipped over and pulled the covers up to her chin. "Who the hell are you? Where's Jason?"

***

After leaving Louie's Flowers, the girls ventured out onto Maple Street to regroup.

Kate pointed down the street. "Coffee. Corner. Let's go." She led the way.

They picked a table on the wraparound front porch and ordered a round of coffees, except for Vivian who got a bottle of water. "I need to hydrate."

A cool breeze rustled the leaves in the huge trees and the humidity wasn't too stifling. A few other customers, some alone reading or working on laptops, occupied the other tables on the porch.

Wendy poured milk into her cup. "We didn't learn much from the flower shop. What next?"

"What are we doing here?" Lucy asked, fiddling with her spoon. "We're not the police, and if anyone's going to find her it's going to be them, not us. I'm not sure we're qualified."

Kate dumped sugar into her double espresso. "We may not be the most qualified, we may not have a badge, but dammit, we're smart girls and I had a dream. I know it means something!"

"Way to get fired up, Kate!" Vivian gave her a high-five. "Let's call Adrienne again, see if anything has happened since this morning."

"And I think we look into that Hairy Harry some more," Kate said and took a big drink. "I don't trust anyone with that many overactive follicles. Maybe he hired those two sleazeballs who took her." Kate looked down at her empty drink. "That was good."

"There's a bookstore across the street that I'd like to run in," Wendy said. "Let's hop over there before we look for follicle man."

Vivian pulled her phone out and dialed as they walked to the Maple Street Book Shop. Adrienne answered on the third ring, so Vivian sat on a rocker on the front porch while the other girls went inside.

"Hey, it's Viv. We were just checking in."

"Hold on a sec."

Vivian heard shuffling and noise in the background. After a minute Adrienne came back.

"Sorry, we're at Mosca's talkin' to the guys about what happened. They're on it. In fact, one of them knows the lead detective on one of the missing girls. Gonna get us some details. What are you up to?"

"We just went to Louie's Flowers. Didn't learn jack other than Harry paid in cash and extra for the guy to deliver at exactly 10:30. Now we're trying to figure out what to do next. You have anything else?"

"I spoke to Antonio about 30 minutes ago. Based on the crime scene recreation, they've determined that the kidnappers are both about 6 feet tall, around 220 pounds, possibly Hispanic. They've pretty much dismissed the two young guys we saw on the video who were trying to get in. They still want to find them and talk to them, though."

"How are they going to find them?"

"I don't know, but they got Harry's cell number off the flower receipt. They've tried to locate him with that, but so far they haven't gotten any pings. But they got a warrant and are going through his life, including his financials."

"And?"

"And guess who withdrew $20,000 two weeks ago?"

Vivian stopped rocking. "No way. Really?"

"Yep."

"That's a chunk o' change."

"Yes it is. Antonio hasn't figured out what he bought with it, so it definitely falls into the suspicious category."

"Hell yeah, it does."

"Other than that, the guy is pretty much a loner. Never married. No kids. He's a facilities manager with an oil company and he evidently missed a meeting today for some big deal they're putting together. I'm not sure who wants to find him more, his boss or the police."

"Sounds like a super freak to me. Where's he staying?"

"Hmmmm, Antonio will kill me. Besides, the cops are all over that place."

"Oh, come on. We won't interfere." *Too much.*

Adrienne hesitated, then said, "It's the Roosevelt Hotel, but you didn't hear that from me!"

"We'll be good, I promise."

They both laughed at that.

"This is really great info, Adrienne. Thank you."

"If you see that hairy beast, call the cops. Don't approach him. I don't want to fish you out of the Mississippi."

18

Vivian went inside the Maple Street Book Shop and found Lucy at the cookbooks and Wendy in history. "Where's Kate?"

"I think she's in children's," Wendy said.

"Lead the way, I've got news."

She followed Wendy through the old house, the wooden floors creaking with every step. A thin man with gray hair and black-rimmed glasses rounded a bookshelf and asked if they needed help with anything.

Wendy held out *Fabulous New Orleans*. "I think we're good, but I'll be gettin' this in a few minutes."

He took the book from her. "It'll be at the front when you're ready."

They walked to the back of the house and found Kate bawling.

"Oh my gosh, what's wrong?" Wendy asked, pulling a small tissue packet from her purse and handing it over.

Kate took the pack, then held up a book entitled "Love You Forever." On the cover, a gleeful toddler proudly held a piece of toilet paper over his head. "This book is so poignant. The little boy grows up and the mom... the mom..." She burst into tears.

"Boy, you are trying to have a baby, aren't you?" Vivian gently took the book from Kate and placed it on the shelf. "It's a wonderful story, one of my kids' favorites, and they make me read it way too often, but there's no need to get upset."

Lucy, Miss Say No To Having Kids, which sometimes equated to no sympathy, took control. "We need to focus here. Vivian got some info from Adrienne. What is it?"

Vivian patted Kate's arm, then told them about the phone call. The connection with the murder case, the big cash withdrawal and where Harry was staying.

Lucy, phone always in hand, looked up the Roosevelt Hotel. "We need a cab."

"I'll go buy my book," Wendy said. Kate tried to give her the tissue pack back, but Wendy waved her off. "Keep it, I've got another."

As they left the room filled with hundreds of children's books, Kate glanced back, teary-eyed, at the little boy on the cover.

"No more double espressos for you." Vivian gave Kate a little squeeze.

***

The well-dressed stranger sat on the chair and calmly looked at Daisy.

"Who are you?" she yelled.

He threaded his fingers together and said with a Middle-Eastern accent, "There is no need to yell, Daisy. I will not harm you."

"How do you know my name?"

"You were quite impressive last night. I think you could have won that competition."

Her stomach clenched. "I still plan to win it."

He said nothing.

What's up with this high-rolling asshole? "You still haven't answered me." Daisy gave him her toughest look, the one that makes most men behave.

Someone knocked on the door and a familiar face looked in. "Time to leave."

Where have I seen him?

The man in the chair stood and walked to the end of the bed. "I am Sonu and you are going to be very happy with me. You will see." With that, he left.

She jumped out of bed and ran to the door but it was locked. She banged on it but no one answered.

***

The girls rocked on the porch at Maple Street Book Shop for a few minutes until a cab pulled up to the curb. They hopped in and Lucy told the driver where to go. The drive to the central business district didn't take long, and soon they were walking up to the hotel's entrance.

"What are we going to do in here?" Wendy asked. "We don't know what room he's in."

"I haven't figured that out yet," Vivian said.

Lucy walked toward a sitting area in the lobby. "Let's just hang here and see what happens."

"Or we can ask around," Kate said, looking into the lounge. "Maybe the bartender knows something. Or the door guy."

They sat for a while, people watching. Vivian watched a family with a stroller fumble to get a kid strapped down. She laughed. Apparently that toddler didn't want to be in there. Several businessmen came and went, then she noticed a young, sandy-blond bellman looking at her. The stern look on his face made her feel uncomfortable. She switched seats so that her back was to him. "I wonder if he's an undercover cop," she said, tilting her head back.

"Who?" Lucy said, much too loudly and looking in his direction.

"Shhhhhhhh!" Vivian said, waving to quiet her.

"Who are you talking about?"

Vivian looked up at the ceiling. "The bellman behind me who looks a little too clean-cut."

Lucy looked at him. "Oh, he's cute." She sat up straight, sticking her chest out. "He can frisk me any time."

Kate ran her fingers through her hair and casually used her pointer. "And what about that guy busing tables in the bar? That's totally a cop."

The girls casually looked that way and all agreed. He had that look. Cop.

Wendy looked toward the front door. "Uh oh."

Vivian glanced up and locked eyes with Detective Leffall, who made a beeline for them. He had on a navy blazer, navy slacks and a bad tie.

"Girls," he said, hands on hips. "You shouldn't be here."

"We're just relaxing. You know, enjoying the A/C," Vivian said, smiling sweetly. "Nice tie."

He ran his hand down the tie. "My kids gave me this." He gave her a stern look. "You don't understand, this guy could be dangerous. You need to leave."

The girls accepted their fate and stood up.

"We're just trying to help," Kate said.

"I know, but we've got it under control."

The girls shuffled out the front. "Now what?" Wendy asked.

Vivian looked at the time on her phone. "It's beer thirty."

Lucy snapped her fingers. "I concur. Let's go find a three-for-one."

Wendy held up her 300-page book. "I'd like to drop this monster off at the hotel."

The girls swung by the Hotel De Lis, freshened up and were walking down Canal Street toward Bourbon Street when Kate pointed. "Look! Gray Mustang!"

The car, full of squealing teenage girls and blaring hip-hop, turned right in front of them. The rear window had big white lettering that said, "Spring Break NOLA here we come!"

"I somehow don't think they abducted anyone," Vivian said, dancing to their music a little. "I remember my spring break days, headin' to the beach on South Padre Island."

After they thought about how long it had been since any of them had had a spring break, everyone decided hurricanes from Pat O'Brien's were in order.

They walked in the main entrance off St. Peter and passed the main bar and the piano bar on their way to the courtyard. The centerpiece was a large fountain shooting blood-red flames, making the water look like their hurricanes.

They took a seat and ordered a round from a girl with hair almost as red as Daisy's.

Drinks arrived and they cheersed to Daisy's safe return.

The waitress delivered a tray of food to the table next to them.

"They serve food here?" Lucy asked.

Wendy finished a sip. "I've been here a million times and I never knew."

Vivian laughed. "You've always been too focused on these." She held up her drink and they clinked glasses.

They sat for a while, watching the fountain erupt and people get stupider and stupider.

After the last, long sweet sip, Vivian said, "I've gotta get some souvenirs for the kidlets."

"It's not like there's a shortage of shops," Wendy said.

Lucy set down her big hurricane glass. "Yeah, there's a place a couple of doors down."

"First, I think we should go to where we had our psychic reading and see if maybe that gypsy lady is there," Kate said. "If she's not, I think we hit the voodoo shop."

Vivian didn't like the sound of that. "Why do you think the gypsy can help?"

"Some of them have a gift," Kate said, then she looked at Vivian. "You, of all people, should be more open to this. She was spot-on about Rick, even though you didn't want to hear it at the time."

"It scared the hell out of me — she was able to see it so easily. So as long as you keep her and the voodoo people away from me, I'll go."

They finished their drinks, then headed toward the gypsy lady's spot. She wasn't there, so Lucy walked up to the door guy at a nearby club and asked about her.

"She's just here once in a while," he answered. "The cops run her off."

Disappointed, the girls walked up Bourbon to Marie Laveau's House of Voodoo.

Vivian's stomach flipped at the idea of walking in the door. "Y'all go ahead. I'm going to stay right here."

Lucy decided to hang with her, so Kate and Wendy went to see what they could find out.

The smell of incense hit Wendy and made her cough. Skeleton masks glared from the walls, and voodoo dolls hung on chains from the ceiling. A bookcase lined one entire wall.

A tall, black woman wearing a silk purple muumuu laced with gold thread and a matching head scarf came out from behind a black velvet curtain. Her bracelets jangled as she walked, and the red gem in the eye sockets on her skull ring reflected off the light. The woman's right eye stared right at Wendy, while her left eye wandered off to the side.

The sight of the googly eye unnerved Wendy. *This lady has a gift, all right. The gift of freaking people out!*

Kate took a step back as the woman said to Wendy, "I see you are in turmoil. Come, I will help you." Then she walked back behind the curtain.

Wendy gave Kate a look and they both followed.

"I'm not in turmoil," Wendy said. "It's a friend of ours. She's in trouble and we need to find her."

"Your friend is at peace," Googly-eye said.

Kate drew in a quick breath. "Are you sure? The friend we're looking for is Daisy."

The woman sat for a moment nodding and clicking her fingernails on the table. "Daisy, yes. The flower. Hmmmm." She waved her hands over the crystal ball sitting in front of her. "Yes, I see her, she's in trouble. She needs help."

Wendy looked at Kate out of the corner of her eye. Kate's eyes were narrowed and her chin was down.

I'm going to call her bluff, Wendy thought. "Is she still in Mexico?"

The lady gracefully moved her hands around the ball, then in a circular pattern in front of her. "Yes, I see sombreros and maracas. She is definitely on a sandy beach. She's sick, though, holding her stomach."

Wendy, ready to walk out, said, "Oh no, Montezuma's revenge."

The woman held her arms out wide in a V above her head. "Yes! That's it! Revenge!"

Kate and Wendy stood simultaneously. Kate threw down a five. "Not a lot we can do about that. Thanks for helping us with our turmoil."

Googly-eye called after them as Wendy pushed through the curtain. "But wait, let me do individual readings. Only $25!"

"We'll pass," Wendy said over her shoulder as they ran past the skeletons and out of the store.

19

Daisy searched for a phone but found only an empty wall jack. She tried the two windows in the room but they were sealed shut. There was no balcony, and the street was at least 12 stories below. Her fight or flight instinct kicked in. Pulling out every drawer, she went through the bathroom, but couldn't find any sharp instruments to pick the lock. She kicked at the door but it didn't budge. The desk and nightstand were clear of pen and paper. No writing a note and sticking it in the window. She grabbed the desk lamp. It wasn't very heavy, but it could be used as a weapon in some capacity. *What else?*

All the while, she concentrated, not on what Sonu had said but on the face of the other man. She had seen him, but it was foggy and she couldn't remember where. She gave up her escape attempt for the moment and sat at the desk. She checked the seal on the water, cracked it open and took a sip. Then it hit her.

Pink martini. Desert Glitter. He fucking roofied me! She'd known others who'd been slipped the date-rape drug. *I shouldn't have taken that stupid drink.*

She looked in the closet and found several Middle Eastern-style, long-sleeved dresses and a black burqa neatly folded. She flung the garments to the floor but did not find anything useful to help escape.

How the hell am I going to get out of here?

A glimmer of silver caught her eye, and she knelt to look under the bed. Her Shoe-Be-Do shoe lay on its side, wooden heel just asking to be beaten into the window. After several blows to the glass, nothing happened except to flatten out the little plastic tip on the bottom of the heel.

Must be some special kind of glass to protect against hurricanes. Or prevent jumpers. Dammit!

Flinging the shoe to the floor, she walked into the bathroom and took a closer look at her reflection. Her face had been scrubbed of makeup. She touched the few freckles across her nose, then looked at her hair. The black dye completely covered her red. Not a speck remained.

She closed her eyes and sank to the floor in heaving sobs.

***

"What a load," Kate said, frustrated. "Obviously that Voodoo woman didn't have the gift. Or any gift other than bullshit."

Lucy and Vivian stood across the street next to a walk-up daiquiri stop. "Whatcha drinkin' there?" Wendy asked.

Vivian swirled her frozen turquoise drink around, then took a big sip. "Mmmm, it's a blue Hawaiian, and it's fantab. Want a sip?" She took another big drink, then got a brain freeze. "Ouuu! My dent!"

Vivian had an indention in the middle of her forehead that was only noticeable in pictures, especially if there was a flash. Everyone else in the picture would look great, but she'd end up with a glowing circle on her head.

Kate walked to the counter. "After that experience, I could use one of those."

"Guess it didn't go well," Lucy said, swirling her drink with the straw.

"No, it did not," Wendy answered. "The lady was just makin' stuff up as she went along. She said Daisy was in Mexico and had the runs!"

"Maybe she meant she's on the run in Mexico," Vivian said, though she didn't really think that.

"No, I fed her Mexico and Montezuma's revenge. She took it from there. It was a joke."

Kate turned around sucking on a purple concoction. She smacked her lips. "This is yum-ola."

"If y'all are gonna be drinkin' those, I vote for some food," Wendy said, then grabbed Vivian's blue drink and took a sip. "Mmmm, that is tasty."

"Hang on to that while I text Adrienne and tell her we're going to Kitty City tonight. See if they want to join the fun."

They sipped and walked a few blocks and saw a place on the corner at Dauphine called Deanie's Seafood.

"I could go for some fried shrimp," Vivian said. "Let's give it a whirl."

There was no wait and the girls were seated right away at a bench that lined a large aquarium displaying glass fish, plants, crabs, shrimp and egrets.

They munched on the boiled potatoes that were served instead of bread, and ordered an array of shrimp. Fried, barbecued, blackened, stuffed. By the end, they were stuffed, too.

Kate put down her fork. "That hit the spot. We've got time to kill before Trikki comes on at Kitty City."

"I'm not looking forward to this," Wendy said. "We better find out some good info on this chick."

"I have a feeling we will," Kate said.

Vivian reached for her phone. "Let me call Jason, see if he has any updates." He answered on the second ring. "Hey, Jason, anything new?"

"I think the cops have finally ruled me out as a suspect. They're trying to find that dipshit Harry and now they're looking into Vikki, too. Turns out she's got two brothers in town who are big like the two fuckers who took Daisy. They're trying to get warrants to look at Vikki's financials along with her brothers and boyfriend."

"We're going to Kitty City tonight. Kate had a dream and we thought we should check Vikki out."

"If the brothers are there, call the cops, then call me, then get the hell out of there."

"Ouuu, watching their sister strip? That would be gross, but don't worry about us, we'll be on guard. Is there anything we can do for you?"

"No, Daisy's family should be here first thing in the morning. My mom and dad will be here on the red-eye tonight, and the guys from my band are all on their way. They live local and we have a pretty big following. I've been doing a vlog and everyone is sharing it on Facebook, Twitter and among the music community. People are coming in from all over the country to look for her."

"I'm glad you're pushing the issue. Based on what little we've seen in the media, these other two girls haven't gotten much attention, and Daisy needs all of our help. But she's going to be okay, hang in there."

"Thanks, Vivian. I've also gotten a local printer to donate 10,000 fliers. We're going to plaster this town with her picture."

"Damn, you've been busy!"

"She's my everything. I'm going to find her. In the meantime, you guys stay out of trouble."

"We'll be fine. We use the buddy system!" That got a small laugh out of him and they disconnected.

Vivian shared the conversation with the girls. "He's on a mission and sounds fired up. He has a purpose."

She paid their dinner tab with their trust fund card and they headed back to Bourbon. A few doors down was a souvenir shop.

"Let me run in here and knock out gifts for the kids," Vivian said.

The doors of the shop were lined with funny T-shirts. "I got Bourbon faced on Shit Street." "FEMA – Fix Everything My Ass." "I put Ketchup on my Ketchup."

Vivian took a minute to read a few before moving to the kids T-shirts. She didn't find anything for her kids, so she went back outside empty handed.

"Strike out?" Kate asked.

"Nothing reached out and grabbed me. Gotta keep looking."

"There's a neat shop on Royal that I've been to before, Forever New

Orleans. Let's go there," Wendy said and led the way.

"So how are things with the kids, Rick, the…uh hum…marriage?" Lucy asked.

Vivian threw her head back. "Uhhhh. It's stupid. The SPS interjects herself into everything. I swear she goes to the kids' activities just to make herself look like the good stepmom. What she looks like is an idiot. A rude idiot, at that."

"Stupid swimming pool slut," Lucy said.

"What do you mean?" Kate asked Vivian.

"She came to Audrey and Lauren's dance recital, but left early. She came to the Audrey's PTA performance, but looked beyond bored. I seriously think she's going just to show the world 'I'm here so suck it.' "

"Is she nice to the kids?" Wendy asked.

"They don't really talk about her, which I guess means she's not beating them or anything like that."

Kate gasped. "You don't think?"

"No, Rick wouldn't let that happen."

Kate was relieved. "Okay, good."

They arrived at Forever New Orleans which had an excellent, kid-friendly section. Vivian picked out a cute *Alex the Alligator* book for Ben, a stuffed sea turtle for Olivia, hair bows with crawfish on them for Lauren, and a Mardi Gras mask decorated with peacock feathers for Audrey. "The kids are going to love these."

"Good job, momma," Wendy said. "I was thinking about getting something for Lizzie."

Wendy's niece, Lizzie, had been diagnosed with a rare form of adrenal cancer at six-months old and not given much of a chance to live. Her parents didn't accept that fate and took her to the Burzynski Clinic where she had been getting Antineoplaston treatment for the past two and a half years.

"How's she doing?" Kate asked.

Wendy smiled and showed them a picture. "The tumors in her liver are gone and there are only two left in her lungs, but they're shrinking. She's going to beat this!"

Lucy took Wendy's phone and enlarged the picture. "Wow, she looks great. Doesn't even look sick."

Wendy looked at the picture again. "She doesn't act it either. Into everything." She turned her attention back to Vivian. "What do you suggest for her?"

"Look at the little book I bought." Vivian pushed a lever on the side of the alligator head at the top of the book and its mouth opened and closed. "Hours of entertainment."

"Special book for a special niece. Sold."

20

S hopping out of the way, Vivian, Wendy, Lucy and Kate walked to Bourbon and down a couple of blocks, and there it was. Kitty City. Hot pink neon lights reflected off the murky puddles in the street.

"This isn't going to be one of those live sex act places, is it?" Lucy asked.

"Guess we're about to find out," Vivian said.

Standing outside the door and trying to lure in dollar bills was a dancer in high-heeled, black patent leather boots with a string around her neck, the middle of her back, top of her waist, around her thighs and down her crack. She turned to greet the girls when they walked up, revealing the thin strap in front, barely covering her nipples, and a small flap of fabric covering her coochie.

"We love the ladies, no escort needed," String girl said and handed them a postcard of Trikki Vikki. "We have a special treat tonight, but there is a two-drink minimum."

Vivian said thanks while Lucy snickered and Wendy started to laugh, then tried to cover it up with a cough.

Once inside, they found a table close to the stage. The current feature, a spiky-haired, flat-chested girl, looked stoned. She was using the pole more to hold herself up than to dance.

Vivian couldn't help but think of Josh Weathers' song, "What Does It Mean To You," as she looked around. His lyrics rang true for the girls here, *You know your momma raised ya better*. None of them looked happy to be there. *Eight hundred dollars a night, opens up your days. And you got them bills you just...got to pay. Brand new Benz sittin...in the driveway*, but that's probably why they were.

Vivian laughed to herself. *I doubt these girls are pulling in $300 a night, much less $800.* Her attention was diverted by the waitress in a red pleather dress with keyhole cutouts around the navel and cleavage. The girls ordered a round of beers, and Vivian looked at the waitress like she must have misunderstood the order when she set glasses not much bigger than a shot glass in front of them.

"Sixteen dollars, please," Pleatherette said.

"Uhhh, we ordered four beers," Vivian said.

"Yep, that's it. Sixteen dollars."

The girls paid, shot their beer, then ordered their mandatory second round. Vivian scanned the crowd for big guys. Instead she saw two big girls in matching shirts, Bitch 1 and Bitch 2. They sat stage left and had their attention focused on the stoned dancer. One of them noticed Vivian looking at them and waved.

Vivian gave a hesitant smile.

The music changed to Marcy Playground's "I Smell Sex and Candy." A big-busted, solid black dancer sauntered on stage wearing a candy-striper outfit and carrying an oversized candy cane, the kind in yards around Christmas. She shimmied, swiveled and swung, never dropping her prop.

The Bitches were front and center, ready to give Candy a treat. Bitch 1 was tall, probably 5-9, with dirty blonde hair. She frantically waved a dollar in the air as Candy danced over, removing her striper layer and revealing a G-string as yellow as a banana Laffy Taffy.

Lucy leaned over to Vivian, nodding her head in approval. "You have to admit, that's a good color for her."

Bitch 2 was shorter with dark, country-girl plain Jane hair. She was more discreet with her dollar, gently placing it in Candy's taffy string.

Instead of walking back to their table, the matching Bitch set took the spot next to Vivian and the girls, who all looked at each other and shared a moment of mortification.

It won't last long, Vivian thought.

Bitch 2 leaned over to Vivian. All Vivian could see was the giant cold sore on her lip.

"Hey there, I'm Tereza. This is Susie." Bitch 1 lifted her chin in a nod. "Are you here to see Trikki Vikki?"

"As a matter of fact, we are," Vivian answered, trying to look at her eyes and not her nasty lip. "We saw her last night, too. She's something else."

"Can I buy you a drink?"

Vivian held up her shot glass of beer. "I'm set. Thanks, though."

Bitch 2 rubbed Vivian's arm. "If you change your mind, let me know."

Bitch 1 hit 2's arm. "What the fuck are you doing? Flirting with this straight bitch right in front of me?"

Bitch 2 shoved her chair back, which fell over. "I'll talk to whoever I want to talk to. What's your problem?"

The bouncer was suddenly between them. "That's it. You're out."

Bitch 1's eyes flashed and she shoved her girth against him. "This is bullshit. We haven't done anything. We bought our two stupid drinks."

"Out." The bouncer stood his ground and pointed to the front entrance.

Bitch 2 stormed off and Bitch 1 got in his face. "You're messing with the wrong bitch." She turned and walked out.

At the door, Bitch 1 broadsided a familiar face.

Adrienne shoved her back. "Watch where the fuck you're goin'!"

The bouncer jumped between them and kept shoving the Bitches out the door. Al pulled another table and two chairs over to sit with Vivian and the girls.

"I can't believe I'm in this place," Adrienne said, inspecting the surroundings. "I feel like I should disinfect the seat."

Lucy passed her an antibacterial wipe. "I used one, too."

Adrienne took it and cleaned her hands. "Thanks, sugar."

Vivian took in the sticky residue on their table and cringed, then hugged Adrienne's neck. "So good to see y'all! Thanks for meeting us at this sleazy joint."

Al smirked. "I've been in worse." He looked up at the current feature on stage. "On second thought," he joked.

The stripper was too thin, too drunk and too uncoordinated.

"I think she's the in-between entertainment," Kate said as she finished off her itty-bitty beer.

"We need something better goin' on over here," Al said, looking around for a server. She arrived and he ordered two bottles of champagne. "Don't give me the cheap shit, either."

After the waitress walked off, Wendy asked Al, "Any updates from your friends?"

"Word on the street is there is no word on the street. My guy that knows the lead detective on Simone Hitchens' case got some info, but it's nothing Antonio hasn't told us."

A man emerged from a metallic fringe curtain hanging near the back of the stage and sat down at the table the Bitches had vacated. Vivian immediately recognized him from the security video.

21

Vivian leaned forward at the table at Kitty City, being careful not to lean her arms on the sticky surface, and said as quietly as she could to the girls, Al and Adrienne, "Look who just sat down!" She casually tilted her head toward Trikki Vikki's boyfriend.

Wendy said under her breath, "Vikki must be coming on soon."

Trikki Vikki's boyfriend looked over at Vivian.

They locked eyes and she smiled. *We need this guy.* "Hey there," she said, holding up her tiny beer.

"Hey."

Vivian discreetly pulled her shirt down to flash more cleavage as the waitress poured her a glass of champagne. She waited for Vikki's boyfriend to get his bottle of beer, then she leaned over with her champagne. "I'm Vivian."

"Clint."

She held up her glass to toast his. "To a great show."

He seemed to like that and clinked her glass, then took a long draw. After a moment he said, "You don't seem like the usual crowd."

I need an excuse, quick! Oh! "We work for Gino over at the French House. He's got us scoping new talent."

"This next girl will be the best of the night. Vikki can pull some tricks out of her hat, that's for sure."

"Yeah, we saw her last night at Gino's. She rocked the house."

Clint puffed his chest out. "Yeah, that's my lady."

"Are y'all just passing through town on the exhibition tour?"

"Yeah, Vikki's gonna win that title in Vegas."

"She winning enough to put y'all up somewhere nice while you're here?"

"It's some little place in the Quarter. We only need it to fuuuuh - sleep."

Vivian laughed and toasted him again, then got up. "I hear ya. Be right back." She ran her hand across his shoulders, letting her fingernails tease, and looked at the girls. "Buddy system."

Lucy and Adrienne popped up, then followed her to the back, where the facilities left much to be desired.

"What the hell are you doin' flirting with Trikki Vikki's boyfriend?" Lucy asked. "She'll kill you."

"I'm trying to get some information. They're the enemy, remember. I just want to know where they're staying so we can check it out."

Adrienne checked her lipstick in the mirror. "Antonio will know, but after y'all showed up at Harry's hotel today, he's not going to tell either of us."

"Dammit," Vivian said, using her foot to push open a stall. "I wish I didn't have to go!" Her thighs burned from the hovering. As she washed her hands, she was grateful there was soap in the dispenser.

The three of them went back together, and as Vivian walked through the club she was surprised at the crowd. She did a double take at Antonio sitting at a table, alone, in the far right corner. She instinctively started to wave but Adrienne pulled her hand down.

Vivian pulled her chair closer to Clint as she sat down. "Is Vikki coming on soon?" Before Clint could answer, Gwen Stefani's "Holla Back Girl" started playing.

Trikki Vikki strutted across the stage, hair in pigtails, hot-rod-red lipstick, cheerleading pom-poms in each hand and the little cotton ball kind on top of her high heels. Vivian squeezed Clint's knee. Trikki shot daggers of death at Vivian and threw a pom-pom in front of Clint. He smiled at her and she kept working her act, which included crotch-flaunting back bends and the splits. The song transitioned to Toni Basil's "Oh Mickey, You're So Fine" and the cheerleader act turned into full-blown stripper. The royal blue and red top came off, revealing pasties that shot out confetti.

Vivian laughed and clapped, then rubbed her hand on Clint's thigh. Vikki saw that and ripped her red bloomers off. She had a wardrobe malfunction in the process and ended up yanking her G-string off, too. She picked up the pom-pom from in front of Clint and strategically placed it. She had to drop the prop a few times to swing around the pole, and the tips came flying in. She picked up the cash from the stage floor, waved to the crowd with her free hand, blew some kisses and stomped backstage, her shoe pom-poms flopping.

"Wow!" Vivian said to Clint. "That was even better than last night."

He grinned. "I don't think everything went as planned, but she pulled it off."

Vivian laughed. "That she did!"

The next act came on and Vivian was determined to get some info out of Clint about Daisy. "Did you hear about what happened to that other dancer last night?"

"Yeah, I heard about it." He shrugged.

Vivian shifted in her chair, looking back for Antonio but didn't see him. "I heard it was two guys from the club who took her."

Clint sat back in his chair and took a long drink from his beer. "She probably just took off. Her boyfriend is a dick."

"I don't know, the police are taking it pretty seriously. Aren't you worried about Vikki since they're up for the same award? Maybe there's some crazy guy out there kidnapping dancers."

"I'm not worried at all. Nothing's going to happen to Vik."

The dancer on stage tripped over her giant high heels and did a dive toward their table. Lucy's quick reaction earned her a handful of boob while Al got a crotch full of ice from the champagne bucket. He did manage to save the bottle, though. The poor girl's fall was broken by not only Lucy but their table full of drinks as she ended up across both tables, spread-eagle.

Kate peeled her purse from the sticky floor and looked at Vivian. "That's our cue."

***

Night fell and Daisy's stomach grumbled. She hadn't touched the fruit on the desk or taken another sip from the bottled water, just in case. She had rinsed a glass from the desk in scalding hot water and drunk only tap water all day.

She lay on the bed, scared, mad, bored. Nothing on TV helped to take her mind off the situation. She had the volume cranked up, hoping to draw some attention to the room. Get a noise complaint. She watched the local news that reported about her disappearance, but this only made her more upset. Hearing about the two other girls who were missing freaked her out.

She kept thinking of Jason and how upset he must be, wondering where she was and if she was all right. Her stomach ached from hunger and she eventually cried herself to sleep.

The sound of the TV clicking off woke her.

Sonu set the remote on the nightstand. "I have brought dinner but you are not dressed. Get a shower and change." He indicated one of the dresses on the floor in the closet.

Daisy crossed her arms over her chest and stared at the blank screen. "I'll never put that head-to-toe crap on. Let me go."

He didn't respond to that but said, "It will be easier for you if you do as I wish."

"Why me?"

He ran a finger down her arm.

She jerked away from him. "Don't ever touch me."

He grabbed her chin and turned her head to face him. "I will do what I please." He let go of her and took a few steps toward the door. "I will be back in 15 minutes. If you are dressed, you may eat. If not, you will go hungry."

"Where are the other two girls?"

He didn't answer and left the room.

Daisy didn't move from the bed. She was not going to do what he wanted. She clicked the TV back on and turned up the volume on "Pretty Woman."

Fifteen minutes passed and Sonu returned, a frown on his face. "I hate that you are upset and will not be allowed food." He paused. "I think you will find life with me can be very pleasing. You will be well cared for, expansive houses, the best jewels, beautiful clothes. In time, you will love me."

She tore her eyes from Julia Roberts wearing the brown and white polka-dot dress and finally looked at him. "Are you insane? I have plans for my life, and you'll never be part of them. I love Jason."

He shook his head. "It is best if you forget about him."

She got out of bed and looked him in the eyes. "I don't know who you think you are, but I will not spend my life with you. I'll die first."

He put his hands on his hips and blew out a breath, then turned away from her. He bowed his head and said, "Get a shower, brush your teeth and put on one of your new dresses. I will be back in the morning."

He started walking to the door, and she ran to beat him to it. He had a head start and reached it first, slipped through it, then slammed it behind him.

Daisy reached for the knob and heard the lock click.

"I hate you, you crazy bastard!"

22

The girls and Adrienne waited outside as Al paid the bill. He emerged a few minutes later and Vivian tried to hand him $40.

He waved her off. "Forget it."

Adrienne squeezed his full frame. "You're such a sweetheart."

He winked at her. "You ready to call it a night and thank your sweetheart in a more appropriate way?" She snuggled close, then pointed him in the direction of their hotel.

"Where to next?" Wendy asked.

"I am NOT going into any more places like that," Lucy said.

"I second that," Kate said. "I need some serious sanitizer for my purse."

Lucy handed Kate two wipes, and she went to town wiping down.

"We need to follow Trikki Vikki and her boyfriend," Vivian said, glancing into the club. "He was too confident that nothing would happen to Vikki."

Kate chunked her two wipes into a sidewalk trash can. "Trikki was eyeing you during her confetti-popping show. I'm not so sure you want to get close to her."

"Yeah, she'll stuff her skanky stripper shoe up your sphincter," Lucy said.

Vivian bent over, cracking up. Kate was mortified. "Oh my gosh, Lucy! That was so crude! I can't believe you said that."

"She seems like a crude kinduva gal," Lucy said, then hiccupped.

"Woohoo! Here we go!" Vivian said. "What all did you drink in there?"

"While you were flirty with Trikki Coochie Clint, Al and I had ourselves a little shot of tequila." Lucy giggled for a moment. "Actually, it was pretty big."

"I think we could follow Trikki and Coochie without them seeing us," Wendy said, looking around. "There's so many people out here, we can probably get away with it. Let's see where they go."

They rounded the corner to hide themselves from the club entrance.

Wendy and Kate went to get Vivian a Big Ass Beer, and they shared a Big Ass peach daiquiri. They bought Lucy a bottle of water, but she occasionally sipped off the BAB.

It took about 20 minutes before Clint and Vikki walked out of the club and up Bourbon. The girls fell in about 15 feet and lots of people back. The couple walked a few blocks and stopped at a bar called the Bump and Hump. "I Got a Feeling" by the Black Eyed Peas blasted from inside.

Lucy went to the bar to keep an eye on Clint while the other three girls grabbed a table just inside the door so they could see the dance floor and Vikki, who let loose gyrating, pulsating and insinuating. Vivian thought she was about to be dislocating — a hip. One guy tried to make his own moves on her, but she shoved him off.

Lucy walked back to their table with four green shots and passed them out.

"What's this?" Kate asked, giving it a sniff.

"Dunno, Bump and Hump special."

Everyone shot a shot, except for Kate. "I'm not drinking this. Smells like sour apples."

Clint finished up at the bar and brought two plastic cups filled with clear beverages to the dance floor. Vikki sucked one down, then tossed the cup of ice toward Mr. Moves, hitting him in the chest.

Moves threw his hands in the air and lunged in her direction, but Clint stepped in the way, forcing him back.

The bouncer brushed past Vivian, got to the dance floor and grabbed Mr. Moves by the back of his shirt, dragging him toward the front door.

Vivian watched as he was thrown out and saw Antonio standing just outside the doorway. She grabbed Kate's un-drunk shot and threw it back. "I gotta go get frisked."

She ran her hand down Antonio's muscular arm. "You look like a pervert out here, by yourself watching everyone. Come on." She grabbed his hand and drug him to the dance floor.

Clint and Vikki were on the far side of the floor, so Vivian and Antonio stayed on the other.

Antonio leaned in close. "What are you doing?"

His breath on her neck gave Vivian chills. "You can be under cover right here. It actually looks more convincing than you being a stalker outside. Trust me, I've had one."

He laughed and went along with the charade. He had some good moves. Excellent hip action.

Vivian stepped in a little closer and worked some hip action of her own. She noticed Vikki and Clint moving closer on the dance floor.

"I better go outside," Antonio said, close to her ear and tingling all the right places.

She reached up, wrapped her hands around his neck and drew him in for a kiss. Their bodies moved together for a few beats. He pulled back and looked at her with passionate green eyes. She'd hit the nerve she was going for.

A grin spread across his face. "This is my kind of undercover work." He glanced up, looking for Vikki and Clint, who were walking out of the bar. "But I better get back to it."

Antonio walked Vivian to the table and squeezed her hand before walking out the door.

"What was that?" Lucy exclaimed.

Vivian grabbed her purse from Kate. "Hooker Vikki left. We gotta go!"

The girls walked out of the club just in time to see Vikki and Clint turn on Toulouse. A few doors down they walked into The Dungeon.

"Oh my gosh, I've been here," Wendy said. "It's super dark inside. We can definitely follow them."

They waited a few minutes, then went through a door and into a courtyard, passing a tall, bearded, nose-ringed guy who didn't ask for any IDs but grunted at them as they entered the bar.

Because of the darkness, Vivian stopped after a few steps. Lucy ran into the back of her, then bounced into Kate, who helped steady her.

"Dammit, it's like a dungeon in here! I can't see anything!" Lucy grabbed onto Vivian's shirt. "Lead me, seeing-eye bitch!"

Vivian's eyes adjusted to the reddish glow that barely shone on the bar. No Clint or Vikki. "Where could they have gone?"

Wendy took the lead. "Follow me." She weaved through the crowd to the back of the bar and led them up a narrow, wooden staircase to a dance floor. A D.J. played alternative rock in one corner, and a bar was in another.

Vivian still didn't see them.

Wendy pulled them onto the dance floor and nodded toward one of two jail cells at the far end of the small room. "There they are, making out."

Sure enough, Clint and Vikki were goin' at it like an inmate and a visitor at a conjugal.

The girls danced for a few songs while Clint and Vikki did their own jailhouse rhumba.

"Isn't that the bellman from Harry's hotel?" Wendy nodded toward a guy standing by the bar, alone.

"I knew he was a cop!" Kate said.

They kept dancing until the song transitioned to a new one. Vivian stopped. "My legs are tired, they've had enough, and I've had enough of the jail cell rock over there."

"Only way out is down the stairs," Wendy yelled over the music. "We can hit Tropical Isle and still see the entrance here if y'all want to go there."

Everyone agreed and they made their way out of the bar and across the street.

Weird Al and his band were on stage again, singing Van Morrison's "Moon Dance." The Blue Ball special had been replaced by the Pink Pussycat, which made the girls giggle.

"I want one of those!" Lucy yelled.

Kate insisted, no, she would not be having one.

Instead, Wendy ordered a round of beers and two bags of hot nuts for snackage. They staked out a spot at the bar where they had a clear shot of The Dungeon door.

"These hot nuts rock," Vivian said, peeling and popping two peanuts into her mouth.

Everyone agreed, digging in.

After about 45 minutes, another round of beer and hot nuts, Vikki walked out looking disheveled. Her pigtails were no more and her miniskirt was sideways. Clint was right behind her, shirt unbuttoned and wearing a smile.

Lucy pointed to the street. "There they are!"

Vivian shoved her hand down. "Shhhhh! We're being spies here!"

"Oh yeah, I forgot, we're secret agents."

The girls followed behind, being loud with the crowd, stopping to grab the occasionally tossed beads from up above. Eventually the couple turned off Bourbon, walking toward Rampart.

"I don't like the feel of this area," Kate said. "It's spooky."

"I can't believe you, of all people, think this is spooky," Vivian said. "Ooooooooooo…"

Kate nudged her. "It is. I've got goose bumps."

"It's just not the touristy part of the Quarter," Wendy said. "We'll be fine."

23

Vivian, Lucy, Wendy and Kate stood in the shadow of a giant oak tree in front of Louis Armstrong Park. Clint and Vikki went into a room of a small motel across the street. Some of the windows of the motel were covered in foil, and clothes hung off the second-floor balcony that ran the length of the timeworn building. Cash was probably king.

The light in their room clicked on and shadows passed back and forth in front of the window. Vivian heard them yelling. *So much for the lovey-dovey act from moments ago.*

"We need to see if Daisy's in the room," Wendy said. "Let's go try to peek in the window."

"No way, José," Kate said. "I'm not going."

"You have to," Vivian said. "Clint is more likely to recognize me than you. Please?"

"I'll go!" Lucy yelled, then stepped off the curb.

"Hold it there, Lushy Lucy," Wendy grabbed her arm and pulled her back. "We've got to be discreet, and right now, you're not. I'll go with Kate. You stay here with Viv."

Wendy and Kate ran across the street and hid behind a hedge of boxwood bushes that stood between a sidewalk and the concrete stoop.

Wendy heard loud voices on the other side of the sliding glass door. "Unless Vikki's voice now resembles that of Barry White, I swear that sounds like two guys in there." She concentrated for a moment, then asked Kate, "Can you make out what they're saying?"

Kate tilted her head. "Somebody's definitely mad. I think I hear Vikki yelling."

"I'm getting closer," Wendy said, then she started to get up. Just as her head popped over the bush, the door opened. Her heart pounded ninety to nothing as she ducked back down.

"You're such a screw-up, Kevin," Vikki yelled into the room, holding the door open. "Get the hell out of here. We'll clean up the fucking mess you've made."

Wendy craned her neck, looking through the bush, but couldn't see anything inside.

A voice came from inside the room. "Sorry. I fucked up. I'll fix this."

"No, don't do anything, just leave." Vikki slammed the door, then muttered to herself, "Stupid idiot. I can't believe we're related."

A lighter clicked several times, and the scent of a freshly lit cigarette wafted through the air.

Panic started to set in about the same time Wendy's thighs started to burn and quiver from the awkward position she was crouched in. She reached over to Kate to steady herself.

Kate mouthed the words, "Oh my god!" She was in a less precarious pose, sitting on her knees.

A bottle crashed across the street and Vikki looked in that direction, squinting, then went back to her cigarette.

What are those girls doing over there? They're going to blow this! Wendy thought.

Two or three long minutes passed and the fire in Wendy's legs was too much. She fell back onto her butt, her shoulder brushing against the bush. Rustling started, and a moment later a bird flew out of the bush, right over their heads, startling them.

It took everything in Wendy not to scream, and Kate looked like she was about to lose it. Vikki did scream, loudly, and a second later Clint poked his head out.

"What's going on?"

Vikki flicked her cigarette over the bush, landing it in Wendy's lap. "Dumb-ass bird scared me."

"Come on, we've gotta take care of this shit."

Wendy heard the door close, so she jumped up, swatting at her pants. "Let's get the hell out of here!"

Kate was already on her feet.

Vivian heard footsteps and hoped it was Wendy and Kate. She and Lucy were hunkered down behind the oak tree and too scared to look.

"What are y'all doin' back here?" Wendy asked.

They stood up and Vivian butt-bumped Lucy. "When Grace here knocked over the beer bottle we decided to move around back here."

"Who leaves a beer bottle on the sidewalk!" Lucy defended. "I mean, come on!"

Kate looked petrified. "Wendy almost caught on fire and a bird almost gave us away. I thought we were goners."

"Did y'all see into the room when Vikki came out?" Wendy asked.

"Not really, too far away," Vivian answered. "Just the TV flickering in the background and a guy, I think Clint, standing beside it."

"We couldn't see from where we were sitting, but we heard two guys and a girl."

"Who was the other guy?"

"I think it might have been one of her brothers. She called him Kevin, then mumbled something about them being related," Kate said. "More importantly, Clint said they had a mess to clean up."

"What kind of mess?" Lucy asked. "Think it was something to do with Daisy?"

The door to the motel room opened and a big guy in a T-shirt and athletic shorts stumbled out.

Vivian said, "He's big like one of the guys who took Daisy. Do y'all think she's in there?"

"I think you should text Adrienne and let her know what we heard," Kate said.

Vivian typed out a quick message, and they watched Kevin slowly work his way toward Bourbon.

A minute later Vivian's phone vibrated.

Antonio said they're on it and that y'all need to LEAVE. NOW.

Vivian looked around. "The cops are watching us watching Clint and Vikki. Adrienne says we need to leave."

Kate hitched elbows with Lucy. "Well, if they don't want us here, let's follow the other guy."

They set off after Vikki's brother. The streets were empty, and following him onto Bourbon wasn't a problem. He stopped at a pizza-by-the-slice place.

"Oh my gosh, that sounds good," Lucy said, walking faster. "I'm so in."

Kevin sat at a small table in the window, working quickly through three slices. Lucy drug Kate into the line while Wendy and Vivian grabbed a table.

Kate ordered a slice of cheese, but Lucy ordered a slice of Italian sausage from a muscular, baby-faced slice of Italian sausage behind the counter.

Lucy was in love. She couldn't get enough of her Italian stallion, Jonathon. She flirted with him at the counter while Kate picked up the pizza and took it to the table. The sausage slice slid off the paper plate and onto the floor.

Kate looked at the slice on the floor, then up at Vivian and Wendy. "Whoopsie."

Wendy hopped up. "It's okay, five-second rule." She grabbed the plate from Kate and used it to scoop up the slice. It had fallen crust-side down.

Vivian was horrified. "We can't let her eat that." No telling the last time the tile floors were cleaned. Bourbon Street black-traffic tracks made clear paths through the place. Tomato sauce and God only knows what else was stuck under their table.

Wendy sat back down. "It'll be fine. It's nothing her immune system can't handle."

Kate laughed and sat down with the pizza. "She's too wrapped up in pizza boy to notice."

"I think he's outside the decade rule," Vivian said. "He is awfully cute, though, and I bet he's spunky and energetic."

Kate took a bite of her cheese slice, then offered it to Wendy and Vivian. "This is pretty good."

Lucy walked over, Jonathon in tow. "Let me check out your handiwork." And with that, she took a big bite of her Italian sausage. "Mmmm, fantastic."

Vivian tried not to cringe as Lucy playfully fed Jonathon a bite. She also tried not to laugh.

Jonathon reached for a packet of red pepper. "I like to spice things up."

"Pour some pepper on me, baby," Lucy said, then took another big, dramatic bite.

Wendy got out her phone. "Lucy, you and lova boy skooch over to the left a little so I can get your picture."

Jonathon picked up the piece of crust and fed it to Lucy. "Open wide."

Wendy angled the camera just right and snapped a couple of shots. "Got it."

"Let me see," Lucy asked and reached for the phone. "You chopped off Jonathon!"

Kevin got up, leaving his trash on the table, and walked onto the side street. Vivian followed him out. He hailed a cab and was gone a second later. She looked for another cab, but none was around. She went back inside and sat down. "Dammit, that's the end of that."

Wendy held up her phone. "I got a picture of him, though."

Kate finished her slice. "What we need is his address."

"I'll call Adrienne in the morning," Vivian said, then looked at her watch. It was 4 a.m. "Or maybe right about noon."

Wendy yawned and stretched. "I think it's time to call it a night. I'm done."

Lucy ran a hand down Jonathon's arm. "We have to go."

"I'll walk ya back," he said and stood.

Jonathon didn't bother to let his boss know he was leaving; he just walked out with the girls and escorted them to their hotel. By the time they were in the lobby, he'd gotten a text. He glanced at it and said, "I'm fired. But it was worth it," then he bent down and gave Lucy a kiss.

The other girls woo-hoo'ed and Lucy blushed. She and Jonathon exchanged numbers, and the girls went up to their room.

Lucy flopped onto the bed, not bothering to get ready for bed. "He's awesome. I bet he's good in the sack. I could feel what he's got goin' on in the package department, and it's definitely something I want to unwrap."

Vivian grabbed her jammies out of the drawer. "Lucy, he's at least a dozen years younger than you."

She started laughing. "He doesn't think so! I told him I was 25." She almost rolled off the bed cracking up. "He's *nineteen!*"

24

Day 4

Daisy slept poorly, her dreams filled with people chasing her, of trying to break out of rooms and of searching for a key, seeing one appear, then fade. She awoke and felt worse than when she had drifted off. She couldn't live with the smell of herself much longer, so she brushed her teeth using a plastic wrapped toothbrush and a sealed tube of Colgate and showered, but she put her clothes back on. She searched for her other shoe but couldn't find it, so she went barefoot. She wanted to be ready to run.

I'm not wearing those fucking dresses.

She sat in the blue-and-tan-striped chair and watched the local morning news. It had an update but not much, basically saying there had been no new developments.

How can three of us disappear in a month and the police don't have anything to go on? Maybe they're not telling the media everything?

The man who had given her the drink in her dressing room pushed a cart with covered dishes into the room. She smelled eggs and her stomach growled. Sonu walked in just in time to hear it.

He looked her up and down. "I see you showered but still have not dressed in appropriate clothing." He walked over to the window, then stopped in front of her. "You must learn to do what I ask. I will not tolerate insubordination."

"You can't keep me prisoner. This is wrong."

"I can do what I please. You do not know the power I have. No authorities will touch me."

"You're crazy if you think you're getting away with this."

He started walking toward the door. "Enjoy your breakfast. You will not eat again until tonight."

Daisy followed after him, trying to get a look at the rest of the hotel suite. "How long are you going to keep me here?"

"Until my plans come together." He closed and locked the door.

***

The curtains never block all the light, Vivian thought as soon as her eyes opened. *So annoying*. She lay there for a minute going over the last three days. Good food, good music, good times. *Daisy!* She sat up with a start, head pounding and a little dizzy. "Ouch." She sank back into the pillows.

Wendy, wrapped in a towel with wet hair, brought over a cup of water and three ibuprofen. "Life-savers."

"I need more than this one cup of coffee." Kate sat on her bed, cup in hand. "Like caffeine from 20 cups of coffee. The late night and lots of walking yesterday got me."

"Sure it wasn't the peach daiquiri or all the beer?" Wendy asked and held out the ibuprofen bottle to her.

Lucy rolled out of bed and shuffled to the bathroom. "I need a 5-Hour Energy, some Spark and a Monster. All at the same time."

The girls laughed, and Vivian said, "Sure you don't just need your 19-year-old?"

Lucy paused in the doorway and smiled. "Was he for real? I kind of thought that was a dream."

Wendy showed her their picture. "He was real, all right."

"Mmmm, mmmm."

Wendy pulled a shirt and capris out of her drawer. "What we need to do is call Adrienne and figure out our game plan for today."

Vivian sat up, slowly this time, and reached for her phone. "True. And we would have heard by now if Clint and Vikki had Daisy, so I guess that wasn't the case."

"Ask her for Kevin's address or last name," Kate said.

"Hey, Adrienne," Vivian said when she picked up. "What happened last night at Clint and Vikki's motel? Anything?"

Adrienne laughed. "Sounded like you girls were a hot mess, but other than that, the police were able to determine they weren't holding Daisy there."

"How'd they do that?"

"One of the undercover guys pretended to be drunk and tried to open their door. When Vikki cracked it, he stumbled inside. He was able to look around enough before Clint threw him out."

"Which one?" Vivian asked. "Because we've seen one guy a couple times."

"I don't know," Adrienne said. "What's he look like?"

Vivian described the blond guy they had seen at the Roosevelt and The Dungeon.

"He sounds cute. I'll see what I can find out."

"Any other updates? They find Harry or figure out what he did with the $20,000?"

"I'm meeting Antonio for brunch at The Camellia Grill on Chartres in an hour. Why don't y'all meet us there? We can quiz him."

"Sounds great, thanks!"

Vivian relayed the info to the girls, and they got ready quickly, as they had the bathroom sharing routine down. They decided that it was definitely a sundress kind of a place. Vivian, despite Lucy's warning about her well-endowed chest falling out, wore a strapless floral print knee-length number, while Kate, Wendy and Lucy went with more modest sleeveless, not strapless, versions.

"At least put some sunscreen on your shoulders," Wendy said and handed Vivian some SPF 15.

Vivian loved a good tan, but didn't want to fry, so she slathered up, being careful not to get it on her cute dress.

They walked up Chartres, past the courthouse a block to Camellia's. Adrienne and Antonio sat at the end of one of two long countertops. She read the local paper, the *Times-Picayune*, and he typed on his phone. The girls hopped onto the stools on either side of them, Vivian beside Antonio.

He brushed her hand with his and smiled. His touch was warm and he smelled like he'd just stepped out of the shower. His freshly shaved face was irresistibly kissable, but Vivian didn't want to explain anything to Adrienne, so she held off.

Damn, he's hot. I wouldn't mind waking up to that in the morning!

The six made chit-chat while they ordered breakfast. The waiter had everything for their drinks right behind the counter and served them quickly. Kate looked happy about the coffee.

Adrienne got right to it, tucking the paper into her purse. "So, Tone, catch us up. Any news on Harry and his 20k?"

He gave her a disapproving look.

She waved him off. "They know everything. They're trying to help."

Antonio shook his head and looked at the four girls. "What were y'all doing following Clint and Vikki last night? I don't want y'all getting into something you can't get out of."

"We had to see if they had Daisy," Vivian said. "We had to follow them around, see where they were staying or who they talked to."

"You knew we were on it, and we're following up on every possible scenario. We are aware of the bad blood between the dancers."

"Seemed like more than just bad blood to me," Kate said. "Vikki hated her."

Antonio dismissed that. "That was friendly compared to Laura's hatred of her."

Everyone was quiet for a moment, shocked.

"Who the hell is Laura?" Vivian asked.

"The other dancer. I think she danced with lollipops?"

"Ohhhh, Lala Lollipop," Lucy said.

"We didn't know she hated Daisy," Wendy said.

"We interviewed all the dancers and employees. Other than the bar fight, which was quickly broken up, nobody noticed anything out of the ordinary. But by far the one who disliked Daisy the most was Laura."

Vivian raised her eyebrows and looked around him at the other girls.

Antonio put his hand on her arm. "That doesn't mean she kidnapped her. Don't go off chasing after another stripper and getting into trouble."

Vivian changed the subject. "So what did Harry spend that money on?"

"We're still looking into it, and again, you stay out of it."

Wendy put down her coffee cup. "Something was going on in that room last night. What's the deal with Vikki and her brother, Kevin?"

"Daisy was not in that room."

"Could they have her somewhere else?" Kate asked.

"Kevin's a drunk and a few notes short of a song."

Vivian set down her chocolate milk. "Did y'all follow him last night to the pizza place?"

Antonio smirked but didn't respond.

The waiter refilled drinks and then delivered their food, which had been prepared just beyond the counter, in the open kitchen. Antonio's breakfast of eggs, bacon, sausage, pancakes, grits and hash browns took three plates. Vivian's ham and cheese omelet only required one plate and was delicious.

Kate used her whole-wheat toast to sop her eggs over easy and asked Antonio, "What is Kevin's last name?"

"Smith."

"Really?"

"No."

"I guess that means you won't tell us where he lives?"

"Correct."

Adrienne popped a piece of cantaloupe into her mouth. "What about Vikki's financials, and her brothers?"

Antonio stacked his pancake plate on top of an empty one. "We got the warrant, but this stuff takes time." He liberally poured on the syrup.

"But it's past the first 48," Lucy said, then took a sip of orange juice. "I watch that show, and they say if you don't find them within the first two days, chances are you won't."

"Chances do diminish, but this city has a lot of eyes and ears. Someone knows something, and we'll find that person. Then we'll find her."

Vivian found Antonio's confidence comforting, but she still wasn't dissuaded from trying to help. Kate had a dream, after all.

"Did y'all find the two younger guys who tried to break in?" Kate asked.

"Not yet, still working on it."

Adrienne pulled the newspaper out of her purse. "There's a mention of the abduction, but I'm a little surprised at the lack of detail. Why didn't they put the guys' pictures in here?"

He pushed the paper away. "I'm not in the PR department, A."

"Are y'all going to show the video on the news?" Vivian asked. "That'd probably help. There's hardly anything in the news about the other abductions. Three girls in less than a month."

Antonio threw his fork down, clanging loudly. He wiped his mouth, pulled out his wallet and put some money on the table. "We don't have anything conclusive that proves they're all linked." He turned to Adrienne. "I've gotta go. See you later."

He turned, but Adrienne grabbed his arm. "What the hell? You can't be pissed about that."

He threw his head back, angry. "Some of the fucking evidence has disappeared. Something's not right."

"Before you go, who is the blond undercover guy that was at the Roosevelt Hotel and at The Dungeon yesterday?" Adrienne asked.

"I don't know, some guy I've never worked with. He asked to be on the task force. I'm done answering questions. Next time you ask me to breakfast don't have an agenda."

The girls sat stunned for a minute as he walked to the door. He shoved it open, then turned around and pointed at the girls accusingly. "I can't believe y'all let her eat that pizza last night." He nodded to Lucy.

Lucy gasped. "What was wrong with my pizza?"

25

The shit hit the fan after Lucy learned her pizza hit the floor.

"It had some extra Bourbon Street flavoring," Adrienne said. "There're worse things. Remind me to tell you about the time I went to Detroit when I was a Luvabull for the Chicago Bulls. Now *that* was a nasty experience."

It took some time, a paper sack and a trip to the bathroom to rinse out her mouth, but Lucy calmed down. Finally able to concentrate, the girls worked out a strategy for helping Daisy, even though they weren't supposed to be helping.

Adrienne gave the girls the newspaper. "I'm going to sic Al on this lack of press bullshit. I've seen it before in New Orleans, the media ignoring crimes involving strippers. I'm not going to let them ignore this."

"It's a shame they've not done more," Vivian said. "Maybe Gino would have had more security on staff if he'd known this was going on."

"Perhaps. And one other thing, before y'all got here, Antonio said he and Eddie's team have gone over video from the club and eliminated a bunch of people who don't match the description. They're still looking at videos from the surrounding businesses, trying to find the car she was loaded up in." Adrienne grabbed her purse. "You girls keep at it and we'll work on this media thing. See ya later."

Adrienne walked out the door, and Vivian decided they needed to call Jason.

He answered on the second ring. "Hey Jason, just calling to check on you. How you hanging in there?"

"Every minute sucks worse than the one before, but at least I have some help now. I have people handing out fliers in the Quarter and going door to door in other parts of the city."

"That is fantastic. The more people who see her face, the better." Vivian then told him about their adventures the previous day, from Trikki Vikki's show to following Kevin to the pizza place. "Do you happen to know his last name or where he lives?"

"The cops aren't telling me shit. I think the news people know more than I do, and that ain't much."

"We just talked with Antonio, and he said they're working all the leads. The tip line is evidently bringing in some information, too." She wasn't about to tell him Antonio thought there was a problem with the investigation. "He mentioned something we thought was odd. He said Lala hated Daisy. Did you know that?"

Jason groaned. "No, she's usually very friendly toward her."

"That's not what Antonio got."

"I guess I shouldn't be surprised. I slept with La once about three months before I met Daisy. It wasn't a big deal, you know. I got the impression she wanted more but it just wasn't happening. I have another call, gotta go."

Vivian turned to the girls. "Oh my god, he slept with Lollipop!"

"No wonder she hates Daisy," Lucy said. "She was a jilted stripper."

Kate got out her phone. "We've gotta find Lala and the brothers. We need to know if she's dancing tonight and where, and their real last name and an address."

"Even if we did get that," Lucy said, "what are we going to do?"

"I am *not* going to another strip club," Wendy said. "I've seen enough."

"If she's dancing somewhere you don't have to go in, I will," Vivian said. "We can follow her when she leaves."

"I'm having flashbacks of cigarettes in my lap. I'm not sure this is a good plan."

"It'll be fine," Vivian said. "We've gotta help Daisy."

Lucy whipped out her phone. "Let's just see what we can find on little Miss Lala." She Googled Gino's strip club and used it to get Lala's Twitter handle. She checked her tweets and found out Lala was dancing tonight at Rick's Cabaret on Bourbon, main stage at midnight.

"That's easy enough," Kate said. "We'll be there."

Wendy threw her napkin on the counter. "All right, fine. I can stand out on Bourbon with a drink at least."

"You could get into more trouble doing that than going in the club," Lucy said and laughed.

"True, but I'll take my chances."

"That's decided, but for now, on to the brothers." Lucy pulled up Trikki Vikki's Facebook fan page.

Kate fiddled with her empty coffee cup. "What exactly are we going to do with that information?"

Lucy kept clicking. "Go to their house. Look around. Clint said they have a mess to clean up, and I want to know what it is."

"You heard what Antonio said. Do you really think we ought to be doing that?"

Vivian shrugged. "We gotta do something. She's a page six story right now. Below the fold."

"That's not going to cut it," Wendy said. "Let's go snoop."

Lucy held out her phone. "You're never gonna believe this. Check it out."

She had pulled up a picture of Clint, Kevin and another guy on an airboat in a swamp. The caption read, "Gator huntin' with the bros." Kevin and Devin Smith were tagged.

"His last name is Smith," Vivian exclaimed. "That damn Antonio!"

"Shut the front door," Kate said.

"Last time I fall for that!"

They all got a good laugh. Lucy looked the brothers up on White Pages, then mapped it.

"This is in mid-cities," Wendy said. "We can hit the streetcar and get over there pretty quick. We should probably wait until it's dark."

"What are we going to do in the meantime?" Kate asked.

"Where are the dream notes?" Lucy asked.

"Vivian has them," Kate said.

Vivian pulled the crumpled paper from her purse. "I almost forgot to take this out of my skirt, but I remembered right before we left the room this morning." She placed it on the table.

Lucy read it aloud. "Don't be tricked. Flower petals will float and fly. You must look through the dense forest to see into the mirrors."

Vivian tapped her fingers on the counter. "I feel like we've covered the tricked and flower petals as best we can, except for checking out Vikki's brothers."

"I don't know what the dense forest is," Kate said, frustrated. "Or the mirrors."

"And what about float and fly?" Wendy asked. "Any other thoughts?"

Everyone was quiet.

A sound similar to a slot machine rang out next to Vivian. A lady down the counter answered her phone.

"Wait a second!" Vivian said, thinking about her numerous nights gambling down the street. "Harrah's has a big wall of mirrors at the escalator going from the casino to the hotel. Maybe that's it."

No one seemed excited about this revelation.

"Maybe the dense forest is the swamp?" Lucy said. "A boat floats."

"Yeah, but there's a lot of swamp around here," Wendy said. "Where do we even begin to start?"

Kate closed her eyes for a minute, then opened them. "Okay, Harrah's is walking distance and the four of us can cover the casino. The swamp, I'm afraid, is beyond what we can do."

Vivian stood up, clapped, then rubbed her hands together. "Ladies, break out your wallets. It's time to go gambling!"

"Just keep in mind, we're on a mission to find Daisy," Wendy said.

"I know, I know, but the sound of slot machines is in my future."

The girls paid the check, then made their way to Decatur, then North St. Peter to Canal. The bright lights of the giant Harrah's globe beckoned Vivian, and she walked faster the closer they got.

She ran up the steps. "Take my picture!"

Kate pulled out her phone. "Only you would want a picture with a giant ball."

Vivian could not deny this.

They went in but weren't carded by security.

"Damn, we're getting old," Wendy said.

Once inside, Vivian led the way to the mirrored escalator. They rode down, then back up, then down again.

"Let's take a picture like in that movie!" Lucy squealed.

"Like in *The Hangover*?" Kate asked.

"That's it," Lucy said and snapped a few shots.

"Excuse me," Vivian said. "This was actually from *Rain Man. The Hangover* made a spoof of it."

"Whatever," Lucy said. The pictures didn't get everyone in, so they rode up, then back down and tried again. Lucy was more successful the second time, so they rode the escalator up and stopped to regroup.

"The mirrors talking to you, Kate?" Wendy asked.

"The slot machines are drowning out everything. I got nothing."

Lucy waved her hand in front of her face. "The smoke's killing me. Let's go."

"Whoa ho ho ho," Vivian said. "No need to rush this. I say we split up and search the casino for more mirrors. Or a forest. You know, these casinos can have some weird themed crap around. I'd hate to hurry and miss something."

Lucy smiled. "You're not fooling anyone."

"I don't have any idea what you're implying."

"Vivian, we know you're just dying to throw some money into a machine. Any machine."

Vivian pulled her best shocked look. "*Moi?*"

Wendy looked around. "I gotta go to the bathroom anyway. You've got 30 minutes."

Vivian jumped up and down.

"Show us where you'll be," Kate said. "We'll hit *el baño*, then walk around."

Vivian took them to The Hangover slot machine and sat down. "I'll be right here. I like looking at Bradley Cooper, and that Asian guy cracks me up." She whipped out her player's card and put it in the machine, along with $100.

The display lit up. Welcome, Vivian!

"Anyone want a drink? I can order one on the slot machine!" Vivian worked on her order of rum and Coke as the others turned and walked away.

"Where's the restroom?" Kate asked Lucy and Wendy, looking around. She felt a need to go toward the high-limit slots, she didn't know why. They found the restroom and met right outside afterward.

"Is that slot machine a $100 minimum?" Lucy asked, pointing to a Lucky 7s nearby.

Kate walked over to it. "Actually, if you bet the max per spin, it's $300."

"Wow," Wendy said, "Who does that?"

A purple-haired woman with tubing wrapped around her face connecting to her oxygen tank sat at another Lucky 7s. She stared intently at the spinning reels, continuously pushing the max spin button, lit cigarette in hand.

"That's an explosion waiting to happen," Wendy said, then directed them out of the area.

A loud crash to the right got Kate's attention. She looked toward the commotion and stopped in her tracks, shocked at who had a hand of cards and a pile of chips.

***

Daisy devoured her breakfast but didn't drink the coffee or orange juice that had been delivered. She didn't trust them not to roofie her again. The food made her feel better physically, but as the day wore on, she felt worse and worse emotionally. She had searched the room again, looking for anything to help her break out, use as a weapon or write a note to post in the window. Nothing had magically appeared.

Having no resources other than herself, she could think of only one other option. She opened the curtains and took off her shirt and bra. Maybe she could catch the attention of someone in the two-story building across the street, or on Chartres, who would be offended and call police. Either way, surely security would come to the room and she could escape.

Daisy waved frantically for 20 minutes, always listening for the lock. No one noticed her. Arms tired and getting frustrated, she dragged the desk chair to the window and stepped up. She pressed her chest against the glass and looked down. A tourist had a camera with a long lens pointed down the street.

Point it this way! Point it this way!

He slowly turned and angled the lens to what seemed like her direction. She started jumping on the chair, waving and boobs bouncing. He lowered the camera and looked at the hotel, then lifted it again and adjusted the focus.

He saw me! She started waving frantically again and mouthing the words help me. She pointed to him and drew an S-O-S in the air. She clasped her hands together under her chin and begged for his help. He lowered the camera, then lifted it again toward her. She repeated everything, but this time instead of S-O-S, she indicated 9-1-1 with her fingers. He let his camera hang around his neck and pulled his cell phone from his shirt pocket.

Daisy put her shirt on and felt a wave of relief when a police car pulled up and her favorite tourist walked over to it. Then came a quick click of the lock and the door opened. She flinched and was too scared to get off the chair.

"Get down, now!" a burly Middle Eastern man yelled, running into the room.

When she didn't move, he slung her over his shoulder and threw her onto the bed. She squirmed trying to get away. The doorbell to the suite rang and he threw his hand over her mouth and whispered, "I will end your life right now if you move."

The pressure of his weight was already choking her, so she stayed still. The door to the room closed and she heard muffled voices and eventually laughter. A tear slipped from her eye and rolled into her hair.

The guy eased his hold on her and whispered, "Do not do that again. Sonu will not be pleased. He will kill you."

The calm the man exhibited as he lay on top of her and the coolness of his voice scared her.

He shoved off her and stormed out. She saw the handgun in the small of his back and decided to stay away from the windows, knowing that Sonu's men were keeping watch outside. Instead she paced the room, ran in place, did some lunges and a few pushups to keep herself from going crazy. She listened at the door for any noises in the rest of the suite but couldn't hear anything but the television.

26

Kate swatted at Wendy and Lucy. "Look! Look! Look! It's Hairy Harry!" She pointed to the hairy guy at a poker table, drenched in the drinks the waitress had been carrying. He looked like the only sleep he'd had was between hands at the poker table, and he still wore the same clothes as the night Daisy was kidnapped. His hair, which was bad to start with, didn't need any gel to stay slicked back it was so greasy. Harry was crumpled, crusty and cranky.

He threw in his hand and stormed off to the restroom.

"I think freshening up is a lost cause at this point," Lucy said, scrunching her nose even though they were too far away to smell him.

Wendy looked shocked. "We've got to get Viv."

"Y'all stay here. I'll run get her," Kate said and took off.

Vivian kept hitting the spin button, even though she saw Kate darting across the casino in her direction.

Dammit, she found the dense forest or something. She pretended she didn't see Kate coming.

"Viv! We saw Harry!"

Vivian pushed the max bet button. "Who?"

"Hairy Harry! Come on!" And with that, Kate hit the "cash out" button.

"This thing was about to hit!" Vivian yelled.

"You're about to get hit if you don't get up!" Kate said.

Vivian recognized Kate's kick-ass voice and stood up, grabbing the receipt and her player's card before she was hauled away.

They made it back to the restroom just as Harry emerged, stumbling a bit, looking down at his shirt.

"Harry, what are you up to?" Vivian asked in a friendly manner.

He looked up, not able to focus, blank look on his face.

"It's me, Vivian. I met you at the club the other night." She lied.

"Oh yeah, how ya doin'?" He looked at the other girls, not recognizing them, either.

"Looks like you've been on a poker streak," Wendy said. "You been winning?"

He pointed his index finger at her. "Yeah, baby. Winning." Then he stumbled to the left.

Vivian reached for him, then thought better of it. "Why don't you join us for a few minutes at the bar? We'll buy you a drink since you got us one the other night."

He put his arm around Vivian and Wendy. "I'm buying, baby."

Vivian gagged but walked with him. *It's for Daisy. It's for Daisy.*

They sat down at the bar in front of the video poker machines.

"Round of Goldschlager," Harry yelled at the bartender, then said to the girls, "It has real gold in it."

The bartender grabbed the bottle from the freezer and poured five shots.

"Wow, Harry," Wendy said. "You must be loaded."

Harry didn't catch the sarcasm. He shrugged and picked up the clear liquid with gold floating flakes.

"To wishing Harry good luck," Vivian said and slammed it back.

Kate took a sip, then set the drink down on the bar.

Wendy winced. "Cinnamon's not my thing. Can't do it."

Lucy licked her lips, then said to Harry, "So whatcha been doing? Because I've gotta say, you look like you've been run over by a Mardi Gras float."

Harry hung his head. "It's been a rough few days. Rough few days."

"Do you not have to be at work today?" Kate asked.

"The fucking deal… just can't."

Vivian asked, "Is everything okay?"

"The love…love." He started blubbering.

Vivian felt sorry for him and shoved a few napkins his way.

He dabbed at his nose. "She was taken from me."

"Who?" Kate asked.

"My Daisy."

"That's horrible," Vivian said. "Who took her away from you?"

His cheeks flushed red and he wadded up the napkin, throwing it to the ground. "Ever since that drummer, she's been different. I shoulda known he'd take her away. One way or 'nother." He picked up Wendy's shot and threw it back. "Jerk."

"You poor thing," Lucy said.

Vivian eyed Kate's un-shot shot. *We gotta get outta here. This guy doesn't know squat.*

He started crying again. "She was the only one who cared. She loves me, I know it. After I got divorced she would listen and make me feel better. I love... I love... I love her."

Vivian placed Kate's shot in front of him. "Harry, you hang in there. We gotta go see somebody about something."

He just nodded, staring into space, and wiped away a tear.

Vivian cashed in her receipt, then led the way to the Canal Street exit. When they sat down on the steps outside, Vivian pulled out her phone and texted Adrienne.

**Just ran into Hairy Harry at Harrah's.
Drunk, depressed and desolate.
Def not the kidnapper.**

"Well, that's that," Kate said. "The mirrors brought us to Harry. We're down to the last of my dream. The forest."

None of them had any new ideas there, so they walked across Canal, heading back into the Quarter.

Just past the yogurt shop, an obnoxious guy at a kiosk waved brochures of some local attractions at them. "Where y'at? I have the tour for you." He handed Kate a brochure, and the girls kept walking.

Kate flipped it open and stopped a moment later. "Wait, maybe we do need to do this."

She held out a pamphlet for a cemetery tour. The inside of a tomb adorned with mirrors in all shapes and sizes was the centerpiece.

Kate tapped the picture. "I feel like we need to go here."

Lucy and Wendy were okay with it, but Vivian hesitated. "It's just a bunch of people put to rest above ground, as opposed to six feet under. It's because the ground is below sea level."

"But look at all the mirrors," Wendy said. "It could be something to do with her dream and we just don't know what. She's had these freaky dreams before, and they seem to work out."

Vivian closed the brochure and handed it to Kate. "Just seems a little far-fetched to me."

Mr. Brochure bounded up next to her. "I'm telling you ladies, this here is the crème de la crème of tours. You'll see some amazing things. Things you'll never experience anywhere else."

"How much?" Wendy asked.

"For you beautiful ladies, $30 per person."

Vivian started walking. "No way in hell am I paying 30 bucks for that."

"Wait wait wait. How about I give you a discount? A deep discount."

118

"How deep is deep?" Wendy asked.

"For you sexy ladies a 50 percent discount. That includes transportation to and from."

"Does that mean we walk there?" Wendy asked.

He started laughing. "Have you been on this tour?"

"As a matter of fact, I have."

"Okay, you ladies drive a hard bargain. Ten each."

Wendy pulled out a hundred and he had to go back to his kiosk to make change. When he returned, he handed each of them a sticker. "Y'all meet your tour guide at the corner of Bourbon and Conti in an hour. Gives ya time to have a hurricane. In fact, take one for the tour."

"I'm not ready for a hurricane, but I could use some yogurt," Kate said.

They turned to go back to the yogurt shop next to Harrah's, but a fleet of police cars surrounded the entrance. Detective Leffall leaned against his unmarked car, in front of the yogurt shop, across from Harrah's. He locked eyes with Vivian.

"We better go find a different yogurt shop."

27

The girls headed down Canal in search of a yogurt shop for Kate. They didn't find a yogurt shop, but an ice cream shop. Blue Bell, no less. Brenham, Texas, home of the happiest cows in the country.

Vivian bumped elbows with Wendy. "Remember when we went there in elementary school? We took the train."

Wendy opened the door, and the smell of creamy goodness floated out. "I don't remember that at all. I've killed too many brain cells. Such a shame."

Vivian ordered a Dutch Chocolate cone, Lucy a cup of Vanilla Bean, Kate a double scoop cone of Southern Blackberry Cobbler, and Wendy got her top two all-time favorites, Key Lime and Lemon Bliss.

Vivian asked for a sample of the Key Lime since Wendy wasn't sharing. Chunks of graham crackers melted in her mouth. "Mmmm."

The girls ate their ice cream in the A/C and waited until the last minute to walk to Bourbon and Conti for the cemetery tour. Their guide was easily identifiable, as the grave logo on his shirt matched their stickers.

He smiled and checked his watch as they walked up. "Thought y'all might've gotten held up by a three-for-one." The dreads in his goatee jiggled as he talked and matched the long, black dreads he wore pulled back.

"We were held up by ice cream," Lucy said, "but now we're ready to go groovin' with the ghosts."

"Excellent," he said and started walking down Conti, a bounce in his step. He turned back to them. "I'm Lazare, and I'm going to show you some of the coolest and creepiest graves in New Orleans history. And the graves of my ancestors."

He and Wendy talked about their New Orleans ancestry as they made their way to St. Louis Cemetery #1. She had traced her fourth-great-grandparents to living in the Sixth Ward in 1860. Part of his family arrived from the Dominican Republic in the late 1700s; the other side were prominent French Creoles. The mixture of the cultures was as common then as it is now.

120

He led them through the gate and started explaining about New Orleans being below sea level and therefore the need to bury people above ground. "The coffins would just float away."

Kate shuddered.

"That's only part of it," Lazare said, leading them into one of the oldest sections. "A lot of it is due to French and Spanish tradition. This cemetery replaced the older, and no longer in existence, St. Peter burial ground after a fire in 1788 and the city was redesigned."

Vivian heard music in the distance. "Where's that music coming from?"

Lazare stopped in front of an ornate tomb and looked to his right. "It's a jazz funeral. They'll be closer in a minute, you'll see," he said, then got back to his history lesson. "Who here is a gambler?"

All the girls looked at Vivian. She waved.

"Then you would have liked Monsieur Bernard de Maringy. Not only was he a playboy, he brought the game of craps to America."

Vivian rubbed her hand on the stone wall. "Thank you, sir. Wish me luck later tonight!"

Lazare laughed and kept moving, pointing out a grave covered in skulls, one built in brick and crumbling, and one with a guardian angel on top, keeping watch.

Vivian stopped in front of one and giggled. "Who was this? He has a funny name."

"Homer Plessy. He was the plaintiff in the civil rights Supreme Court case in 1896."

Lazare had them scoot back about a minute later as the jazz funeral walked slowly by, playing a dirge. A man in a top hat, wearing a sash and carrying a parasol, led a tuba, three trombones, two trumpeters and a drummer, followed by the mourners.

The band started up a festive tune and Vivian thought, *I wouldn't mind being sent off like that.* She watched as the mourners turned down another row and started dancing, several with feather boas and one with a tambourine.

Kate pulled out the brochure for the cemetery tour and tapped on the picture with the mirrors. "Where's this tomb?"

"It's on the opposite side of the cemetery, but I'll take you there. We'll go past Marie Laveau's resting place on the way." Lazare started down a narrow row and they had to turn sideways to pass another tour group, all wearing bright yellow matching shirts.

He stopped at a tomb with messages scribbled on the walls and a circle of shells in front of the door. Inside the circle was a cigarette, a praline and some loose change.

"It is believed that Voodoo Queen Marie Laveau is interred here with the Glapion family. People leave offerings to her and write well wishes or prayers on the walls."

Lucy tossed a few coins inside the shell circle. "For Daisy's safe return."

Kate snapped a picture of Lazare with the other three girls, then he took them over three rows. "This is where my lighter side originated. Mr. Vignaud met my great-great-great-great-grandmother at a ball and had a little too much fun. He at least put her up in a small shack and made sure she and the baby were clothed and fed."

Vivian looked at the other names, birth and death dates on the crypt. "So it looks like they got married?"

Lazare laughed. "Why, yes, he got married, but not to my grandmother. She remained his mistress, though, for the rest of his life. They actually had three children together."

Kate gasped. "You mean he had a whole second family?"

"It wasn't as rare as you'd think."

They walked for a few minutes before reaching the mirrored grave. Vivian felt like somebody was watching her and looked around. Not seeing anyone, she dismissed it as the cemetery creeps.

Lazare led them to a taller structure with a trio of steeples. "This is the Duplantier family tomb. We'll have to go around the back to see inside."

They shuffled along the pebbles to the back, where a circular opening about the size of a basketball gave view of the inside. Vivian, at 5-4, had to stand on her tippy toes to look in.

"There used to be stained glass here, but it's been long broken out."

All different shapes and sizes of mirrors lined the walls. The window was so high Vivian couldn't see the floor, but she could see several crypts on one side and mementos on the other.

"Let Kate see," Wendy said.

Kate stepped up to the window. Three inches taller than Vivian, she had an easier time seeing everything inside and took a good, long look.

Short little Lucy tried to see past Kate's head. "You getting anything?"

Kate sighed and turned around, looking behind Vivian. "No, nothing. But who is that?" She pointed a few rows over.

Everyone turned to look, but no one saw anything.

"That's one of our friendly ghosts," Lazare said with a smile, then he looked at Lucy. "You want a boost?"

"No, I'm okay."

Kate kept looking around the cemetery. "I swear I saw somebody."

"Let's check it out," Vivian said. "You lead."

Kate walked past Vivian, and the rest of the group followed. "He had blond hair and I swear I've seen him before." She walked several more rows and looked around, then went left. She stopped again and covered her nose and mouth. "Do you smell that?"

Vivian sniffed. "Smell what?"

Kate took a few more steps, then stopped. Slowly, she turned to the group and stiffened. Eyes wide and hands still covering her nose and mouth, she said, "It smells like death."

28

Vivian held her breath and stood frozen in the cemetery. Scared to keep going and needing oxygen, she inhaled quickly but didn't pick up on the scent of death that Kate was experiencing.

Kate walked down the row a little more, stopped in front of a small, crumbling tomb and pointed to the ground. "This is it."

The grass in front of the door was pulled away, but it looked like someone had tried to push it back down.

Lazare followed Kate, examining the writing on the entrance. "I don't recognize this family name, but regardless, something's not right."

"Exactly," Kate said and took two steps back. "You should look inside. I'm not going any further." She walked to Lucy, grabbed her arm and pulled her away. "I might be sick."

Lazare tugged at the door, which opened a crack. He stumbled backward, turning his head and gagging.

Vivian threw her hand over her nose from the stench.

He got up, pulled the door open more and peeked inside. He walked away from the tomb and covered his nose and mouth with his shirt. "We need to call the police."

They moved down a few rows, trying to escape the stench emitting through the partially open door of the tomb. The scent was burned into Vivian's memory forever, no matter how far away she walked.

Lucy sat down on the grass and leaned against a stucco-covered grave. She put her head in her hands, then looked up at Kate. "Do you think that was Daisy?"

Tears welled in Kate's eyes and she started to say something, but her voice caught. She shook her head.

The sight of Kate crying got to Vivian, and she started crying, too. This experience was traumatic, but Vivian was an empathetic crier anyway. She could see a stranger crying in a restaurant, and she'd start in, too.

"What did you see in there?" Wendy asked Lazare.

He ran his hand down his face, then did the sign of the cross. "It was dark, but it was a body that didn't belong. It wasn't properly entombed."

Vivian cringed and heard sirens in the distance.

"I'm going to meet the police at the entrance," Lazare said. "Are you okay staying here?"

"We'll be fine," Wendy said, though two out of the four were still crying.

As he walked off, Vivian sniffled and said, "We've got to go see Jason. He's going to be devastated."

"Hold on, Viv," Wendy said. "We don't know for sure that's Daisy in there."

Lucy wiped a tear. "But Kate's dream brought us here. It's got to be her."

Kate let out a long sigh. "I don't know. I don't know."

Lazare returned along with two uniformed police officers and explained what happened. "I do this every day and this isn't part of the regular tour, but she," he pointed to Kate, "noticed an odd smell and led us over here." He walked over to the tomb where the door was ajar. "This is it," he said, then walked back over to the girls.

Vivian watched between the rows and saw one of the officers pry the door open a little more. He threw his arm over his face and backed up. Not wanting to see inside, she turned away.

Two other officers arrived shortly, then a few more. A female officer walked over and got names and ID.

The girls were moved toward the entrance and sat there about 30 minutes before Antonio walked past them toward the tomb. A little while later, he approached the girls. "Tell me what happened."

Vivian explained, Lazare by her side confirming what she said. She grabbed Antonio's arm. "Is it Daisy?"

"We're still waiting on the medical examiner."

She nodded.

"Come over here with me," he said, and led her a few rows over. "Listen, Adrienne told me about what happened in Mexico and now you're around another murder? It doesn't look good, Vivian."

She was shocked. "I didn't have anything to do with Mexico! And Kate's the one who found this poor person. I was just here!"

He looked skeptical and didn't respond, so she continued. "What are you trying to say?"

He stepped closer. "I'm not saying anything, but this is not normal." He ran his hand down her arm and stopped on her elbow. "You need to lay low and stay away from this investigation."

"We were on a cemetery tour! Thousands of tourists do this every year!"

He looked down at the ground and shook his head. "Dammit. You're frustrating, but you're cute!" He grinned, then led her back to the group. "Everyone's given a statement, right?"

All the girls and Lazare nodded.

"You can go, but stay around town, and please," he looked at Vivian, "stay out of trouble."

The girls left the cemetery and stood outside the arches to regroup.

"I'm going to call Jason and find out where he is," Vivian said. When he picked up she tried to pull herself together and sound normal. "Hey there. How are things?"

"Good here. We've already distributed almost 5,000 flyers and I just got a call from the local ABC affiliate. They're coming to the hotel soon to interview me and Daisy's parents."

"That's awesome, I'm happy to hear it. Listen, the girls and I want to come by, if that's okay." The lump in her throat was growing and her eyes began to water.

"Yeah, sure. I'm at the Marriott on Canal, 1422."

"Okay, see you soon." She clicked off and wiped a tear from her eye.

Wendy handed her a tissue. "Are we going to tell him about the body?"

"No way," Lucy said. "Nothing has been confirmed. For all we know some stupid tourist got drunk, passed out and died in there."

Vivian put the tissue in her pocket. "I'll pull it together before we get there. I just feel like we need to go."

As they made their way to the hotel, Vivian's phone rang.

"What's this I hear about y'all finding a body?" Adrienne asked.

"Kate's nose led us to it," Vivian said. "But we didn't actually see it. We were too chicken to look inside."

"Just your luck."

"I know. We're freaking out thinking it might be Daisy. We're headed over to Jason's hotel."

"You can't tell him!" Adrienne yelled.

"We know that. We just want to be there for him if something bad goes down." Vivian switched ears. "He said he's got an interview with a local news station."

"Good. Al's been working on that. Sounds like he's making some headway."

"Let us know if you hear anything from Antonio," Vivian said.

"I will. 'Bye."

They arrived at the Marriott and went up to Jason's room. Kate knocked on the door.

Jason answered holding an energy drink. He smelled of soap, his bald head was sleek, and his eyes were clear. "Come in, come in."

Two suitcases were on the floor beside the dresser. One was open with a dress and high heel hanging out. There was some paperwork on the dresser, and Vivian couldn't help but notice it said "Marriage Certificate."

"My parents and hers are downstairs getting a quick bite to eat before the reporter gets here." He opened a cooler. "Anyone want a drink? I've got beer, water, more of these." He held up his caffeine bomb.

"No, thanks," Lucy said.

Jason pushed a pizza box off one of the two beds. "Here, sit. Sorry it's such a mess. I haven't let housekeeping in." He noticed Vivian looking at the papers. "Yeah, I went and filed for a marriage certificate today. Only one of us had to be there, and I had her driver's license and her mom helped me get the birth certificate and social security stuff. That way, when I get her back, we're ready to move forward with our life together."

Vivian sat on the edge of the bed, a knot in her stomach. She tried to smile at him, but couldn't. "We saw Harry today. He was at Harrah's. He was pretty torn up, looked like total crap. We called the police and they showed up. Detective Leffall was there, so I'm sure they got him."

"Finally that piece of shit has been found. I can't believe the cops haven't called me." He pulled his phone out of his jeans pocket and checked his call history.

Vivian looked over at Kate, who looked down at the floor. Wendy quietly cleared her throat and gave a slight shake of her head. Lucy's eyes portrayed a silent message to Vivian. *Don't!*

Jason noticed the exchange. "What the fuck is going on? What aren't you telling me?"

Vivian couldn't help herself and started crying. He turned pale and clenched his soda can.

After a moment, she took a deep breath. "We took a cemetery tour this afternoon and there was a body in a grave."

He looked confused. "It's a cemetery. There are going to be graves with bodies in them."

Kate walked over to him and touched his arm. "This body wasn't buried. It was just inside one of the tombs."

He wrinkled his brows. "What?"

"It wasn't buried, Jason."

He stared at Kate, not blinking, then he looked at Vivian. His face was no longer just pale, it had gone white. "Was it Daisy?"

Before anyone could answer, he threw his hand over his mouth, ran to the bathroom and slammed the door.

"We don't know!" Vivian jumped off the bed and yelled through the door. "We never saw who it was." She heard him retching on the other side, so she sat back down on the bed.

A few minutes later he emerged, shirtless, covered in sweat, eyes bloodshot. He sat in a chair next to the window and stared out.

"I'm sorry we upset you," Vivian said.

Wendy went into the bathroom and came back with a cold washcloth. "We don't know who that was, it could have been any — " She was interrupted by a loud knock on the door.

Jason put the washcloth on his head and showed no sign of getting up, so Lucy answered it.

Antonio scowled as he walked into the room.

29

Antonio stopped in front of Vivian, who still sat on the bed in Jason's hotel room. "What have you told him?"

"I didn't mean to, I just couldn't keep anything from him."

Jason stood, a little uneasy. He grabbed the chair for support. "Was that Daisy? Tell me the truth."

Antonio turned to face him and kept a professional demeanor. "The ME needs to do a complete autopsy, but initial findings are that the victim has been dead at least a week, maybe longer. It's not Daisy."

Jason started crying and sat back down, rocking back and forth, covering his face with the washcloth.

"Thank god!" Lucy said.

Vivian went to Jason, looking at the Wizard of Oz characters tattoo across his back. "This gives me hope we can still find her."

Jason nodded and sighed, using the washcloth to wipe away tears.

"I need to talk to him alone, so if you don't mind." Antonio waved his arm toward the door.

"Jason, call us if you need anything. We're here for you no matter what." Vivian hugged him as he sat almost in a trance.

The girls left the room and walked outside. The streetlights on Canal flickered, then blinked on.

"I feel so bad we upset him," Kate said.

"I didn't mean to go there," Vivian said. "I just couldn't keep it in."

"Let's go find Vikki's brothers' house," Lucy said. "We need to keep up the hunt."

"I agree," Wendy said. "I'm just so relieved it wasn't Daisy. I feel bad for whoever it is, though."

Kate held her hands up. "Are we sure this is the best plan? These guys could be murderers."

"We're just going to look around," Vivian said. "You can be our lookout. And I'll let Adrienne know where we're going to be, just in case."

Kate shifted from foot to foot and hesitantly agreed. "Fine, I'll keep watch, but I may be half a block down."

Lucy pulled up the map to the brothers' house. "We need to hop on the Canal streetcar. Who's got ones? We need six bucks."

"Me," Wendy said.

They walked a few blocks down Canal, just in time to meet the oncoming streetcar. Wendy fed the meter while the others crowded in with commuters on their way home from work and a few touristy folks.

The streetcar made several stops along Canal. Since the weather was nice, most of the windows were down. As it passed a two-story pink house that had been converted into a restaurant, Vivian got a big whiff of something good. "Holy crap, something smells delicious." She tugged on the chime cable. The streetcar stopped two blocks down and they got off at Carrollton.

"This was our stop anyway," Lucy said, putting her phone into her purse.

Vivian was already walking back the direction they'd come toward the Pepto pink house.

Lucy caught up to her. "Guess we're checking out the brothers' house after you satisfy your taste buds."

"Yes we are," Vivian responded, tummy rumbling. "All this emotional stress is driving me to eat."

A red neon sign that read Mandina's lit up the front windows and made the pink house glow a little red. A hostess greeted them and led them past a long wooden bar to the upstairs dining area.

A waitress went over the specials, then mentioned the bottle of Sangiovese as a pairing.

"I may need a whole bottle to myself," Vivian said, and they ordered one.

After perusing the menu and tasting the wine, Wendy ordered the house special, Trout Meuniere, Kate got the Grilled Shrimp Pasta Bordelaise, Lucy ordered Miss Hilda's salad, and Vivian got the fried chicken with two sides of mashed potatoes, hold the vegetables.

"They have green beans," Lucy pointed out.

"It says 'string beans' and in my mind, it ain't the same. I'm not risking it."

Kate offered a toast. "The cemetery mirrors didn't quite work out the way I was hoping, but at least it wasn't Daisy."

They touched glasses and polished off the first bottle before dinner was served and ordered a second. The meal was remarkable, Vivian shared her mashed potatoes, and even Lucy was glad she'd gotten two scoops. Wendy insisted everyone try the Meuniere sauce, including Vivian, who didn't like fish but had a bite anyway.

"Mmmm. That sauce could make anything taste good." Vivian winked.

They finished dinner and their second bottle of wine but passed on dessert.

"I may be feelin' beignets later," Kate said and tugged on her expandy pants. "I've got room."

They paid the bill and Vivian pushed her chair back. "Can we take a cab? I had too many mashed potatoes."

"It's only three blocks," Lucy said. "You can work off 20 calories of fried chicken." She led the way and they slowly walked by Kevin and Devin's. They stopped a few houses down and Vivian texted Adrienne where they were, then put the phone in her pocket. The girls watched the street and the house for a few minutes.

A dog barked and Vivian jumped, then she started giggling.

"Shhhh!" Wendy said.

"I'm sorry, it's nerves, and maybe the wine. And now I need to pee!"

"You're gonna have to hold it," Lucy said.

"Screw that, I'm going to knock on the door." Vivian said, then marched toward the house. The overgrown grass brushed against her legs and the screen door hung loosely on one hinge. The girls waited on the driveway while she walked onto the porch and rang the doorbell. No answer, no sounds coming from the house.

She carefully moved the screen door and jiggled the door handle but it was locked. Hopping off the porch, she waved for the girls to follow and went around back. She bypassed the dilapidated detached garage and walked up the back stoop.

"What are you doing?" Kate asked as Vivian tried the back door.

It, too, was locked. "I've gotta go and we might as well check out the inside." She leaned over and tried the window. Locked.

"You're probably better off in the weeds back here," Lucy said. "I bet these boys are disgusting."

"Are you insane?" Kate said, "these guys could be killers. No way, you're not going in there."

Vivian walked to another window on the back of the house and tried it. Locked. "They're not home and we'll be quick."

"What if they're not answering for a reason? Like they have Daisy?"

"Then we need to get her."

Wendy started walking to the detached garage. "I'm going to see if there's a gray Mustang in here before we go into this house. If there is, we're calling the cops and they can go in."

She peered through a dirty window on the garage door. "Nothing but a bunch of junk. We're clear."

Lucy looked at Kate. "Aren't you supposed to be the lookout?"

"Oh yeah," Kate snapped her fingers. "The wine made me forget." She walked to the corner of the house. "I'll call if there's any movement."

Vivian tried the knob again, then kicked at the doggie door. The plastic flap swayed back and forth, and she suddenly really regretted those mashed potatoes. "We need Kate."

Lucy hustled around the house and came back with a reluctant Kate. Vivian pointed to the doggie door.

"No way, not happening, not in a million years. Never."

"Oh come on, it's for Daisy."

Vivian looked to Lucy.

"Screw you, my boobs would never fit in there."

Vivian nodded in agreement, then looked at Wendy.

"Have you seen these hips?"

Kate sighed and dropped her shoulders. "Dammit, you girls need to lose some weight or boobs or hips or something. This is total crap. I'm supposed to keep watch in case they come home. If I get abducted, killed or eaten by a dog or some other animal, you totally owe me."

With that she dropped on all fours and lifted the flap, then turned to Vivian. "It's dark, I can't see anything."

"See if you can reach the door handle."

Kate reached her arm in and frowned. She sighed again. "Fuck it." Then she disappeared through the doggie door.

30

The lock clicked on Kevin and Devin's back door and Kate swung the door open. "Let's get this over with."

Lucy stepped inside. "It's dark in here. Where's the light?"

Vivian hit a button to wake up her phone. "We snuck in here, we can't turn on any lights."

Just as she finished saying that, Lucy hit the wall switch and a dim light over the kitchen sink flickered. A roach skittered across the floor and they all screamed.

"Turn off the light!" Wendy yelled. "I have a flashlight app on my phone, but I don't know how much of this nasty-ass house we want to see."

Lucy flipped the light off and Wendy pulled up her app. They let their eyes adjust to the darkness before they moved into the living room.

"What are we looking for?" Kate asked, clinging onto Vivian's shirt.

"Any sign that Daisy's been here or that they have anything to do with her disappearance."

Beer cans and a pizza box sat on a coffee table in front of an orange, yellow and green plaid couch. A gaming console and two controllers sat on the floor beside it. The smell of stale beer, musty carpet and body odor drove the girls upstairs, to the bedrooms, which didn't smell any better, though one had a faint scent of weed.

Vivian opened the lid to a cigar box on the dresser. "What do we have here?" Inside the wooden box sat a package of Zig Zag rolling papers, a lighter, a glass pipe and a baggie of pot. Vivian pulled the seal apart and sniffed. "This could be Maui Wowie."

Wendy snatched the bag and took a whiff. "What? How can you tell?"

"I can't. I just like to say Maui Wowie."

"Y'all put that back," Kate said, taking the baggie and returning it to the cigar box. "We get into enough trouble as it is. Don't need to get busted with pot, too."

Wendy shone the phone light around the room. A guitar sat propped in a corner and pornographic magazines were strewn next to the bed. Dirty clothes lay all around.

"Check out this monster flashlight," Lucy said. She picked it up from the nightstand and tried to turn it on. "I think it's broken, I can't even get the switch to move."

Vivian saw a bottle of lubricant on the nightstand and gasped. "Oh my gosh, Lucy, put it down! Put it down!"

Lucy dropped it and the end popped off. "What the — "

A skin-toned blob was exposed.

"Eeeew! Gross! It's a Fleshlight!" Vivian hopped up and down, shaking her hands. "Go disinfect yourself, Lucy! Hurry!"

Lucy ran into the bathroom, flipped on the light and reached for the hot water knob. "This place is disgusting!"

"I suddenly don't need to pee anymore," Vivian said and turned off the light, using her phone to search for the soap.

An orange and blue container sat on the back of the toilet, "GoJo pumice hand cleaner." While Lucy lathered up, Vivian looked around, searching for any sort of feminine products. Not seeing anything, she waited for Lucy to finish up. After a few minutes of intense scrubbing, she declared her hands as clean as they could be under the circumstances, and wiped them on her shirt.

Wendy hovered over the Fleshlight with her flashlight. "This thing freaks me out. I've never seen anything like it."

"Is that for what I think it's for?" Kate asked.

"Uh, yes," Vivian said and nodded toward the bottle on the nightstand. "That's some quality lube he's got there. He doesn't skimp."

Wendy moved to the door. "We need to wrap this up. Let's not touch anything — nothing, nada — in the other bedroom."

The girls agreed and moved to the second bedroom, looking for anything that indicated Daisy had been there.

A shrill ring pierced the quiet. All the girls jumped and Lucy knocked over a glass bong that sat on the dresser. Dark, stale water poured out of it. The stench was overwhelming.

Vivian looked at her cell phone screen and answered the call. "Hey, Adrienne, I can only talk for a second. We're in the house looking for clues."

"Get out of there now!" Adrienne yelled.

Vivian had to hold her phone away from her ear. "We're going, we're going."

"I'm serious. Right now."

"Okay, okay." She moved to the stairs. The other girls followed.

"Antonio said those guys are known to shoot first, ask questions later. Get out."

Vivian hit the bottom stair as headlights glared through the front window. An old truck pulled into the driveway and continued to the back of the house.

"Shit, gotta go. We've got brother trouble." Click.

"Out the front!" Wendy whispered and led the way with her phone light.

The engine turned off and the hinges of the door squeaked.

It was hard to see, and Vivian kicked a beer can across the room. The crash reverberated, sounding much louder than it actually was.

Wendy fumbled with the front door lock as a key was inserted into the back door.

"Open it! Open it!" Kate squealed.

Wendy yanked the door and the four ran out, leaving it open behind them. Lucy took the lead, hauling ass down the street, then turned on the corner and ducked behind a parked car. The other girls caught up, gasping for breath, listening.

One of the brothers yelled into the darkness. "Stay the fuck outta my house, mothafuckers!" He ratcheted a shotgun. "Sonsabitches!"

31

Vivian, Kate, Wendy and Lucy took off again, back toward Canal. They came to a place called Venezia's, decided they needed a drink, and took a small table in the bar.

"Geezus hell, that was close!" Vivian's heart raced and she wiped at her forehead with a napkin. "That's the most running I've done since I thought I was going to be bear kibble in Colorado."

Kate shook her head. "I can't believe I crawled on that floor and had to look at some nasty guy's sex toy." She stood. "I'm going to go wash my hands. Get me a water, please. That wine earlier messed with my head. I went through a *doggie* door."

Wendy laughed. "It got a little hairy, but we made it. Way to go, girls!"

Lucy hopped up. "Thanks for reminding me. I've got to go wash again, too. Order me a vodka tonic. Double."

The bartender was on his way over when he was stopped by a man with silver-white hair and wearing a navy blue suit. He scribbled in the air, then reached for a napkin.

The bartender handed him a pen and walked over to the girls. "What can I get for y'all?"

Vivian was about to order when she heard the man at the bar repeat the address they had just fled from.

The man said, "I'll go check it out. I'm leaving right now. Call you back." He walked out the door.

Vivian turned her attention back to the bartender and ordered a Dos Equis and Lucy's double.

After the bartender walked off, Vivian looked at Wendy. "Did you just hear what that man said?" Wendy looked around. "What man?"

"The older guy who was just at the bar. He was talking to someone on the phone and repeated Kevin and Devin's address, then said he'd go check on it."

Lucy and Kate came back to the table.

"What's up with those freaks' address?" Lucy asked. Vivian caught them up.

"Hmmm," Kate said. "What's he going to check on? Did we miss something to do with Daisy?"

"We're not going back," Lucy said. "He had a gun."

The drinks were delivered and the girls began to relax a little. The first drinks went down smooth so they ordered another round. Lucy only got a single this time.

Midway through drink two, the silver-haired man came back into the restaurant. He glanced at Vivian as he walked by. He then got out his phone and said to someone, "What did you say they looked like?" He listened for a minute, then said, "What's her name?" Then he looked back at Vivian and said, "You Vivian?"

She nodded.

"You need to call Adrienne."

"Oh shit, okay. Thanks." She pulled out her phone, which said she'd missed seven calls, all from Adrienne. "Oops." She dialed and Adrienne answered on the first ring.

"You scared me to death," Adrienne yelled.

"Sorry, sorry. I had put my phone on silent after your earlier call scared the hell out of us! We're even."

"What happened?"

"We ran out the front as they came in the back. Then one of the brothers came out with a gun. Needless to say we won't be going back."

"Hell no, you aren't going back," Adrienne said. "That was too close, but I'm glad you're okay."

"Did Detective Leffall get Hairy Harry at Harrah's?"

"Sure did and promptly interviewed him. He says he paid $15,000 for a boat and gambled away the rest of the 20 large at the casino."

"Have the cops been able to find the boat?"

"They're working on it. Antonio said Harry, though sleazy, seemed like he was telling the truth. They asked about the money several different ways and his answers were all the same."

"Thanks, A." Vivian signed off, then told the girls about the money.

Kate set down her glass of water. "That story ought to be easy enough to prove."

"A bill of sale and the actual boat," Wendy said.

Vivian took a sip of her beer. "He did seem genuinely upset about her."

"Poor Harry," Lucy said. "He's just a big hairy mess."

"I wonder how Jason's holding up?" Kate asked. "Maybe we should call him?"

"Good idea." Vivian dialed his number.

"Hi, Vivian."

"Hey. How you doing?"

"Daisy's story is going to be on the 10 o'clock news. They interviewed me about an hour ago."

"That's awesome! Hope it turns up some leads."

"And the cops were able to track down the two guys who tried to break in the back door to the club. They're about to go bust their apartment."

"How'd they figure out who they were?"

"Searching cameras from nearby stores. These guys stole a case of beer from a convenience store and they were able to get a license plate number."

"Well, that's something." *They don't seem like the most savvy criminals.*

Jason sounded a little dejected after saying it out loud. "Yeah, it's something."

"We'll be looking for you on the news." Vivian clicked off and relayed his info to the girls.

"Guess Adrienne lit a fire that Al is fanning," Kate said. "It's about time the media took notice."

"Hell yeah, but what are we going to do tonight?" Lucy asked. "We have some time to kill before Lala Lollipop rips off her wrapper at Rick's, and Jonathon wants us to meet him at Tipitina's. He said a really great band, Trombone Shorty and Orleans Avenue, are playing tonight. He knows someone and can get us in."

Wendy smacked her hands together. "Oh yeah, we need a little break, and that's just the band to give it."

Lucy checked the website on her phone. "They start in an hour. Let's ask the bartender to call us a cab."

They paid the tab and started to walk out the door. The silver-haired man turned on his stool and yelled out as they left, "You girls are lucky Al's on your side. You gotta watch your step in this town."

32

The cab pulled to a stop in front of Venezia's. The girls piled in and told the driver Tipitina's Uptown. He nodded and took off. A short while later, they were at a banana-yellow bar at Napoleon and Tchoupitoulas.

Jonathon opened the cab door for Lucy and kissed her while the other girls got out. He came up for air and said, "So glad you could make it. Follow me." He walked up to the bouncer at the front door, shook his hand and gave him a bro-hug. They bullshitted for a minute, then the bouncer waved them all in.

The club was packed with people dancing to the music of legendary Professor Longhair, even though the stage was dark. The girls followed Jonathon to the bar where he shook hands with the bartender. A few minutes later, the bartender set a draft beer and four pink concoctions on the bar and gave Jonathon a nod.

"What is this?" Lucy asked as Jonathon passed each of them a pink thing.

"It's free, drink it!"

Lucy shrugged and held up her high-ball glass. "To hookups!"

The girls cheersed her back, then Vivian checked her phone. Jason had texted that he didn't feel like getting out, no other news from the cops. Her pink drink was okay, a little too watermelony. Next round she was getting a beer, even if she had to pay for it.

Lucy seemed to be enjoying hers. She had her drink in one hand and Jonathon's bicep in the other.

Jonathon pushed through the crowd, the girls following, as he made his way closer to the stage. He stopped about three rows of people back and started making out with Lucy.

Kate leaned over to Vivian. "I'm not sure I approve of this."

"Oh, loosen up. The poor girl has been sexless for how long? She can make out in New Orleans."

"Ehhh," Kate said.

"Look, I've been telling her to do something about it. Either to get a divorce or make it work. She's been trying the latter, and dammit, it's not working. I'm not going to stop her from kissing some guy on vacation."

"You're right. I'm not going to judge." Kate sucked down her entire pink drink and handed it to Vivian. "I need another."

With Lucy and Jonathon occupied, Vivian only took a drink order from Wendy, who wanted a Shiner Bock. Drinks procured, Vivian made her way back to the girls and Jonathon and handed them out. As she did, the lights in the club dimmed and a green and blue spotlight shone on the stage. Trombone Shorty walked out with a trumpet in his right hand and a trombone in his left.

The crowd went crazy, shouting and clapping.

He stepped up to the mic. "Where y'at?" he shouted. The crowd cheered even louder to the standard New Orleans greeting. The rest of his five-piece band got into position and started into his tune, "Suburbia."

Vivian got past the fact he was wearing a wife-beater, especially since he was super ripped. A few lines into the first song, she looked over at Wendy. "Damn, he's good."

"Told ya!" she said and kept dancing.

The band played several of its own songs and a few tributes and the crowd sang along. It got more and more packed down front, but the girls held their ground.

The musicians took a break and Vivian checked her phone again. A text from Jason read:

Those guys are petty thieves. Knew nothing about Daisy.

Vivian felt badly for him. He was having a tough time. She showed the text to the girls to catch them up. Lucy looked sad for a split second, then went back to dancing with Jonathon.

Wendy made a bar run and brought Vivian a new beer. They cheersed with Kate and the band came back on, joined this time by Kermit Ruffins. Kermit and Trombone Shorty played their trumpets to a couple of Kermit's originals and Shorty's "Neph," then more crowd favorites. During "The Craziest Things," Vivian happened to glance toward the bar. The undercover cop from Harry's hotel and The Dungeon moved behind another patron. She scanned the club looking for him, but he seemed to have disappeared.

She nudged Kate and Wendy and thumbed toward the bar. "I just saw the bellman from Harry's hotel. Remember, blond buzz cut?"

"Where'd he go?" Kate asked, straining her neck to look around.

Wendy kept dancing to the music. "I remember him, he was cute."

Vivian shrugged. "I don't see him anymore." She pulled out her phone and texted Antonio, asking if NOPD had something going undercover at Tipitina's.

A few minutes later, he texted back two words: No. Why?

Kate grabbed Vivian's arm. "I just saw him walk out the door. That's who I saw in the cemetery."

"We saw a lot of cops today, Kate. I'm not surprised."

Her eyes were wide. "No, I saw him *before* we found the body. He was watching us when we were at the mirrored tomb."

Vivian texted that to Antonio.

He responded:

LEAVE. Don't know him. Don't trust him.

Vivian looked at the time on her phone, 11:30. They needed to leave soon anyway to get to Rick's. She nudged Lucy, who was bumping and grinding with her 19-year-old, and pointed to the door. Lucy got the hint, grabbed Jonathon's belt loop, and they all made their way to the door. Trombone Shorty played the last notes of "Big," and the crowd showed no signs of leaving as the band walked off the stage.

Cabs lined Napoleon Avenue, and Wendy waved to the closest one.

"Where y'all going?" Jonathon asked as Vivian opened the front door to a black and white cab.

"Titty bar," Lucy said and shimmied her ta-tas. "Wanna come?"

"Hell to the yeah!" Jonathon said, jumping into the cab next to Kate and Wendy. "Which one?"

Lucy climbed onto his lap and yelled out, "Take us to Rick's!"

***

By 9 p.m. Daisy was hungry again and her fear had turned to anger. She couldn't concentrate on anything on the TV, but the news report at 10 compounded her anger and brought back the fear. The body of one of the missing dancers had been found in a tomb in St. Louis Cemetery #1. Murder was suspected.

The door to her room opened and the pink martini, roofie asshole pushed a tray in.

I hope the other "Desert Glitter" guy isn't behind him. She tried to run past roofie asshole but Sonu was behind him and caught her. She struggled to get free but the guy from earlier grabbed her in a bear hold, easily

Joan Rylen

overpowering her. There was no escape. He dumped her on the bed and left the room.

Sonu signaled for the cart-pushing roofie asshole to leave, then looked at Daisy. "You must understand, you belong to me now. You are never again to publicly display nudity, and you will dress appropriately tomorrow, or there will be consequences."

Daisy jumped off the bed, fists flying at his face. "Let me go, you fucking dick!"

He was incredibly strong for his trim size and easily gripped her wrists and held them together. He raised his voice and shoved her onto the bed. "You will not conduct yourself in such a manner. Do not ever attempt to strike me, nor should you use such language. Do not make me hurt you to teach you a lesson."

She lashed out at him again, managing to scratch his arm before he slapped her. The force propelled her back on the bed, and the entire right side of her face stung. She knew he could easily overpower her, but she wasn't ready to give up. She leapt off the bed again and aimed a kick at his groin. His reflexes were quick and he grabbed her leg, laying her flat on her back. He pinned her arms over her head and held her legs down with his knees.

He lowered his face to just inches from hers and said, "One more attempt like this and you will remain drugged until we are ready to leave. Do you understand?"

Daisy thrashed underneath him and yelled.

He tightened his grip on her wrists, and his knees pressed harder into her thighs. He kept her like that until she stopped and her outburst had turned to sobs. He moved off of her and sat on the side of the bed. She rolled away from him and curled into a ball.

He listened to her cry for a few moments, then reached over and yanked on the shoulder of her shirt, ripping it. "Get out of these disgusting, Western clothes. If you do not take them off, I will."

Daisy flinched and cried even harder.

He stalked out of the room.

33

I t's a good thing you have me along," Jonathon said as they rode in the cab to Rick's Cabaret on Bourbon. "You have to have a male escort to get in."

"I'm surprised any of those joints on Bourbon require you to have a man with you," Kate said.

"The nicer ones do, and I'm your man."

Lucy settled further into his lap. "And you're man enough to escort all of us. I like that."

Vivian, Wendy and Kate cracked up laughing as Jonathon pulled Lucy in tight.

Vivian pulled up the local ABC affiliate and found a new story about Daisy and the other two girls. She held her phone so everyone could see and turned up the volume.

A lot of what was reported, the girls already knew. The story cut to a reporter standing in front of the arches to St. Louis Cemetery #1. Spotlights lit the area behind her, casting an eerie glow and shadows on the screen. "The police are still at work, searching for evidence of who could have committed this crime and desecrated these historic grounds. Though the victim has not been identified to us, sources tell us it is one of the three missing dancers who have disappeared during the past month."

Pictures of all three victims flashed across the screen. "Police are requesting the help of the public and have established a tip line." The phone number was displayed, and the reporter continued talking. "I had the opportunity to speak to Jason Pitts, the fiancé of Daisy Easley, to discuss what he and others are doing to help bring Daisy home."

The story cut to the interview with Jason, microphone in his face. He said, "I've had an unbelievable response to my pleas for help. People have come from across the country to cover the city with flyers, ask questions and just do anything they can to help. I know we're going to find her safe."

Vivian put her phone into her pocket just as the cab pulled to a stop.

Rick's red neon sign cast a glow, making everyone who walked by look sunburned. "We need a game plan," she said as everybody got out. She asked Jonathon, "How do we get Lala Lollipop to talk to us about Daisy?"

"This is the Daisy from the newscast?" he asked.

The girls gave him a quick rundown of the kidnapping and the Lollipop connection.

He smiled. "Leave it to me. I can get any woman to talk."

"Oh yeah?" Lucy said.

"Twenty bucks says I can get this chick to come to your hotel."

Lucy slapped him on the arm. "She's a stripper, not a prostitute."

"Wanna bet?"

Vivian laughed and told him their hotel and room number. "I want to see this process in action. Do you need some cash? How much does this kind of transaction cost?"

"Depends. I'll have to feel her out, literally. I'll buy a lap dance, and the handsier she lets me get, the more likely she'll go to the hotel. I'll know pretty quick how much for the whole shebang." He laughed at himself.

"I'm only supporting this for the cause," Lucy said, tracing her fingernail down his chest to his navel, "but I'm going to be watching you."

Kate looked at the too-tanned woman in a neon-green G-string bikini and 6-inch acrylic platform heels that flashed like a strobe light, standing out front of the club. "I'm good with staying out here. I've about had enough of naked ladies."

"I'll stay with Kate," Wendy said. "Buddy system."

Vivian linked arms with Jonathon. "I got my boy buddy right here. Let's go!"

Lucy linked arms on the other side and they walked to the door. Too-tanned welcomed them in, giggling and jiggling as Lucy paid the cover charge.

The three found a table in the middle of the club, not too close. A girl in hot pants and a highlighter-yellow bikini top asked what they'd like to drink. Twenty-four dollars and three beers later, they were tortured by Trace Adkins' "Honky Tonk Badonkadonk" and a girl in chaps, leather bikini top, cowgirl hat and high-heeled western boots.

Vivian groaned. "And yet another reason why I can't stand country music."

Lucy started singing really loud and Jonathon joined in. Vivian put her head in her hands, then looked up to see Jonathon grinding on Lucy and both of them waving pretend lassos. She put her head back into her hands and turned to the side to slip in sips of beer.

Finally, Lala Lollipop was announced. Her starting music was the same as at the French House, Shirley Temple's "Good Ship Lollipop" gone wild. She strutted on stage in a super-tight navy sailor dress with a white-trimmed collar and red belt. The candy-cane heels fed into red platforms with cupcakes painted on the sides resembling boobs.

"How is she going to get out of that dress?" Vivian leaned over and asked Lucy and Jonathon.

"She'll manage," Jonathon said, never taking his eyes off the stage.

When the music changed to Nickleback's "Burn It to the Ground," Lala threw her belt aside and ripped off her dress, which apparently was Velcroed in the back. She took to the pole and tricked, turned and twisted beyond what Vivian thought the human body could do. She ended the routine in the splits, and the crowd clapped for an encore. She did the next routine to Bow Wow Wow's "I Want Candy."

Vivian stood up and started dancing along with Lucy and Jonathon. "Now this is a great song!"

"I've never heard it," Jonathon said, "but I like it."

That comment hurt a little, and Vivian looked at Lucy. *Dammit! We're not old!*

Lala ended her routine upside down, legs spread-eagle, clinging on the pole. Jonathon whispered something to Lucy, then walked toward a bouncer standing by the stage. He slipped the guy some cash and disappeared behind a velvet red curtain.

Jonathon chose a spot in the far left corner that was nice and dark, although the entire room was much darker than the rest of the club. He sat on a bench seat and pushed the small table that was in front of him away a few inches.

Lala walked out about 10 minutes later. She'd changed into a fluorescent orange string bikini.

I'm gonna enjoy this! he thought.

Lala sat down next to him and ran her hand up his thigh. "You here for me?"

"You are hot, baby," he answered.

She threw her leg across his lap and got down to business. She pushed her bikini top to the side and shoved her boobs in his face.

He went for the handsy moves and Lala let him go... almost to candy land.

Jonathon pushed through the red curtain and walked up to Vivian and Lucy. "I'm in. We might need to stop by an ATM on the way to the hotel. She'll be there in 30 minutes."

"How much is this gonna cost us?" Lucy asked.

"I promised her $200."

"We'll give her $100 to keep her clothes on, how's that?" Vivian asked.

He shrugged. "She ought to be happy."

They made their way outside and found Wendy and Kate covered in beads, laughing with a couple of cute guys holding big ass beers. "Hey, hookers!" they yelled.

"Looks like y'all've had a good time!" Vivian said, grabbing Kate's beer and taking a big-ass sip.

Wendy threw an arm around Vivian's shoulders and danced to the music blaring out of another club. "Woo hoo!"

Vivian danced along and said, "We have a date with a stripper. We gotta get to the hotel."

"Adios, boys," Wendy called to the cute guys and ambled off down Bourbon, still dancing next to Vivian. "I love this town."

They passed an ATM and Lucy halted everyone. "We need to get some phony fuck money." Jonathon stood guard as she completed the transaction.

Once in the hotel room, Vivian started laughing. "I can't believe we have a prostitute coming here."

"No shit," Wendy said. "I'm hiding my laptop."

Kate sat down on the bed. "I can't believe she's a prostitute."

Jonathon put a hand on her shoulder. "Many of them are." He smiled.

Ick!!

"What should we do while we wait?" Lucy asked. "Do we need some mood music?"

"Her mood is going to be ruined the second she walks in and sees y'all. Music won't help."

Lucy fumbled with the clock radio anyway but was interrupted by a knock at the door.

Jonathon rubbed his hands together and whispered to the girls, "Here we go." He cracked the door. "So glad you came." He then let Lala in and closed the door behind her.

"What the fuck is this?" Lala said, then turned to Jonathon and waved her finger around the room. "*This* is gonna cost extra."

34

L ala Lollipop stood in the entry to the room, hands on her hips, glaring at Vivian, Lucy, Kate and Wendy. "I'm not usually into the group thing." She turned to Jonathon and pointed her finger in his face. "Are they watching or participating?"

Vivian handed her five 20s. "Neither. We just wanted to talk to you."

"Honey, I don't get paid to listen." She stuck the money into her bra and turned toward the door.

Jonathon blocked her way. "We've paid for at least 10 minutes of your time. Then you can go."

She rolled her eyes. "Fine, I'm listening. Talk."

Kate approached her. "We're looking for information about Daisy's disappearance."

She crossed her arms. "Like I told the cops, I didn't see shit, and honestly, I couldn't give a rat's ass what happened to her."

"We get that," Kate said, "but have you heard anything? Other dancers have disappeared."

"Again, don't give a shit."

"Do you think another dancer could have played a part in this?" Wendy asked.

Lala cocked her head. "Like who?"

Lucy cleared her throat. "We were thinking maybe Trikki Vikki."

Lala threw her head back and laughed. "She barely knows where her pasties get pasted."

Vivian shifted on her feet. "Do you think Jason really loves Daisy? Maybe things weren't as peachy as he makes them sound."

At the mention of his name, Lala's eyes narrowed.

Hit a sore spot with that one, Vivian thought but said, "Y'all had a thing, right?"

Lala took a step forward but before she could say anything, Kate asked, "You were backstage when it happened. You didn't see or hear anything?"

147

Lala's chest and face were crimson and her fists were clinched. "Other than hearing those camel jockeys, all I heard was the bass thumping." She made for the door. "I'm done here."

The girls looked at each other.

"Camel jockeys?" Vivian asked.

"They sure as hell weren't from around here." With that Lala brushed past Jonathon and was gone.

"It's late but we've got to call Antonio right now," Vivian said, reaching for her phone.

He picked up on the second ring and sounded groggy.

"Hey, Antonio, I'm sorry to call so late but we just found out something!"

The phone on his end jumbled around. "I'm listening."

"That stripper, Lala Lollipop, was just at our hotel, and she said she heard — I'm using her words — camel jockeys backstage the night Daisy was kidnapped."

"What was she doing at your hotel? Never mind. Just tell me what all she said." Vivian gave him the details.

"And she used the term 'camel jockeys'?"

"That was exactly what she said. Does Gino have any Arabic-speaking men on staff?"

"Negative."

"Well there you go! It's a clue!"

"All right, listen, thanks for this, but you have to stop. I don't want to know how the hell you got her to your room, but these types of girls have pimps and they're not nice guys. Don't mess around with her anymore."

"Ten-four."

"I mean it."

"Got it."

He hung up and Vivian said to the girls, "He thanked us!"

They all cheered and high-fived. Jonathon, too.

"Who was there that was Middle Eastern?" Kate asked.

"That place was packed," Lucy said. "There were all kind of ethnicities represented."

Wendy bit her lower lip. "GQ looked like he could be."

Vivian waved her off. "No way. He was too into himself and uppity. He wouldn't be into strippers."

"He was there, wasn't he?" Wendy said.

"True, but I just don't see it. He seems too polished."

Kate agreed. "He was definitely from the area, but I don't see it, either." She kicked off her shoes. "I'm ready to hit the hay."

Vivian noticed Lucy and Jonathon sharing a lusty look. "I'm too wound up. Y'all come with me to the casino." She looked at Wendy and Kate, specifically.

Kate put a shoe back on but groaned. "Okay, but only for a little while."

"Yay! We'll be big winners! Karma is on our side tonight, baby!"

Wendy picked up her purse. "Not long, you promise?"

"Promise!" Vivian said, grabbing Wendy's sash from the desk and slipping it over her head. "You gotta wear this baby to the casino. You might get some last chance kisses from cuties." Vivian popped one of the condoms off and slipped it to Lucy. "You've got an hour to feel his power."

Lucy smiled at her and took the condom.

"Have fun!" Vivian said and left the room with Wendy and Kate.

"You shouldn't encourage this," Wendy said, bumping Vivian on the butt as they waited for the elevator.

"Screw that. And I used those words purposefully. Like I told Kate earlier, that poor girl hasn't been laid in years, ladies. *Years*. I'm just giving her the opportunity to get back into the swing of things."

"Too bad they don't have a swing like Shorty's," Kate said as the doors opened. "Lucy could have some fun with that!"

"I still can't believe you got in that thing," Vivian said, "and I thought I was the adventurous one."

"Y'all needed a product demonstration." Kate laughed with a gleam in her eye.

They went through the hotel lobby and took the underground tunnel to the casino. Once again, they were not carded.

"It's all your gray hair," Wendy said, tousling Vivian's curls.

"I just colored it a week ago!"

"I know, but you're 10 months older than me and I have to remind you occasionally."

"Thanks for that," Vivian said, stepping onto the mirrored escalator where they had re-enacted the scene from *Rain Man* earlier that day.

"Weren't we here about 12 hours ago?" Kate asked, her eyes already red from the smoke, or maybe it was the long day of beers, hurricanes and more beer.

Vivian spied a three-card-poker table that only had two players. "Come on, I'm gonna teach y'all how to play. It's easy."

The girls sat down and pulled out $40 each, except for Vivian who threw her player's card and a hundred on the table.

"Hey big spenda!" Wendy said.

"You gotta play big to win big, baby!"

Vivian explained the game with the help of the dealer, Alyssa. Kate dropped out after losing her money in four hands. Wendy won some, then gave it all back. Vivian, however, hung in there. The young couple at the table kept passing money back and forth to keep one another in the game.

Vivian picked up her hand, set it back down and placed $10 on top. "Watch this," she said and clapped.

Alyssa started with the woman, who didn't have squat. Her husband had a pair of tens, so he got paid on his pairs plus, but the dealer had a pair of queens so he lost on the other bet. Alyssa reached for Vivian's three cards and flipped them over.

"Shazammapuss!" Vivian yelled and raised her arms in victory.

A six, seven and eight of hearts lay neatly on the table.

The girls cheered and Alyssa congratulated her, then called the pit boss over. He confirmed the bonus hand.

Vivian had $25 on the three-card hand and was playing $10 against the dealers' hand. In all, it paid $1,050. Vivian passed Alyssa a $25 chip, put the rest in her purse and stood up. "My work here is done."

35

Day 5

"Wake up! Wake up! Jason's on TV!" Lucy said, shaking Vivian. She unmuted the volume and cranked it.

Vivian shimmied herself up on the bed, plumped the pillow and forced her eyes open.

"Kate, Wendy, wake up!" Lucy said, hopping on the bed. "Matt Lauer just did an introduction. Daisy's story is finally going national!"

"We're going live to the family of the first victim, whose identity was released early this morning, Lisa Miller." Lauer's tone had a sense of urgency. "Folks, I'm sorry for your loss. I know this must be a difficult time and we appreciate you talking to us."

A lady in her mid-20s, who looked a little rough around the edges, held a photo of Lisa. "We just want to find who did this."

"I understand that Lisa was an adult entertainer in New Orleans and that she was missing for almost a month."

"That's right."

"Do you feel like enough was done to search for your sister?"

"We're real appreciative of the police, but we wish they would have found   her before — " The woman paused and lowered her head. "Before, you know."

"Did your sister know the second dancer who was kidnapped?"

"We don't think so, but Lisa had a lot of friends. People loved her. She was always doing nice things for others."

"Have the police found anything common among the three victims other than their shared occupations? Had the women ever met? Worked at the same club?"

"You know, we've talked to her friends, the police have talked to her co-

151

workers. Nobody can come up with anything that connected Lisa to the other two girls."

The shot switched to Jason, his parents and Daisy's parents. Lauer introduced and thanked them.

"This is day three since Daisy disappeared. How are you holding up?"

Jason answered. "We're trying to stay positive. We're lucky we've had a lot of support, friends and family, who are here helping in the search."

"I understand a local printer donated flyers and other groups have come forward to participate."

"That's right. We won't stop until Daisy has been found."

"The adult entertainment business can be a dangerous world. Had Daisy ever encountered problems?"

"Not really. She would get the occasional crazy marriage proposal or overzealous fan. She's pretty good at taking care of herself. That's one of the things I love about her."

"I understand she's been nominated as Newcomer of the Year in the Exotic Dancer National Championships and the two of you were on your way to Las Vegas for the competition when she was kidnapped."

"That's correct."

"Are you second guessing her choice of professions?"

Jason got a bit defensive. "Absolutely not. Daisy isn't just an entertainer, she's a competitor. An athlete. She's worked hard to get where she is and I'm proud of her. We're all proud of her." Their parents all nodded their heads. Daisy's mom wiped a tear from her cheek.

"Have the police shared any new details with you regarding who could have done this?"

"I think you know what we do. They're tight-lipped about the investigation, but I've been told they're following up on all leads."

The shot changed to just Lauer. "Sources tell us the investigation continues into the disappearance of the second dancer, Simone Hitchens, missing for almost two weeks. We requested an interview with her family, but they declined. Sources tell us, however, that video footage shows her willingly getting into a gray Mustang, so authorities have been hesitant to call it a kidnapping."

Lucy muted the TV and looked at Kate. "So it was the first dancer you discovered in the tomb yesterday."

Kate dabbed at her eyes with her pajamas. "Poor Lisa. I hate to think of what she must have gone through."

Vivian groaned. "I can't imagine, but the interview and story were good. Drawing attention to the cases will help."

Wendy stood up and stretched. "Antonio's got to be feeling pressure to find Daisy and Simone, and it doesn't get much bigger than the 'Today Show'."

Vivian smacked Lucy on the butt. "Speaking of big, how was Jonathon last night? Did he meet your expectations?"

Lucy tossed the remote onto the bed. "We had a really nice time. That boy can kiss!"

"And you really mean *boy*, don't you?" Wendy teased.

"What else can that boy do?" Kate asked.

Lucy shook her head. "I couldn't do it. *Dammit!* I wanted to, but it just didn't feel right. I couldn't do that to Steve."

Vivian kicked off her covers. "I commend you for having the willpower, but hell, Steve has put you in sexile. I'd be dying a slow, sexaperating death. Damn, I was expecting the ol' towel on the doorknob when we got back. Not that it would have stopped us."

"Yeah, no. He left about 45 minutes after y'all did."

"Ya big loser." Vivian hip-bumped Lucy on her way to the bathroom. "I, on the other hand, was a big winner!"

"You were?"

"Yep, won over $1,000!"

"Damn, you're lucky! Lunch is on you!"

Vivian's phone buzzed on the nightstand. Kate picked it up and tossed it to her.

"Hello."

"Hey! It's Adrienne. Did y'all see Jason on TV?"

"Yes. He did a great job."

"He sure did. That'll help move things along, I'm sure of it. Y'all need a break from what's going on here. I want y'all to come to my family's place outside the city. We can eat some home-cookin', take a spin in the airboat, just get away for a while. Al's busy, he doesn't want to go. What do ya think?"

"Hold on, let me ask." Kate, Wendy and Lucy agreed.

"We're in. When?"

"I'll give ya an hour. I'll text you when I'm close."

"Okay. Bye." Vivian put the phone on the dresser. "Let's move, ladies."

***

Daisy showered and inspected her clothes. There was no wearing the ripped blouse, and her white miniskirt was so filthy it could probably stand up on its own. It hurt worse than his slap, but she put on the least ugly Middle Eastern dress. It had purple and red swirls against tan fabric; the

153

others were a solid burgundy, navy and brown.

A guy she hadn't seen before brought her breakfast. His gaze held a little more leer than Sonu's other two guys, and it made her uncomfortable. She was almost glad she was covered head to toe in the ugly dress. *Or is that what he likes?*

She flipped on the "Today Show" and caught Matt Lauer's interview with Lisa Miller's family, Jason, his parents and hers. As the camera zoomed in on Jason, she ran to the screen and kissed his face. The camera panned to her parents and she kissed them, too. "I'm here! I'm here!"

The interview over, Daisy pounded on the bedroom door. "Let me out of here! You motherfuckers! I'm going to kill you all when I get out of here!" She screamed, cried and threw the breakfast dishes across the room, splattering eggs, grits, fruit and cottage cheese all over the walls.

***

One by one, the girls took turns getting ready. Vivian waited to the last minute, threw herself into a quick shower and got dressed in her much-loved denim skirt and a chiffon, one-shouldered emerald green blouse. Since she was going to be with Adrienne, she decided some bling was needed. She raided her accessory bag for her crystal chandelier earrings and looked in the mirror. *Need a little more.* Several silver Bengal bracelets and a matching necklace later, and she was ready to go.

Lucy, wearing dark brown shorts, a pale pink top and Cole-Haan sandals, looked at her. "You're aware we're going to the swamp, right?"

Vivian shrugged and smiled, bracelets jangling. They finished up and headed out. Her phone chimed with a message as they made their way downstairs.

Adrienne waited for them at the valet stand in a black SUV.

Wendy adjusted the hem of her black shorts as she reached for the door handle. "I haven't been out to the bayou before. Will my red shirt set off alligators like it does bulls?"

Adrienne laughed. "They'll think you're pretty and want to give ya a kiss."

Wendy pursed her lips and blew a kiss into the air. "Mmmmmmwah!"

"You're gator bait and I'm starving," Kate said as they got in. She wore a much more conservative, and swamp appropriate, ensemble of jeans and sleeveless blue blouse with satin trim. A silver disk inlaid with a gold fleur-de-lis dangled from a thin silver necklace, and a pair of strappy pewter sandals completed her look.

"If you can hold out 30 minutes, my momma will have plenty to eat. She's the best on the bayou."

They rode for a while, talking about Daisy and the case.

Adrienne slowed and made a sharp turn. "I can't believe the first dancer is dead."

"Yeah, and that we found her." Kate stared out the window.

"Terrible," Wendy said.

"It is," Adrienne said. "Antonio questioned the two kids last night, the ones who tried to break in. They didn't have much to say, but one of them mentioned seeing a large, black SUV."

"That doesn't match with the gray Mustang from the second girl," Vivian said.

Adrienne shook her head. "Nope, and they've had no other developments in that kidnapping, if it was a kidnapping."

"We're in a large black SUV," Kate pointed out.

Adrienne laughed. "Yep, I'm gonna feed ya to the gators."

"So it was *you* then," Kate said.

"Ya got me."

Vivian adjusted the air vent. "Surely, after all this, the cops have to know the girl has been kidnapped. Yes, she may have gotten into the car voluntarily, but for her to just disappear. No way."

"I know," Adrienne said, speeding over a short bridge that spanned a waterway. "Too coincidental."

Vivian turned to Adrienne. "Don't know what this means, if anything, but we saw that undercover cop while we were out last night. I texted Antonio and he said he didn't trust him."

"He's usually good at reading people. I'd heed his advice." Everyone was quiet for a bit. They passed over another bridge and Adrienne asked, "Y'all ever been on an airboat?"

"Nope, but I've seen 'em on 'Swamp People,' " Kate said.

"Well honey, you're about to live like a Cajun for a day in the confines of a swamp."

"Are we gonna catch a gator?" Kate asked.

"Nah, it's not gator huntin' season. We'll catch somethin', though. That I guarantee."

36

"W here are we?" Wendy asked Adrienne as they drove down the two-lane road.

"Right now we're on the Delacroix Highway, but we're almost to my parents' camp."

"What do you mean by camp, exactly?" Vivian asked. "As in your mom is making us lunch on an open fire? Are there gonna be s'mores?"

Adrienne laughed. "No. The houses on the bayou are called camps. Just one of those regional things." She turned onto a dirt road and went two miles or so, where the road ended in front of a small, wooden cabin on stilts, set back from the bayou. A weathered deck led from the yard out to the water, where an airboat was tied to the pier.

Vivian stepped out and expected it to be quiet, but the wind rustled the trees and birds sang. Two brown Labradors bounded up to the car, barking.

"Here's Rex and Roux, our friendly, drooling welcoming committee." Adrienne scratched their ears. "Say hey to the girls." She stood up straight and took a deep breath. "I've missed the smell of the cypress. I spent many a day lying on that pier, working on my tan and watching the boys go by."

"Hey, cher," an older version of Adrienne called. She stepped off the porch, followed by Adrienne's dad, who walked with a cane, though he still looked quite fit.

Adrienne gave her parents a hug and made introductions.

"Come on in, girls," Mr. Robichaux said. He beat them to the screen door and held it open for them.

Mrs. Robichaux ran into the kitchen and started ladling up bowls of crawfish étouffée with white rice.

Adrienne gave her mom another hug. "My favorite, you must love me."

Her mom shooed her off and said, "Get our guests some sweet tea."

They sat around the dining room table enjoying the étouffée and listening to stories of Adrienne's antics as a child.

Mr. Robichaux set down his spoon. "I was ready to lock her away when

156

she hit puberty. Those boys were as persistent as coons in the trash."

"Daddy, you just called me trash," Adrienne said.

"My cher, you know what I meant."

Mrs. Robichaux laughed and went into the kitchen. She came back with a hot pan of bread pudding. "Adrienne, go grab the bourbon sauce off the stove, but stir it up first."

Oh yeah, Vivian thought. "That was the best crawfish étouffée I've ever had. Thank you, Mrs. Robichaux. I can't wait for the bread pudding."

"I hope you like it. I don't put any raisins in it, Adrienne doesn't like them."

"Me, neither. Perfect." And indeed, the bread pudding with bourbon sauce was perfect.

After lunch the girls sat in rocking chairs and a swing on the front porch, letting their food settle. In a bit, Mrs. Robichaux came out with a stack of photo albums. They flipped through Al and Adrienne's wedding and pictures of Adrienne and Antonio as children. One of Antonio as a teenager showed him in tight shorts jumping off a tree swing into the bayou.

"Is it safe to swim out there?" Lucy asked.

"You just gotta watch," Adrienne said, "and never swim alone." She closed the last album and stood. "Y'all ready for a boat ride?"

***

Lunch never came and Sonu didn't check on her until late afternoon. She sat against the wall, arms wrapped around her legs, and didn't acknowledge him.

He took in the mess from breakfast. "The sooner you come to terms with your new life, the better."

"This is not my new life. It will never be."

He indicated the mess. "This is unacceptable behavior from my wife. You are not to do this again or you will not eat until we get to our destination in a few days."

The word "wife" got her attention and she stood. "What? Are you really so insane as to believe I will marry you?"

"You are not given a choice in the matter. We will be wed in my country next week."

She took a step toward him. "I will never marry you, asshole."

He slapped her. "My wife will not address me in such a manner."

She covered the side of her face and glared at him. "I will never be your wife!"

He slapped her again and threw her on the bed. He moved on top of her and put his mouth to hers. She tried to twist away from him but he was too strong, even his jaw was strong, and he kissed her harder. She managed to get a knee into his groin. He rolled over on the bed and she hopped up and ran for the door. He grabbed her arm as she went by the bed and shoved her to the ground.

He stepped close, then kicked her in the legs and back. "Do not ever hit me like that again or you will be killed. I will not tolerate such disrespect and disobedience from my wife!"

She scrambled away from him and ran into the bathroom and locked the door. He pounded on it but eventually gave up and left the room.

***

Adrienne and the girls were headed down to the pier and a banged-up, 16-foot airboat. It had two elevated pilot seats and a wide bench with handles. A big cage with two spotlights on top surrounded the giant fan on back.

Adrienne gave them a quick spiel about holding on at all times and keeping arms and legs inside the boat, then she passed out earplugs. Vivian wound up with the big, red earmuff-style.

Just before Adrienne fired up the engine, her dad walked down the pier, carrying a shotgun, a bag of Cheetos and two fishing poles rigged with lures. "I thought you might want to feed the critters for the girls and show 'em how to catch their supper." He handed her the bag and laid the poles in the boat. He checked the gun, then gave it to Adrienne. "It's locked and loaded, safety's on. Never know what you might run into out there."

She took it, double checked the safety, and stored it under her footboard. "Thanks, Daddy. I also have my Lady."

"That's my girl." He pecked her on the cheek. "Have fun out there!" he called and walked back up to the house.

"What's your Lady?" Lucy asked.

Adrienne reached into the console and pulled out a small, silver and pink Lady Smith revolver with a black handle. "It's my .38. Al gave it to me as a wedding gift."

"What a romantic," Vivian said and laughed.

Adrienne put it away. "He loves me." She maneuvered away from the dock and down the bayou. The deeper in they went, the more pungent the smell of decay, rot and just plain ol' funk.

Adrienne pointed out a few pelicans in a cypress tree covered in Spanish moss. Turtles sunned on a log and a crab crawled along the bank. A bullfrog the size of Vivian's head jumped off a floating log and made a splash as they zoomed past. An egret stood in the mangroves, ankle deep, looking for something to eat.

Adrienne cut through the marsh, taking them farther into the swamp. She yelled over the roar of the engine, "We're going to Daddy's favorite honey hole, where he catches the biggest gators."

"I've heard them say that on 'Swamp People'!" Kate said and clapped.

Adrienne slowed as she drew close to the spot. Sure enough, an eight-footer sat along the bank.

"That's a lot of purses," Lucy said, "and shoes!"

Adrienne laughed and opened the bag of Cheetos. She tossed the gator a few and he slowly swam to them, raised himself and snarfed them out of the water. Those down the hatch, Adrienne handed the bag to Vivian, who threw out two handfuls, then ate a few and licked the orange powder from her fingers.

"I knew they liked marshmallows. I didn't know they liked Cheetos," Vivian said as another gator swam up on the other side of the boat.

"It's an ancient Cajun secret," Adrienne joked.

Kate took the bag and dumped the rest in for the new guy. "I heard a tour guide lost his hand feeding a gator *and* got a fine. I'm not risking it!"

Feeding time over, Adrienne pulled up to the bank, where the grass was matted down. She hopped out. "This must be one of the gator's favorite spots. I gotta tell Daddy."

Vivian caught movement out of the corner of her eye and turned in time to see something splash into the water, next to the boat. "What was that?"

Adrienne squinted. "Just a nutria. They won't mess with ya."

"Get back in the boat!" Wendy yelled.

Adrienne looked around. "Why?"

"You're making me nervous. What if one of the gators comes out of the water real quick?"

She laughed. "Then grab the shotgun!"

"We might be from Texas, but we don't know what to do with a gun."

Vivian heard the hum of an engine and turned to see an airboat with two guys in overalls. Their long hair and scruffy beards waved in the wind as they rounded the bend and sped right at the girls. A Confederate flag waved off the back of the boat.

Adrienne got back in and pushed off the bank. "I hate these guys, the idiot Breaux brothers." She grabbed the .38 out of the console and tucked it into her waistband, then handed the shotgun to Wendy, who sat in the other co-pilot seat. Adrienne gave a quick demonstration, flicking the safety on and off a few times. "If I give the signal, take the safety off, aim anywhere in their direction and pull the trigger." She cranked the engine and yelled, "Y'all need to hang on!"

37

The airboat with the two bearded men flew on top of the water, headed straight toward the girls. Adrienne took off, cutting across tall grasses in the marsh.

"Who is that?" Vivian yelled and glanced back. The guys were following them.

"Coupla coon-asses," Adrienne yelled. "Trouble."

The guys were in a smaller airboat and closing in. Adrienne banked a hard right, cutting through more tall grass. The guys didn't anticipate the turn and lost some ground but soon caught up.

Adrienne swerved hard to miss a gator and Vivian lost her grip. She jerked and hit her ribs on the metal handle on the side of the boat.

Kate reached out for her and pulled her back. "Don't fall in! They'll run over you!"

"I'm trying not to!"

The coon-ass boat flew up behind them, only inches away. Adrienne, unable to go any faster, yelled to the girls, "I've got a plan. Hang on!"

The other boat rammed them. Adrienne held up her left hand and gave them the finger. They were so close Vivian could see one of the brothers smirking to the other with a yellow-toothed grin.

Adrienne swerved hard to the left toward an open-water pond lined with cypress trees.

"We're trapped!" Vivian yelled, but then she saw what Adrienne was aiming for — a three-foot wall of sticks and mud, the work of a busy beaver. On the other side of the dam lay more open water.

"Get ready!" Adrienne said as they neared. "This might hurt!"

The airboat launched through the air and Vivian yelled, "Aiiiyyyeeeeeeeee!" She held on for dear life.

The airboat hit the water hard, jolting everyone, but no one flew out. Adrienne let off the throttle and turned to the left.

The coon-asses didn't fare as well. They attempted the dam but went over at an angle and landed too far to the right. The driver couldn't maintain control and veered off course, crashing onto the bank amongst the trees. The airboat landed on its right side, and the brothers flew into the grass.

Adrienne shot them the finger again while the girls cheered.

"Take that, suckas!" Lucy shouted.

Just to show off, Adrienne swung the airboat around and jumped the dam again. The girls yee-hawed as they went by. Adrienne steered them back to her parents' and the girls got off, glad to be on solid ground.

"That was some ride," Vivian said, giving Adrienne a high-five. "Bravo!"

She grinned. "I've been piloting since I was old enough to climb up in the chair. Those guys may have had a faster boat, but they didn't stand a chance. Sorry we didn't get to go fishing, though."

"That was almost like *Deliverance*," Lucy said. "I think I heard banjos."

Adrienne laughed. "I wasn't that worried. I never had to give Wendy the signal."

"Thank goodness for that," Wendy said. "Last time I held a gun, I shot my brother in the butt. It was just a BB gun, but still!"

This got a round of laughs as they walked to the house. The Robichauxs greeted them on the porch and Adrienne told them about their coon-ass adventure.

"I'll have a talk with their daddy," Mr. Robichaux said. "Not that it'll do much good. He's a piece of nutria rat shit, too."

"Those boys are just into all kinds of things lately," Mrs. Robichaux said, wringing her hands on a dish towel. "Just the other day I was at the grocer and somebody they'd been talking to almost hit my car in the parking lot. I waved, trying to be friendly, and tell him it was okay, and you know what he did? He shot me the bird." She raised her middle finger in display.

"You didn't tell me about this," Adrienne's dad said, getting more pissed by the moment and gently taking her hand down.

"Oh, Billy, it was fine." She rubbed his shoulder.

"That's no way to treat a lady," he said.

"Well, it turned out all right. But that boy in the hot rod, I've seen him parked over at the Benoits' camp, which surprised me since it's usually empty. Maybe the kids finally sold it?"

"I don't remember seein' a for sale sign or hearin' anybody talking about it. That kind of stuff usually comes up."

"Well, it's over now, Billy. Don't go messin' with that man in the hot rod or those two Breaux boys. They're trouble."

Wendy, a car buff, asked, "So what kind of hot rod was that guy driving?"

"It's the one that's still real popular with the kids. Antonio had one when he was a teenager."

Adrienne looked at the girls. "Mustang." She turned to her mom. "What color was it?"

"Dark, almost black but not quite. Looked real pretty. Very shiny."

"Damn kids these days," Mr. Robichaux said. "Gets my blood pressure going. I gotta sit down." He went inside and Mrs. Robichaux followed, the screen door slamming behind her.

Vivian turned to Adrienne. "You thinking what I'm thinking?"

Adrienne pulled out her phone. "I'm calling Antonio." He didn't pick up so she left him a message, describing their mother's encounter with the Mustang guy and seeing the same car at the Benoits' place. "I'm driving by there on our way out. I'll call ya after. Love ya, little bro." Click.

"Don't say a word to my parents," Adrienne whispered. "Let's get going."

They all went inside and the girls thanked her parents again for the delicious meal and the hospitality. Rex and Roux followed the SUV down the drive, barking and wagging the whole way. Adrienne took the girls back to the highway but turned the opposite direction from where they'd come, and soon after she turned down a different dirt road, one that was bumpier and full of holes. Overgrown brush and trees lined the path.

The SUV bounced along and Adrienne said, "The Benoit camp has been mostly unused since Maggie and Burt passed away a few years ago. For a while the family would come out around holidays, but lately the place has just sat. I can't imagine the kids selling it without letting folks around here know. A lot of times, neighbors will buy up places like that to expand, you know."

She parked in the grass just after pulling into the drive. "We'll have to walk, need to maintain our element of surprise. It's only a quarter mile, maybe less." She pulled her Lady out of her purse and popped open the glove box. She dug around for a moment, then took out a Swiss Army knife. "Never know."

The girls walked slowly down the road and went around a bend. A dilapidated trailer sat on cinder blocks, right along the banks of the bayou. A sleek, gray Mustang was parked in the grass out front.

Adrienne hustled the girls into the trees, where they ducked down, and pulled out her phone. "I'm texting Antonio the license plate."

Vivian, using her 20/20, called the numbers and letters out to her.

"Let's give Antonio a few minutes to get back with me."

Two or three quiet minutes passed, then a tall man wearing a grungy wife-beater and camouflage shorts walked out onto the stoop. He had a large potbelly, pale bird legs and carried a shotgun. He looked around, then yelled, "I know you out there, motherfuckers, I heard ya. There ain't nothin' here for you, so get the hell out." He cocked the gun and lifted it up, scanning the perimeter.

The sound of glass breaking came from the side of the trailer and he took off in that direction. "Goddammit, sonofabitch!"

A girl screamed and he yelled and cussed some more before coming back around the corner, squeezing Simone Hitchens in a chokehold. She tore at his arm, kicking and trying to break free.

He shoved her up the three steps and into the door. "You better stop this shit, bitch, or you'll end up with the other one."

Vivian's heart raced. She couldn't believe she was seeing the missing exotic dancer whose face had been broadcast all over the news.

After he slammed the door, Adrienne snapped to attention and handed Wendy her car keys and phone. "Keep calling Antonio until he answers. Y'all get back to the car. Kate, you call 911 and tell them what's going on at the old Benoit place on Water Moccasin Lane."

Wendy dug into her purse, pulled out pepper spray and handed it to Lucy, then she and Kate ran back to the car.

"What should we do?" Vivian asked.

A terrifying scream and a crash came from the trailer and Adrienne replied, "This guy's probably going to kill her." She flipped open the Swiss Army knife and handed it to Vivian. "Puncture a back tire but keep the knife. I'm going into the house. Y'all stay behind me and keep low." With that, she took off running across the clearing to the trailer.

38

V ivian's adrenaline kicked in as she stabbed the driver's side, rear tire of the Mustang. Air hissed as she yanked the three-inch blade from the sidewall. She ran to the right side of the step and crouched as Adrienne kicked in the door, .38 pointed in front of her.

"Drop the gun!" Adrienne yelled, then ducked as a shot rang out and the side of the doorframe exploded. Pieces blew onto Lucy, who was to the left of the steps, back flush against the dirty siding.

Adrienne returned fire. Pop! Pop!

Potbelly yelled and shot his gun again, this time blasting out the window beside Vivian. She dropped the knife, then ducked to the ground. Lucy, too.

"Motherfucker!" the guy yelled, and Adrienne advanced into the trailer.

"Throw your weapon down! Do it now!"

The shotgun ratcheted and Adrienne fired another shot. He screamed in agony and Adrienne yelled, "I said drop it!"

He moaned, then said, "You fuckin' bitch, you shot me!"

"Damn right I did. I could've killed you, asshole. Be grateful, 'cuz I still might."

Vivian decided it was probably safe to look inside. She crouched and peeked.

Adrienne kicked Potbelly's shotgun toward the door and well beyond his reach. She asked Simone, who was tucked between the end of the couch and the wall, "Is there anyone else here?"

Covering the side of her face, she answered, "I don't think so."

"Vivian, pick up the shotgun and point it at this piece of shit," Adrienne said. "If he moves, shoot him."

Vivian helped Lucy up, then went inside and grabbed the shotgun. Though shaking, she held it on the guy, who lay partially on dingy shag carpet and partially on crusty linoleum, bleeding from his right shoulder and left arm. Lucy held the pepper spray out toward him, too.

Adrienne walked through the rest of the trailer, then returned to the living room. "Lucy, run tell Wendy and Kate we've got everything under control and we need a couple of ambulances."

Lucy took off down the path.

Simone started crying and Vivian went into the cramped, moldy bathroom, wet a washcloth and brought it back to her. One eye had already swollen shut and the other was on its way. Her black hair was matted, chapped lips were busted, and bruises ran up and down her legs. All she wore was a blood-stained, white T-shirt.

"Was there ever another girl here with you? One named Daisy?" Vivian asked, wanting to reach out and comfort her but afraid she'd touch something that hurt.

Simone shook her head once. "I don't think so. He kept me in a back bedroom but I haven't heard anyone else here."

Adrienne stooped over the kidnapper, gun pointed to his head. "Where's the other girl?"

"Screw you."

She ground her foot into the wound on his shoulder. He screamed in pain. She didn't let up. "Where is she?"

"They already found that whore."

She dug her foot in deeper. "What about Daisy? The girl you took from the French House."

He screamed again. "I didn't take that bitch. Get off me!"

She pushed off, and he rolled over into a fetal position.

Wendy drove up in Adrienne's SUV and came inside the trailer with Kate and Lucy. "Is Daisy here?" she asked.

Vivian shook her head. "No, Adrienne checked the rooms. She's not here."

Kate looked around the torn-up trailer, then said, "The 911 dispatcher has the police and EMTs on the way."

"I spoke to Antonio," Wendy said, carefully stepping over a broken lamp. "He said to call him ASAP."

"I'll deal with him later." Adrienne asked Simone, "Is there anything we can do for you?"

"I just want to go home. Can I use your phone?"

Vivian handed it over and Simone dialed with a shaky hand. "Momma," she said when the call connected. She started crying too hard to speak, so Vivian gently took the phone and explained that they found her hurt but alive. Help was on the way and she'd be taken to a hospital. The police would be calling soon on what hospital Simone was taken to.

"Praise God! Praise Jesus!" her mom said several times before Vivian could hang up. As soon as she did, she heard sirens in the distance.

A few minutes later, two sheriff deputies pulled up to the trailer. Kate and Wendy met them outside.

"I'm the one who called this in," Kate said.

As they walked up to the trailer, one of them saw Adrienne with the gun and started to draw his weapon.

Adrienne held her hands up, the Lady slinging on her finger. "Whoa. Point that at him, not me."

"Drop your weapon."

"Okay," she said, and bent over and slid it across the floor toward the officer. She raised her arms back up.

One deputy called for the ambulances and trained his gun on the kidnapper while the other searched the house.

The sheriff arrived just as the ambulances pulled in. One of the deputies ushered Adrienne and the girls outside so the EMTs could get to work. Soon the kidnapper was loaded up and hauled off in an ambulance, followed by two patrol cars. A female EMT attended to Simone in the trailer.

Lucy had a one-inch gash on her cheek from the doorframe debris and was treated by a stocky, brown-haired EMT. He blew on her cheek after he cleaned her wound with alcohol.

"It's not deep enough for stitches," he said as he gently placed the first of two butterfly bandages.

Lucy looked up at him. "I'll add this to my list of flaws."

He stepped back and looked her up and down. "I don't see any flaws."

The deputies separated the girls and waited for additional units so they could drive them individually to the sheriff's office.

Vivian's anxiety was building and thoughts of Mexico flooded her mind. She started to panic. "We didn't do anything wrong," she said to the nearest deputy. "Adrienne saved this girl. Why are we going to jail?"

"You're not going to jail," the deputy said. "We've got to do this by the book, which means separate interviews. We don't want the prosecutor to have any reason to doubt your friend's story." He helped Vivian sit down on the back bumper of his patrol car.

She took some deep breaths trying to calm herself. *In through your nose, out through your mouth.*

The female EMT and the guy who fixed up Lucy walked Simone down the steps of the trailer and helped her into the back of the ambulance. The female climbed in with her and the guy closed the door and got in the cab, then drove off.

Antonio came hauling ass up the driveway in a black Dodge Charger just as the sheriff put Adrienne in the back of his car. Antonio jumped out of his car and flashed his badge. "That's my sister. What the hell happened?"

"She fired her Lady Smith, hit the guy twice, we've got to take her in," the sheriff responded. "She's not handcuffed and we haven't Mirandized her."

"Did anyone else get hurt?"

"Other than the girl being held here, everybody else is fine."

"If it's okay, I'd like to be present for the interview."

The sheriff shrugged. "Fine by me." He got in his car and headed out, no sirens or lights.

Antonio walked over to Vivian, stern look on his face. "Y'all put yourselves in a lot of danger with this stunt."

Vivian's stomach clenched. "Adrienne was goin' in, we had to have her back. She's had ours."

His eyes softened and his shoulders relaxed a tad. "I know, she is a bit of a wild card isn't she?" He squeezed Vivian's hand. "But I don't want that putting you in danger, so quit getting involved, okay." He dropped her hand and started jogging to his car. He looked back at her. "Please!"

Vivian smiled as Antonio sped off, a dirt cloud trailing after his car. She watched as, one by one, Kate, Lucy and Wendy were loaded into separate patrol cars and taken away. The deputy came for her and opened the back door. She slid onto the bench seat and looked at the cage in front of her. *It's happening again.*

The deputy went to close the door, but Vivian stopped him and pushed it open. She jumped out, fell to her knees and threw up.

39

The interview room at the St. Bernard Parish sheriff's office had gray cinder block walls, one table bolted to the floor and two chairs. Vivian looked at her reflection in the one-way mirror and almost got sick again. Her eyes were bloodshot and her hair was sticking out everywhere. She stared at a vomit stain on her shirt.

The door opened and a state trooper walked in followed by the sheriff, who carried a manila folder and a pen.

"Vivian Taylor, I'm Sheriff James Daugereaux. This is State Trooper Brian Hill. I understand you've not been feeling well. Is there anything we can get you before we proceed?"

This interview is starting out way better than in Mexico. Being accused of murder was a little rough. "I had some water, thanks."

"We need you to go over the events of today. Please be aware this interview is being recorded and could be used as evidence."

Vivian agreed and told them what led the girls to the trailer.

Hill drummed his fingers on the table. "So you went there because Adrienne Russo's mother was flipped off by this guy?"

"No, but her mom saw the gray Mustang and we knew one had played a role in Simone's disappearance. We were hoping to find a connection to our friend Daisy's kidnapping."

Vivian backtracked a little and told them about Daisy, Jason, the body in the cemetery and how she knew Adrienne and Antonio.

The trooper shook his head. "And you're here on vacation?"

"Yeah. Parts of it have been fun."

The officers asked a few more questions about the events at the trailer. Vivian answered and soon the interview was over. They walked her to the lobby where Lucy, Kate and Wendy sat with Antonio.

Antonio stood and asked Vivian, "Oh Jesus, are you okay? What happened in there?"

Vivian felt super self-conscious and pushed her hair out of her face. "I'm better now. I wasted all your mom's good cooking, I'm afraid. So much for a relaxing day visiting your parents and taking an airboat ride."

He shook his head. "From what I've heard, I have a feeling it's always something with you girls."

Lucy looked Vivian up and down. "You look like you've been run over by an airboat. Several times."

"It's just been a long day, and I need a shower," Vivian answered.

Al walked in as Daugereaux said to Antonio, "We're about to interview your sister. You want to come on back?"

"Yes, and this is her husband, Al Russo."

Al stuck out his hand. "Hear my girl's been causing trouble."

The sheriff shook his hand. "That's one hell of a lady you've got. I'll take you to her."

Al went back with the sheriff, and Antonio started to follow. Wendy stopped him. "I've got Adrienne's phone and keys." She handed them over.

"How are we going to get back to New Orleans?" Kate asked.

Antonio looked to the deputy behind the front desk and handed Wendy the keys. "Can you see these girls get back to the SUV on Water Moccasin Lane?"

"Sure, we'll take care of it." A few minutes later a red minivan pulled up to the entrance. "That's my wife, Peggy. She'll take you."

The girls thanked him, especially Vivian, who was afraid she might hurl again if she had to get back into a patrol car.

Peggy played oldies as they drove the few miles to the SUV. "I hear y'all took down the guy who kidnapped that stripper up in N'awlins."

"It wasn't us," Lucy said. "We just watched as our friend kicked ass."

"Well, it's a good thing and I'm glad to have met ya."

Wendy took the wheel and got them back to the Delacroix Highway. Since Wendy and Kate weren't in the trailer for the action, Vivian and Lucy told them everything.

"Adrienne's got some *cojones*," Wendy said. "I don't think I could have done it."

"You sure had some guts on our last trip," Lucy said. "That Colorado cliff could have been the end of us."

"Yeah, I guess so," Wendy said. "Right now I need someone to rescue me with a map, 'cuz I don't know where the hell we're going."

Lucy pulled up directions back to their hotel and the girls made it without incident.

Wendy valeted the car and said in the elevator, "We smell like swamp, sweat and that skanky trailer. We need showers."

The doors opened on their floor and Vivian stepped off. "We've got to go see Jason and tell him Simone was found but the guy didn't know anything about Daisy."

Wendy unlocked their room. "Don't you think we should let the cops handle that? We got in trouble last time we gave him news."

"Antonio has his hands full with Adrienne, and I doubt the sheriff's office will come out here and tell him anything."

"If by chance the police have already talked to Jason, then we can still tell him our version of the incident," Kate said. "And if he hasn't heard from them, then this is not going to be easy news to break. Maybe it's best coming from us."

Lucy opened their door. "I need food for that kind of mission. Let's grab a bite before we go see him."

The girls took turns getting ready and stuffed their swampy clothes in the laundry bag supplied by housekeeping. "I'm tying this bitch up tight," Lucy said, yanking on the plastic strings. "We do not want to come back to this stench."

Wendy grabbed her big purse and said to Vivian, "I'm diggin' that shirt."

"Thanks, my mom gave it to me for Christmas." Vivian straightened her flowy white, purple and turquoise floral blouse. "It's kinda see-through." She tucked her white tank into her black capri pants and grabbed some silver dangle earrings.

"I need more color," Wendy replied, looking at her black and white striped V-neck blouse and black skirt.

"You look cute," Kate said. "Your snazzy purse jazzes you up." Kate had thrown on a long, red maxi dress and grabbed a beige wrap.

"Damn, I wish I could wear those kinds of dresses," Vivian said, looking her up and down. "I think they make me look pregnant."

"Not everyone can get away with that style," Lucy said. "I'm too short."

Kate walked up to her and pulled a thread off the sleeve of her charcoal, V-neck top. "This fits you perfectly. And I like those jeans with their little bit of bling."

"Thanks," Lucy said grabbed her small, black clutch. "Y'all ready?"

"Are you going out with the Band-Aid still on your face?" Wendy asked.

"Oh yeah!" Lucy said and went into the bathroom where she peeled the bandage off her face and inspected her wound. She dabbed some powder around the spot and threw the bandage away. "I don't need this."

"Are you sure?" Vivian asked and inspected her cheek.

"I might have played up my injury a little bit. The EMS guy was really cute."

Vivian smacked her on the ass. "You bad girl." As the girls left the room, she said, "Let's go somewhere close. I'm too tired to walk."

170

"Morton's is across Canal," Wendy said. "I think we need to celebrate being alive. We can grab a quick dinner in the bar."

Vivian's mouth watered thinking about the macaroni and cheese. "Sounds perfect."

40

The girls walked across the street and the Morton's valet opened the restaurant door for them. As they rode the elevator up, Vivian's stomach growled at the sizzling steak and baked bread aromas.

"I'm going to eat an entire filet," Lucy said as she sat down. "I'm not sharing."

"I think I could eat two steaks right now," Kate said, taking a seat next to Lucy.

John the bartender introduced himself and gave them each a bar menu. Two appetizers would hold them over until dinner arrived.

"We'll have the mini-crab cake BLTs and the petite filet mignon sandwiches," Wendy said, closing her menu. "And we'd like to go ahead and order if that's okay."

Lucy, true to her word, got the center-cut filet. Kate ordered the porterhouse so she could get the filet on one side and the New York strip on the other. Vivian ordered the Cajun ribeye and Wendy the Shrimp Alexander.

"And what can I get y'all to drink?" John asked.

Before any of the girls could answer, a man in a tuxedo came over. "They'll have a bottle of Silver Oak cab."

"Ralph!" Wendy said and jumped up and gave the maître-d a hug. "So good to see you!" Wendy bartended at Morton's in Houston during college; Ralph was her manager.

"What a surprise to see you," Ralph said. "What are you doing these days?" They caught up and reminisced about the late nights in the bar playing cards.

John served the wine and the appetizers, which were gone in minutes. He inquired about the scratch on Lucy's face, so they told him all about their crazy ass day in the swamp. From the hicks to the shooting, he was captivated. "Y'all should write a book about this."

The girls laughed and cheersed to that.

The steaks and shrimp were all cooked to perfection. The girls dipped their bread into Wendy's Shrimp Alexander sauce.

"That is the best damn sauce," Lucy said, taking a second swipe and double-dipping.

Wendy shielded her plate. "Back off, sista."

They finished dinner and resisted dessert, but John surprised them and brought out the Godiva cake, topped with Haagen Dazs vanilla. Heaven on a plate.

Vivian's phone buzzed with a text from Adrienne.

This jailbird is free. Hope u made it back ok. Get car 2moro.

Vivian filled in the girls, then threw down her napkin. "I need to walk, y'all about ready?"

Kate set down her fork and wiped her mouth. "I just want to go to bed. I don't want to have to tell Jason anything. It's going to be heartbreaking."

Wendy polished off her glass of wine. "It's not the worst news that could be delivered. It still leaves hope that Daisy will be found."

Vivian tucked her phone back into her purse. "I just texted him and he's good with us coming by. Let's go."

The girls said goodbye to Ralph and John and left the restaurant. Two cop cars were parked facing opposite directions on the streetcar tracks on Canal. The officers talked to each other through the driver's open windows. A street light illuminated the three-sided shelter of the streetcar stop, where two passengers were waiting.

Vivian did a double take as she recognized the blond-haired, buzz cut guy sitting long ways across the bench. She tilted her head slightly in his direction. "Don't look over there, but there's that damn undercover cop again." She started walking toward the Marriott a few blocks down.

"This is officially getting creepy," Lucy said.

Wendy stopped and bent over, pretending to fix her flip-flop. "He left the shelter and is walking down the median."

"You've got to call Antonio," Kate said.

***

Daisy remained hiding in the bathtub until her muscles ached with stiffness. The blows to her legs and back didn't help. Wanting more comfort, she peeked into the bedroom, and finding no one there, crawled into bed. She had left the television on a local station, and the late news was about to come on. She felt around the bed for the remote but didn't find it and didn't have the energy to look for it.

The screen cut to a female reporter, who was having a bad hair day, standing in front of a hospital sign. "We have an update on the murder and kidnappings that are plaguing the adult entertainment industry in New Orleans. Simone Hitchens, the second victim who was taken two weeks ago, is being treated in the Medical Center of Louisiana at New Orleans after being rescued today in St. Bernard Parish by neighbors. According to her family, the kidnapper was shot twice during the rescue. Sources tell us he's in stable condition here. The police have just released the identity of the body that was found yesterday in St. Louis Cemetery #1. We're told it is the first kidnapping victim, Lisa Miller, who had been missing almost a month. The third victim, Daisy Easley, is still missing. We will continue to provide updates as they become available."

Simone being found alive gave Daisy a little hope, though she had no idea if Sonu had anything to do with her or Lisa's kidnappings. She didn't think he did, but what did she really know about him other than he was a delusional jerkwad who thought she was going to marry him in his country? Probably some very hot, sandy country with weird customs and archaic ideas about women. *No fucking way.*

***

The girls walked into the lobby of the Marriott and Vivian called Antonio. She got his voicemail and left a message about the undercover cop being outside of Morton's.

They took the elevator to the 14th floor and Lucy hesitantly knocked on Jason's door.

He answered looking more upbeat than Vivian expected, but that quickly changed once he realized the girls were not too chipper.

"What? What's happened?" he asked as they entered the room. He looked up and down the hallway before closing the door.

Vivian took a deep breath. "It's not horrible news, it's just been a crazy, crazy day. Crazier than we ever could have imagined."

Jason sat on the bed and pointed to a chair across from him. "Tell me about it."

She recounted the airboat chase with the swamp brothers and how that led to Mustang guy. She told him about the gunfight that led them to Simone.

Jason stood up. "You're sure he didn't know anything about Daisy?"

"I'm almost positive. Adrienne crammed her foot into his gunshot wound and was adamant as he answered. He admitted to killing the other dancer but said he knew nothing about Daisy."

Jason sank further into the bed and put his head in his hands. "What does this mean?"

Wendy put her hand on his shoulder. "We feel like Daisy is alive and waiting to be found."

Kate moved to him, placing her hand on his other shoulder. "We won't give up, Jason. We know this isn't over."

Lucy stood next to Kate. "Absolutely. This isn't finished."

Vivian got up from her chair and Jason stood, staring down at her with tears in his eyes. "I can't give up hope."

Vivian squeezed his hands. "We haven't."

41

Day 6

The girls awoke earlier than usual since they had gone to bed before midnight and no one was hung over.

Kate sat on the edge of her bed, TV turned down low, watching the "Today Show." Bobby Flay was grilling post-St. Patty's Day brunch on the plaza.

Wendy had the one-cup coffee maker hard at work. She was on cup number three as she waited for everyone else to get dressed. "I'm ready to take on the Big Easy today. Y'all put it into overdrive."

At 9:25 the channel switched to a brief section of local news. A picture of the Medical Center of Louisiana at New Orleans flashed on the screen beside a blonde with a big smile.

Kate jacked the volume. "Listen up!"

"Authorities continue to investigate the shooting yesterday in St. Bernard Parish that freed kidnap victim Simone Hitchens from her captor, Donny Dickens." A mug shot replaced the hospital picture. "Dickens was shot twice by a neighbor during the rescue. He has previous convictions, including aggravated assault and armed robbery. His injuries are not considered life threatening but he remains hospitalized. New Orleans police are looking for connections between this case and the kidnapping of dancer Daisy Easley." A picture of Daisy was shown. "Easley was kidnapped from the French House three nights ago. Police have established a tip line and are looking for any information in the case." The phone number flashed on the screen. "And now, here's Hank with your weather."

Kate lowered the volume. "Adrienne's the neighbor!"

"Best neighbor ever!" Lucy said, and they high-fived.

"So, Donny Dickens, that was the guy," Wendy said.

"How on earth is a guy who's been found guilty of aggravated assault and armed robbery walking around free?" Lucy asked. "Something is wrong with the system."

"Yeah, and he's probably got more of a record than that," Vivian said, pulling out her mascara wand and examining the brush. "They probably just hit the highlights because of time."

Kate turned off the TV. "Hopefully this time he'll be kept in the slammer, where he belongs."

Vivian ran a last swipe of mascara over her lashes and put the brush away. "I'm ready. Where're we going?"

"We've made a big dent in my list of places to go on this trip," Wendy said and pressed her finger in Vivian's forehead dent, "but we haven't hit the Acme Oyster House yet. Y'all mind?"

Vivian shooed her hand away.

"Sounds good," Lucy said and picked up her purse. She looked over at Vivian, who had made no move to leave. "They serve more than oysters there, ya picky freak."

With that, they left the room, stopped by the valet and gave Adrienne's name so she could pick up the car. They walked past Jason's hotel and two local news vans out front, one with the antenna raised and a woman in her early 30s dabbing powder on her face. A camera man sat in a folding chair facing the hotel's entrance.

"Looks like they're camped out for the day," Vivian commented and they kept going.

***

Daisy woke, tangled in the sheets and sweating although it was not hot in the room. She had been running through the desert in her dreams. She instinctively reached across the bed for Jason but he wasn't there. Reality hit hard and sucked her willpower to get up. The only thing that motivated her to leave the bed was the need to pee.

Her body ached everywhere. She looked at herself in the mirror and cringed. Black was not the best hair color against her skin. She took off the wrinkled dress. The bruises on her back and legs were a lovely purple and green. Since the dress was off, she went ahead and showered, to wash off his touch if nothing else. Thinking about his kiss from the day before made her want to vomit. Even though she was starving, she wasn't sure she could swallow anything if they brought her food.

After her shower, she picked up the three remaining dresses on the floor in the closet. The only one that didn't have yesterday's breakfast on it was

177

the navy. The room had started to stink from the rotting food, and she threw towels over the biggest splatters.

Surely they'll give me new towels. Maybe even have housekeeping clean it up. I may be able to tell them what's going on.

She sat in the chair, as far away from the stink as she could get, and watched TV, her only pastime in the small hotel room. Hoda and Kathie Lee had just come on when the roofie asshole pushed the breakfast cart into the room. One whiff of syrup and she knew she could eat.

"Could you have housekeeping come clean this up?" she asked him.

He looked at the crusty eggs, other white matter and towels, then left. A few minutes later, the leery guy came in the room with a stack of towels. He watched her scarf down breakfast.

This fucking guy digs ugly dresses. The uglier the better. Creep.

She stood up and glared at him. "Why don't you take a picture, weirdo?"

He left the room.

***

The girls made their way to the Acme Oyster House and were pleased they didn't have to wait in line this early in the day. They were seated right in front of the windows so they could watch the goings-on in the Quarter.

"It's mimosa time," Vivian said, looking over the non-oyster section of the menu.

The girls agreed and they ordered a round for the table along with some Boo Fries and fried crawfish tails. They took their time, not ordering more food until the appetizers were polished off but ordering another round of mimosas.

Their cups of seafood gumbo and oysters Rockefeller soup had just been delivered when there was a tap at the window. The Romanian gypsy peered in and continued knocking.

Vivian waved her in but the woman shook her head so Vivian hopped up and said to Kate, "Buddy system. Come on."

They ran outside and the gypsy grabbed their arms and held them tightly. She stared through Vivian and muttered, almost trance-like, "Your friend is in grave danger. Find the mirrors. Find them."

"We found the mirrors when we found Harry at Harrah's, and then we found them again at the cemetery," Vivian told her. "That's where we found the dead girl."

The gypsy shook her head. "You are incorrect. You must find the soaring predator surrounding the ship before she's gone." And with that she took off, running down Iberville.

Vivian took a few steps after her. "Wait, what predator? We don't understand!"

Kate stared after her, flabbergasted.

Lucy rapped on the window and gave them a "what's up?" shrug. Vivian and Kate went back inside.

"What'd she say?" Wendy asked.

Vivian sat down. "It was weird, a bunch of mumbo jumbo. She said something about a soaring predator."

"I need a pen," Kate said. Wendy dug in her purse and handed her one.

They waited for Kate to write several things on a napkin.

"She said Daisy is in danger. Find the mirrors and find the soaring predator surrounding the ship."

"Those damn mirrors are back!" Wendy said, slapping the table. "I thought we had that figured out."

"What the hell is the soaring predator?" Vivian asked.

"Okay, one thing at a time," Kate said, tapping the pen on the table. "Where all have we seen mirrors? I realize they were at Harrah's and the cemetery. Where else?"

"There were a lot of mirrors at both of the strip clubs," Lucy said. "In fact, it's all smoke and mirrors at those places."

Kate wrote that down. "We already checked out all of that. We've got to be missing something."

They sat for a minute. No one had any new ideas.

"So what does this soaring predator shit have to do with any of this?" Vivian asked.

"Let's think about this logically," Kate said. "Eagles, falcons, hawks. What else?"

"I don't know, I'm not National Geographic," Vivian said. "Let's Google it."

Lucy pulled out her phone and searched. "There are vultures and dragons."

"Dragons aren't real," Wendy said.

"Well nobody said the crap that lady was talking about had to be real!" Lucy said.

Kate wrote it all down.

"Should we tell Antonio about the gypsy lady?" Vivian asked.

"He'd probably think we're crazy for even listening to what she had to say," Wendy said. "I mean, even I'm kinda thinking that."

Kate pointed back to the napkin. "What flying predators surround a ship?"

"Eagles are in Alaska," Vivian said. "And don't they nest by the ocean?"

"I think dragons are officially out," Lucy said.

"I get attacked by those annoying seagulls when I'm at the beach," Vivian said.

"Don't feed them and you won't get attacked," Wendy noted.

"This is going nowhere," Kate said.

"Let's check all of our pictures during the trip," Vivian said, pulling out her phone. "Scan through and look for any with mirrors. Or birds."

Everyone pulled out phones and cameras and started searching. They couldn't help but giggle now and then and show the picture.

"I love this one," Wendy said of the fake vomit picture of Vivian. "Classic."

"Ohhh, look." Lucy turned her phone to show a picture she had taken of Jason and Daisy that first night on Bourbon. "You can tell they're in love."

That sobered them up as they continued to flip through pictures.

Kate quit flipping. "I forgot about this one."

"Which one?" Vivian asked.

"It's you talking to Angels, or Angel." Kate showed the picture of the winged dancer diving into Vivian's boob for money.

Vivian grabbed the phone and enlarged the picture. "Holy shit, I have a double chin! Look at that!"

Lucy took the phone and examined it. "You're all hunched over and have your face buried into your chest as she's diving in. Of course you have a double chin."

Wendy looked. "Kate Moss would have a double chin in that pose. Chillax."

Vivian looked at it again and felt under her chin. Satisfied, she moved the picture around and noticed GQ in the background. "There's that dickwad, stuck-up guy who ignored me."

Kate took her phone back and zoomed in. "Oh my god, this is it."

42

Kate showed the girls the picture on her phone as they lingered over an early lunch at Acme Oyster House. "I knew this guy was trouble. Look at his tie tack."

Vivian squinted. "Is that a ship?"

"Yes, that's a ship," Kate said, pointing to the middle of the pin. "And the bird completely surrounds it. See, its head is at the bottom and its wings go up and around the sides."

"Holy shit, you're right, I see it," Vivian said. They showed Lucy and Wendy, who agreed.

"What could he have to do with this?" Wendy asked. "I don't see how he could have taken her. He was still at the table when we went backstage."

Vivian leaned her head back and thought for a minute. "He had those other guys with him, though. We thought they were bodyguards. Maybe they're something else."

"We saw him at Hotél Versailles," Lucy said. "We're close by, let's go see if he's still there."

Wendy asked for the check, then turned to Vivian. "You should text Antonio."

"Uh, I don't think so. If looks could kill we'd be sprawled out on the Delacroix Highway."

Kate put her phone away. "Let's go ask the doorman, maybe we'll get lucky and it'll be the same guy from the other day. He'll remember us."

They paid and walked the few blocks to Hotél Versailles. The same doorman was on duty. They waited for him to help a woman into a cab before approaching him.

Vivian put on her best smile and lifted her head up so there was, for sure, no double chin. "Hey there. We're looking for a little information about one of the guests who's staying here. At least we think he is."

The doorman, Gary, held his hands up and started to walk past them. "I can't give you any info on our guests."

Lucy grabbed his sleeve. "We think one of your guests has kidnapped a friend of ours and we need to know if he's still here. If he's still in town."

Gary narrowed his eyes. "If he's kidnapped somebody, then why are you here and not the police?"

"It's kind of a long story," Kate said and started with Daisy disappearing and ending with the gypsy's message.

Kate was interrupted a few times as Gary opened the door for guests and hailed a cab for one couple.

"We know this sounds crazy," Wendy said, "but we promise we're not making it up."

"Here," Kate said and showed him the picture of Vivian, the stripper and GQ. "Zoom in on him to see the tie tack."

Gary zoomed, but on the stripper. He grinned. "I'm kidding." He then moved the picture to GQ. He handed the phone back to Kate and his demeanor turned professional. "I'm sorry, ma'am, but I'd be risking my job if I told you anything."

Vivian's heart sank. *He's gotta help us!* "Gary, we don't know what this girl is going through. Is he abusing her? Raping her? Worse?"

Wendy chimed in. "And can you imagine the torture her fiancé and family are experiencing, wondering where she is and if she's okay? I worried non-stop about my boxer, Luke, when he went missing a few years ago."

Gary sighed and looked around. He hesitated before saying, "This better not get me fired, but Mr. Surendran's not here right now."

"Thank you, Gary," Vivian said and gave him a side squeeze. "You don't happen to know his first name, do you?"

Gary laughed. "It's Sonofabitch, or something to that effect."

The girls walked across the street to a restaurant with tables on the sidewalk. They grabbed one and sat down.

"I think we've gotta call Antonio now," Wendy said. "He already thinks we're nuts. A little more loony info can't hurt. And now we know GQ's name!"

Vivian agreed and placed the call. He picked up right away. "We think we know who kidnapped Daisy. He's staying at Hotél Versailles and his last name is Surendran."

"And you think this why?"

Vivian told him about the gypsy's message and discovery of the tie tack in Kate's picture.

"So because a street swindler gives you a so-called clue and you see a bird on a guy's tie clip, you think he's a kidnapper."

"It's not just that. Our friend Kate has these premonitions in her dreams. They never make sense at first, but she totally called this one. She said there would be a soaring predator, and look! The tie tack has an eagle or falcon or something."

Antonio didn't respond.

"Can we at least send you the picture of the guy?"

He was silent for a minute, then she heard him take a deep breath. "Fine, send me the picture." He clicked off.

Kate sent it immediately.

"Now what do we do?" Wendy asked. "Just sit here and watch the tourists go by?"

"If I don't hear from Antonio in 10 minutes, we'll move on to plan B," Vivian said.

"What's plan B?" Lucy asked.

"I dunno, but we've got 10 minutes to come up with it."

Eight minutes later, Vivian's phone chimed. She read the message to the girls. "Diplomat from Kuwait. Immunity. Must have substantial evidence."

"What the hell?" Wendy said. "Diplomatic immunity? Does that mean he can just go snatch women and get away with it?"

Vivian's phone buzzed. Another text from Antonio.

Where are you??????

Kate pulled out her phone. "I don't know what all diplomatic immunity entails, so let's look it up." She scanned the internet for a few minutes, then said, "Says it's not a get-out-of-jail-free card and most crimes involving diplomatic immunity are petty, traffic tickets, shoplifting, etc."

"What's it say about more serious crimes?" Vivian asked.

Kate scrolled down the webpage. "It can be revoked, though it's tough and circumstances must be very serious."

"Kidnapping is serious!" Wendy smacked her hand on the table. "Let's get Antonio some proof that Sonofabitch has Daisy, and he can get that shit revoked!"

"I'm totally with you," Vivian said, "but how?"

"I have an idea," Lucy said with a little mischief in her eye. She turned and looked at Kate. "But it's kinda risky."

43

The doorman at Hotél Versailles, Gary, introduced Lea to Kate. "Lea's our new housekeeping supervisor and a very good friend. I've told her the situation and she'll help you find what you're looking for, inspector."

"Thank you," Kate said and smiled at Lea.

"Yes, follow me and we'll make a quick stop in housekeeping so you can review items there. Then we'll move to the 12th floor."

"Perfect."

Kate glanced back at Wendy, who was still across the street. As she walked inside and into the lobby, she saw Lucy sitting on the couch, holding a newspaper. She looked into the *Gallerie de Glaces* and briefly made eye contact with Vivian, who sat at the bar and twirled a curl on her finger. Nervous habit.

Lea used her badge to buzz the security door that led to an employees-only area of the first floor. They walked past noisy kitchens, an engineering office, a security station and banquet area before coming to a large laundry room with several industrial-sized washers and dryers.

"Mmmmm, smells good back here," Kate said. "Thanks for helping us with this. I know you're putting your job in jeopardy."

"This is a really great job, but there will be others," Lea replied. "I just keep thinking, what if it were me? I'd want someone on the hotel staff to help." They approached the long row of shelves with lost and found items. She looked through the odds and ends and pulled out a briefcase. "This should work." She yanked off the identification tag. "What else do you need?"

Kate felt her iPhone in her pocket. "A clipboard and paper, pen, tape measure, bobby pins, ponytail holder, a stepstool, and perhaps, that?" she asked, pointing to a black suit jacket.

"Sure." Lea pulled it off the hanger and held it up to her. "It's going to be big, but it'll work well enough."

As Kate used bobby pins to hold her hair in a bun, Lea clicked around on the computer. "Looks like Mr. Surendran hasn't received any housekeeping services in the last four days other than requesting extra towels."

"That time frame coincides with when Daisy was taken." Kate slid on the jacket and adjusted her sleeves. "How do I look?"

"Like no inspector I've ever seen." They both snickered.

***

Vivian sat at the bar in the *Gallerie de Glaces*. A trifold mirror was across from her and she could see Lucy in the lobby, fanning herself with the *Times-Picayune*. Vivian hopped up and went over to her. "I'm going crazy in there, worrying about Kate. We shouldn't have sent her up."

Lucy quit fanning. "She's smart and she's with Lea. They can bullshit their way through this."

Lucy's confidence didn't help Vivian feel any better. She looked at Gary, who looked away, and she could see Wendy at her post across the street. She scanned every car, every face that went by. Sonofabitch wasn't getting past her.

Lucy flipped through the paper. "I can't believe there's no mention of Simone being found yesterday."

"They probably didn't find out about it until past deadline," Vivian said. "I'm going back to my spot."

"I only have great ideas. This is gonna work. Don't worry."

***

A do-not-disturb sign hung off the doorknob to suite 1217, registered under Mr. Sonu Bhavesh Surendran.

That does sound like Sonofabitch, Kate thought.

Lea knocked. "Housekeeping." The door wasn't answered right away, so she rapped again.

A stocky Middle Eastern man in a suit answered.

Lea flashed her badge and said, "Sorry for disturbing you. This is Inspector Kate Jameson with City Code Compliance. There was a fire here last month and she needs to verify we have corrected all issues. We need to come in."

The man studied Lea and then glanced at Kate, unimpressed.

Kate stood on her tippy toes, trying to look into the room. "The fire started in this very room, and I'm here to ensure that the hotel is in full compliance with the fire code." She flashed her library card.

185

"That will not be possible," he said.

Kate quickly conjured a list of fire code sections specific to transient lodging from her early days at the architecture firm. "If the corridor partition is not per ASTM E 1966, and the undercut on this FM-rated door is not within the specified tolerances, and the smoke alarm is not installed per IBC Chapter 9, Section 204.1.2, you could be in trouble as we speak. I mean, someone *died* last month." Finger pointed, articulating every syllable, Kate added emphatically, "In. This. Room."

The man sighed and said, "One moment," and closed the door.

***

The guy who had pulled Daisy off of Sonu two days prior ran into the room and ordered her into the bathroom. He had a roll of gray duct tape in his hand. She hesitated to get up from the chair, so he ran over and picked her up onto his shoulder and carried her in there. He shut the door and slammed her down onto the toilet. Then he pulled a gun on her.

"Do not make one sound or you will die."

He looked like the kind of guy who had no qualms about killing people.

He pulled a strip of duct tape off the roll and put it over her mouth. He motioned for her to get into the bathtub. She didn't want to die, it would interfere with her plans to escape, so she climbed in. He kept the gun trained on her.

***

The man opened the door to the suite and motioned for Kate and Lea to come in. "Please be quick."

Kate pushed past him. *Those years working on hotel prototypes finally paid off!*

Lea followed behind, stepstool under her arm and with a pleased look on her face.

Kate scanned the suite and assessed three bedrooms, the nearest door of which was closed, and a bathroom with the door open. Dirty towels littered the floor. She looked back at the closed door, and the man placed himself between her and it.

Lea unfolded the stepstool. "Where do you want this?"

"Under that smoke alarm, right there, please."

Lea set it in the middle of the living room, under the chandelier. Kate took the three steps up and reached for the smoke alarm but couldn't get to it. She stepped down and glanced at the man. "Would you mind pushing that little button up there?"

He scowled but did as she asked. The alarm shrieked for a second.

"Excellent! Sounds like it is in perfect working order." Kate pulled out her iPhone and continued the fake inspection around the living room. She opened the flashlight app and waved the beam up and down at the curtain as if it were a metal detector. "Looks like these curtains just barely pass the Class A flammability rating for a Type R occupancy."

She then moved into the nearest bedroom and rapped on the walls and inspected the curtains. She nodded to the man, then repeated the action in the second bedroom.

Back in the living room, Lea pointed to the closed bedroom door. "She'll need to inspect in here."

The man gave a tight smile, opened the master suite door and walked in first.

The smell of sour food hit Kate and she coughed. Towels were piled against the wall near the closet. She did the wall tapping and curtain charade, then stooped at the end of the king-sized bed. She pounded on the floor and loudly proclaimed, "This floor-ceiling assembly is sufficiently fireproofed!" She took a good look under the bed, and there it was, Daisy's Shoe-Be-Do shoe.

44

W endy tapped on the table, watching everything that moved and even things that didn't. She couldn't help but laugh at a person dressed in jeans and a T-shirt and a giant, brown dog head. He was slumped against the lamp post, tallboy of Keystone in one hand and a sign that read "Ruff nite" in the other. A top hat was flipped over in front of him, and she watched as people dropped money in.

People can make a living here doin' nothing!

The waitress delivered a glass of water and Wendy tipped her $2, then took a sip. She almost spewed it everywhere as a limo pulled up and two guys stepped out, followed by GQ. Gary rushed to meet them and started talking to GQ. Wendy couldn't hear the conversation, but she could see it was mostly one-sided. She quickly texted Kate, Lucy and Vivian.

***

Vivian looked around the bar, glanced in the mirror above it and felt worse and worse about sending Kate to meet her fate. She decided to text Antonio. He needed to know where they were.

We're at Hotel Versailles. We might have screwed up.

She started to put her phone away when another text came in, this time from Wendy.

Red alert! Red alert! The Eagle has landed!!!

Vivian's heart raced and her stomach flipped. She stared at her phone until the screen went blank. She looked into the trifold mirror and almost fell off her stool. GQ was in the middle mirror, walking toward the elevator. Lucy was in the right-hand mirror, newspaper covering all of her face but her eyes, which looked into Vivian's with fear. Gary was in the left mirror, trailing after GQ.

***

Kate's heart raced but she kept her cool as she walked around the room, pretending to further inspect. "There are definitely signs of leakage under these demising walls. I've got to check under the corridor baseboards in here."

The man didn't move away from the door. "Someone is in there."

"The corridor wall is in the bathroom. It's pertinent that I inspect it." He shook his head, and the angry look in his eyes convinced Kate not to push him. She turned to Lea. "I have no choice but to red flag this suite."

Lea let out an exaggerated sigh. "Are you sure? Is there nothing else we can do?"

Kate tapped her clipboard with her pen. "I'll have to re-inspect next week when my schedule opens up. You know, I'm a very busy woman."

Lea's walkie-talkie beeped and Gary's voice crackled. "Has the lavatory on the seventh floor been cleared?" Lea looked at Kate. "I've got another issue I have to clear up."

Kate tucked her pen behind her ear. "My inspection is as complete as it can be for now. I'll write up my report and send it to the fire marshal."

Lea and Kate hustled to the door. Lea called over her shoulder just before the door closed, "Thanks for your cooperation!"

***

Daisy heard a knocking on the walls and woman talking about something being fireproof. She looked down the barrel of the pistol and contemplated screaming behind the tape. The jerk read her, pressed the gun to her forehead and tilted her head back. She trembled and kept quiet. She heard radio chatter and then another woman speak into it. Moments later she heard them leave. Tears spilled from her eyes.

***

After GQ got onto the elevator, Vivian and Lucy rushed up to Gary, who was talking into his walkie-talkie. "Has the lavatory on the seventh floor been cleared?"

"You've got to get them out of the room!" Vivian said.

His walkie-talkie beeped. "That's affirmative. The drain has been cleared."

"Ten-four," he said, then looked at Vivian. "They're out of the suite." He rushed to the front door, put on a fake smile and held it for a couple walking in.

Vivian and Lucy waited in the lobby for Kate. Vivian sighed in relief as Kate walked off the elevator. She walked through the lobby and out the door without glancing at them. Vivian and Lucy waited a couple of minutes, then met Wendy and Kate inside the restaurant across the street.

"She's in that room," Kate said as soon as they walked up. "I saw her Shoe-Be-Do shoe tucked under the bed. He's got her!"

"Did you see her?" Lucy asked.

"No, but they wouldn't let me go into the bathroom in the master suite. I know she's in there."

"I'm not sure that's the proof Antonio needs, but he's gotta do something," Vivian said.

***

Daisy paced the room and looked out the windows every few steps. Something was up. She heard Sonu shouting in a foreign language in the other room.

A short while later, Sonu and the pistol-toting nutcase came into the room. Crazy guy shoved a glass of water into her hand and pointed his gun on her.

"Drink this," Sonu ordered.

Daisy looked at the chalky water and didn't want to drink it. She frowned.

Sonu raised the glass to her mouth. "This will be your last warning to obey me."

Crazy guy inched closer.

I'm never going to get away with this motherfucker around.

Daisy took a tiny step back. "What is this and will it kill me?" *Could their plan be to give me an overdose?*

"It will only help you deal with our departure," Sonu answered.

Fuck it, she thought, and chugged the water.

***

Vivian sat in the restaurant facing the hotel and pulled out her phone. Antonio answered right away and she said, "He has her."

"What'd y'all do?"

Vivian gave him the rundown. She was just getting to the shoe when a limo pulled up and one of GQ's goons started throwing luggage into the trunk. A purple-fringed, horse-drawn carriage sporting a fleur-de-lis emblem clip-clopped to a stop behind the limo. The driver was decked out in a lavender dress shirt and purple pants, vest and top hat. He hopped down and Gary walked over and took the reins. The driver indicated five minutes, then went inside the hotel.

"They're loading up the luggage," Vivian said into the phone. "They're getting ready to leave. You've got to do something."

The goon slammed the trunk, then looked to the hotel. Another came out arm and arm with a woman wearing a full-bodied brown robe and a scarf wrapped around her face and head, almost like a burqa. A third guy followed.

"I gotta go!" Vivian yelled, then threw her phone into her purse.

The girls ran onto the sidewalk, but traffic prevented them from crossing, "Daisy!" Lucy yelled.

The woman looked up.

One of the bodyguards opened the back door to the limo and shoved Daisy toward it. Gary tried to reach for her, but the bodyguard pulled him aside and punched him with a hard right. Gary went down.

Daisy was shoved into the car, and a goon got in behind her. Another got in on the left side and slammed the door. The third sat up front with the driver.

The girls started to run after the limo, but it sped off. Vivian knew there was no way they'd catch them.

The midnight-black horse whinnied and Vivian stopped, then turned and looked at him. She could tell by the spark in his dark eyes that he wanted to run. He was tired of the slow pace that was forced upon him in the streets of New Orleans day after day. He stamped at the concrete with his front hoof and bit at his bridle.

"Jump in!" she yelled to the girls, pointing to the fringed buggy. She stepped onto the running board, snatched up the reins and sat on the bench seat.

The girls changed course and hopped in behind her, onto the rear bench seat.

Lucy crawled over the short railing and sat shotgun. "Who's driving this thing?"

Vivian cracked the reins on the horse's back. "Meeeeeeeeee!"

191

45

The purple carriage raced along Chartres, trying to catch up to the limousine that held GQ's goons and Daisy. Cars screeched to a stop and pedestrians jumped out of the way as the limo barreled down the road.

Vivian flipped the reins up and down on the horse's back. "Giddy up, horsey! Go, go!"

"Do you even know what you're doing?" Lucy yelled as they zoomed past the Shoe-Be-Do.

"No, but I watched 'Little House on the Prairie' when I was a kid!" Vivian smacked the reins again. "Yah! Yah!"

A gold sedan with dark tinted windows began to pull across the intersection right before the big courthouse but the limo swerved around it.

"We're gonna crash!" Lucy covered her eyes.

"Where's my 'oh shit' handle?" Wendy yelled and gripped the side railing.

The horse expertly veered to the right and they missed the car by inches, but Vivian saw who was behind the wheel. "It's that undercover cop!"

"What the heck?" Kate said and strained her neck to look back.

Purple fringe was flying as they passed the courthouse. As they neared the Camellia Grill, a herd of Japanese tourists stepped off the sidewalk into the street. The limo driver honked and the herd scrambled. As the girls flew past, the tourists snapped away at the excitement.

"We're coming up to Jackson Square!" Lucy yelled. "The driver is going to run over people!"

The limo's brake lights flashed and the tires screeched as he approached the square. He tried to make a sharp left onto St. Peter but fishtailed and skidded to a stop, metal crunching as the front end of the limousine crumpled and jammed into the back of a Dos Equis truck.

"This is our chance!" Vivian yelled as the horse slowed.

The reverse lights came on, the engine revved, and the back tires

192

squealed and smoked, but the limo stayed put.

"He's trying to get away," Kate shouted.

Vivian pulled up on the reins. "Whoa, horsey. Good boy!"

The carriage came to an abrupt halt. The girls jumped down, then ran toward the limo.

The driver got out of the car and slammed his door, then put his hands on his hips, looking at the front of the car.

The Dos Equis truck driver ran out of Le Petit Théâtre. "Hey, man, you all right?"

"What the hell? You're blocking the whole damn road."

The truck driver stopped. "I have my flashers on and this is perfectly legal. I heard the tires squealing. You were coming around the corner too fast."

Kate tried to open the back door to the limo, but it was locked.

"Let me try this side," Lucy said and tugged on the other door handle. It, too, was locked. "I'll fix this." She reached down and pulled off her Shoe-Be-Do wooden pump. She reared back, but the limo driver grabbed her arm.

"Don't even."

Lucy yanked her arm away. "Don't touch me!"

The Dos Equis driver intervened. "Take it easy, take it easy." He stepped between them.

"He has a kidnapped girl in there!" Vivian yelled. "Let her go!"

A small crowd had gathered and the same cop who had helped apprehend the pickpocket whizzed up to the accident. "What's the situation here? Anyone injured?"

The limo driver started in. "This guy is blocking the whole intersec — "

Wendy interrupted. "He has a kidnapped woman in the back of his car! We saw them put her in there! It's Daisy Easley, the dancer!"

The goon in the passenger seat of the limo got out and walked up to Robocop. "Officer, I don't know what she's talking about. We are not holding anyone against her will."

"They've probably got Daisy drugged!" Vivian yelled. "And they're making her wear a headscarf so you can't see who she is."

"There're two other guys in there, too," Lucy said. "They're pretty damn big, you might want to call for backup."

Robocop parked his Segway and talked into his shoulder radio as he brushed past the goon and walked to the limo. He knocked on a back window. "Everyone out of the car."

The locks clicked and both back doors swung open. The other two guys got out of the car, but not the woman.

"Everyone out," Robocop said again, peeking into the car.

The goons shared a look, then one of them reached inside and grabbed the robed woman, who emerged and stood quietly by the car.

Robocop walked up to her. "Ma'am, are you being held against your will?"

She shook her head, no.

"They've probably threatened her life!" Kate said.

The purple-clad carriage driver ran up, huffing and puffing from the run. "Those are the girls who took my Midnight."

"Oh geez," Vivian said, who had started to walk toward Daisy. She turned around to Purple guy. "We just needed to borrow him to save Daisy. He did a great job!"

The man nuzzled the horse. "Of course he did a great job. He's Midnight the Magnificent. You should have seen him in his prime." He turned back to the girls. "But you shouldn't have taken him."

Robocop spoke up. "Milton, are you going to press any charges?"

Milton petted the horse's nose. "He seems okay, so I guess I'll let it slide. Can I go now? I've still got a fare to pick up."

"You can go."

Milton put his purple self into the purple carriage and clip-clopped down the street. Midnight held his head high, his ears straight up and alert. He arched his tail and swished it repeatedly and he raised his front legs a bit more, almost prancing. He knew he'd saved the day.

Robocop turned back to the accident and kidnapping. "Ma'am, do you have any identification? In fact," he said, turning to the three goons and the two drivers, "let me have everybody's."

A squad car pulled up and Robocop told them the situation. One of the officers started collecting IDs.

Vivian looked at the woman, trying to make eye contact, but she stared at the ground. Finally, Vivian couldn't take it anymore. "This is bullshit!" She ran over and flung the woman's headscarf off.

46

"Who the hell are you?" Vivian asked, looking at the Hispanic woman wearing the brown robe, but now missing her headscarf.

"Maria Montejano, I work at Hotél Versailles."

"What?" Wendy asked. "Where's Daisy?"

"I do not know a Daisy."

Robocop stuck his arm between everyone, making Vivian back up. "Let me ask the questions here. Ms. Montejano, what are you doing with these men?"

She looked down at the ground. "They paid me $50 to do this for them. I didn't know it would cause trouble."

***

The pistol-toting asshole stayed in the room with Daisy and wouldn't let her leave the chair. She wanted to get the drug out of her system, but he wasn't going to give her the chance. By the time she started to feel woozy, another man walked in. Daisy squinted at him, trying to place him, but her thoughts wouldn't come together. The guy with the gun left and Daisy got up from the chair, only to be pushed down by the familiar face.

A few minutes later, Sonu walked in and pulled the black burqa out of the closet and tossed it to her. Daisy made no move to put it on, so he roughly draped it over her head and put her arms through the sleeves. He pulled her to her feet and she wobbled, so he led her by the elbow to the elevator and out a side entrance of the hotel. A tan car waited at the curb, and he steered her toward it as the familiar-face guy opened the back door.

It's now or never. Daisy lurched to the side, away from Sonu, and ran to a large planter filled with red flowers. She stuck her fingers down her throat and heaved up everything she could.

The guy holding the back door grabbed her around the waist and tossed her into the car.

195

She had a sudden moment of clarity. *He's the other fake Desert Glitter guy.*

***

A shrill whistle pierced the air and Vivian looked down the street to see Adrienne waving her arms frantically.

Vivian turned to Robocop. "You don't need us, right? Since Milton isn't pressing charges?"

"I've got your contact information if I need you. Go on."

Vivian and the girls ran down the block to meet Adrienne.

"What are you doing here?" Kate asked.

"Antonio called me, said something was going down with Daisy at Hotél Versailles. We hauled ass over there and the doorman said y'all stole a carriage."

"We just borrowed it," Lucy said.

"What happened down there? Did you find Daisy?"

"No, it was a decoy! Those fuckers tricked us!" Wendy said.

"But GQ wasn't with them," Lucy said. "He must have Daisy."

Vivian snapped. "We almost crashed into that undercover cop we've seen all around town. He may have been going to the hotel."

"I bet he's on the take," Adrienne said.

"GQ must have known we were on to him with the building inspector charade," Kate said. "I bet he called the cop and GQ and Daisy are long gone by now."

Vivian looked at Adrienne. "If you were loaded and needed to get out of town quick, what would you do?"

"How loaded?"

"Super-rich loaded."

"You'd charter a plane and leave out of Lakefront. Low security, close by. It's perfect."

"How do we get there?"

"Al's parked around the corner. Let's go." Adrienne took off and the girls followed.

They hopped into the SUV, Vivian and Lucy in the middle seat and Wendy and Kate in the back.

Adrienne told him where to go and Al hauled ass through the side streets, heading to the small, private airport. They called Antonio and put him on speaker phone in the car, filling him in on the decoy and where they thought GQ might be taking Daisy.

"I'll send a couple of cars, A, but I can't call out the cavalry," Antonio said. "Not on a wild guess."

196

"I just saw your undercover guy. He was driving by the courthouse and we almost ran into him with the carriage."

Antonio groaned.

"Is he the problem in your investigation?" Adrienne asked.

"It's certainly starting to look that way. Dammit!"

Al punched the accelerator. "Our ETA is seven minutes."

"Okay, I'll call in some help and will do some checking around. *Dammit!*" Antonio hung up.

Al raced across town, blowing through red lights. He drove 90 mph on I-10 before exiting for the airport. He turned onto Stars and Stripes Boulevard.

"We're almost there," Adrienne said. "Shit! Turn here!" She pointed left.

Al hit the brakes but couldn't make the turn and sped by the main entrance.

"It's okay, just go on down to the service entrance," Adrienne said. "We can turn around there."

They whizzed by palm trees and came up to a beige cinder block building.

"Hang this left and we can do a U-turn," Adrienne pointed.

Al slowed and had to wait for a car before he could make his left.

Vivian screamed and leaned forward over Al's shoulder. "There's the car that almost creamed us in the carriage! It's the undercover cop!"

Kate looked back. "I don't see anyone else in the car with him."

"He's already dropped them off," Adrienne said. "That asshole. I *hate* dirty cops!" She slammed her hand on the dashboard. "We're running out of time."

Al turned into the service entrance.

"Wait!" Lucy said. "I think I see them!"

Al slowed down and Lucy pointed to a woman who was being supported by two men, walking from the main building to a plane on the tarmac. The woman wore a black burqa and was completely covered except for the slit at her eyes.

"Those fuckers have drugged her!" Kate said. "We've got to stop that plane!"

Rather than do a U-turn to go back to the main building, Al headed straight toward the service entry to the tarmac.

"Al, the gate's closed!" Adrienne yelled.

"Not for long!" He hit the gas and gripped the wheel tight. The SUV blew through the gate like it wasn't there.

The door to the airplane closed, and the plane soon started taxiing toward the runway. "How are we going to stop them?" Kate asked.

"Whatever we do, we've got to do it quick," Al said. "That's a G650. It'll be airborne in no time."

Adrienne reached into her purse. "Damn, the sheriff took my gun as evidence! Where's yours, Al?"

"Shit, lost mine in Gino's poker game last night."

"Al!" Adrienne slapped his knee.

"I'll win it back tonight!"

She shook her head as Al pulled behind the plane.

"We need something heavy to throw at the plane," Kate said and reached over the back seat into the cargo area. "What's in this orange and black bag?"

"Oh, nothing," Al said.

Kate unzipped it. "Bowling balls?" She tossed aside tape, scissors and playing cards, along with a pair of bowling shoes, including a slipcover on one.

"Can we get close enough to the plane and use those to damage it?" Vivian asked.

Al's eyes flashed in the rearview mirror. "Not my bowling balls! Those are custom!"

Kate passed a black and red one with a yellow flame up to Lucy as Adrienne opened the sunroof to the SUV. "Geez, how heavy is this?"

"Wait, throw Vapor first, the blue one," Al said. "Save my Ultimate Inferno!"

Lucy put Inferno down and took the blue one from Kate. "Wow! What's this one weigh?"

"It's a fifteener," Al said sadly.

"You've got some serious balls, Al!" Wendy said.

Lucy steadied herself in the sunroof, then leaned in and said to Al, "Get me close enough to throw this at the wing. I can damage it or something."

The plane slowed and turned onto the runway and Al pulled alongside.

Lucy had blue Vapor at the ready. "You've got to get in front of the wing, Al! Speed up!"

He gunned the SUV.

The plane also sped up, but Al kept pace. Lucy chunked Vapor, but she overshot. It flew completely over the wing and crashed to the ground. Blue shards flew everywhere.

"Shit! I missed!"

Vivian handed her the Ultimate Inferno. "This is your last shot, Kingpin! Don't miss!"

"Ahhh! The pressure!" Lucy went back out and steadied the ball.

The plane sped up and the wing almost passed them. Al redlined the SUV and got back in front.

Lucy reared back and heaved the ball with all her might. "Geronimo!"

47

The black and red bowling ball flew through the air, hit the leading edge of the wing, bounced, then hit the flap and took out a chunk before crashing onto the tarmac. Red liquid began spewing from a hydraulic line on the plane's wing, and Al jerked the SUV to the left and slowed down.

Lucy, still standing up in the sunroof, raised her arms in victory. "Strike!"

Vivian tugged on her shirt. "Actually, that's a spare. You got a gutter ball the first time."

"Whatever," Lucy said. "Mission accomplished."

The girls and Al gave high-fives all around as the plane slowed down. Al followed the plane to the end of the runway, where it lurched to a stop.

"What do we do now?" Kate asked.

Al looked in the rearview mirror. "We don't have to do anything. The reinforcements are here."

A few moments later, a police cruiser and airport security, lights and sirens going full force, pulled up behind them.

A policeman yelled over the loudspeaker, "Driver of the SUV, move your vehicle away from the plane."

Al gave a thumbs up out the window, then circled behind the two cruisers. He rolled the rest of the windows down, but everyone stayed inside the car.

"Occupants of the plane," the policeman said over his loudspeaker, "lower the stairs and deplane."

"We've got to call Antonio," Adrienne said and Al dialed over Bluetooth.

He picked up immediately.

"You're not going to believe what happened!" Adrienne said.

"I'm pulling up on the tarmac. Stay in the car." Click.

After several minutes with no response from the plane, the officer repeated the order. Four more police units, a news van and Antonio arrived, and still nothing.

199

Antonio and Detective Leffall walked up to the SUV.

"Do you know how many people are on the plane?" Antonio asked.

Vivian leaned out the window. "We saw a goon and Surendran dragging Daisy into the plane. We think she's drugged. Didn't see anyone other than them, though."

"Did you see any weapons?" Leffall asked.

"Nothing, but we were pretty far away," Al replied. "With these guys, you can bet they've got some firepower on board."

Antonio looked at Al. "I want y'all to move away from this scene. Drive over to that hangar and stay put." He pointed to a blue metal building 200 yards away. Then he looked at Vivian sternly. "Stay in the car." He walked to the officer using the loudspeaker.

Al flipped the SUV around and drove to the hangar.

"I want to see what's going on," Kate said.

"Me, too," Lucy said.

Al turned the SUV so they could watch the action, then he killed the engine. Nothing happened except three more police cruisers arrived and two ambulances.

"What's with the medics?" Lucy asked.

"Probably here just in case," Al said.

A gray-haired man in blue, oil-stained coveralls walked away from the plane he was working on in the hangar and to the SUV. He pointed a greasy finger toward the mass of lights on the tarmac and said to Al, "What's goin' on with that plane?"

Al was cool. "Hostage situation."

Lucy stood up again in the sunroof. "I brought 'em to a stop with a bowling ball!"

The man wiped his hands on a rag. "I was wonderin' what damaged the wing on that beauty."

"Screw the wing," Lucy said. "He kidnapped our friend. He's goin' down!"

"They've been there awhile," Kate said. "At first the cop was using the car's loudspeaker to communicate, but now, nothing."

"They're probably using the radio to talk to them."

"What radio?" Vivian asked.

"I've got a VHF handheld over there." The man pointed into the hangar. "There's a ground frequency and a tower frequency. Anyone can listen if you're tuned to the right channel."

"Can we listen?" Adrienne asked, opening her car door.

He walked the group inside and picked up a radio from a workbench.

"What you got here?" Al asked, gesturing toward a white plane with a turquoise underbelly and tail.

"Learjet. Had to check the engine igniter, had a hard time starting her last time. I'm 'bout done," the mechanic said and clicked through several channels. "They weren't on the tower frequency so it must be the ground." He clicked the radio one more time and a deep voice crackled on the radio.

"This is New Orleans Police Department trying to reach Golf three two four Victor. Do you copy?"

Static.

"This is New Orleans Police Department trying to reach Golf three two four Victor. Do you copy? Come in, over."

"We copy. I want another jet. I have diplomatic immunity."

"This is Sergeant Fred Womack of the New Orleans Police Department. I'm here to help you through this and make sure everybody stays safe. Who am I speaking to?"

"You don't need my name. What you need to know is I have diplomatic immunity and I want another jet."

"We can work on that, sir. However, it will take some time. Do you, or anyone on board, need medical attention?"

"No, but they will if I don't get another plane."

"Let's see if we can keep this peaceful so everyone comes out okay. Sound good?"

Silence.

"Who all is on board, sir?"

"Myself, my wife, my bodyguard, a flight attendant and the pilot."

"We can get you another plane but we're going to need all hostages released," Womack said.

"There are no hostages. This is my staff."

"Sir, we have reason to believe that Daisy Easley is on board the plane. We need her and the others released."

Silence for a few beats, then: "I'll give you the flight attendant when I get my jet."

"What flight plan can we file for you, sir?"

"No flight plan."

"We will agree to that if we get the pilot, your wife and the flight attendant."

"I need the pilot, and my wife is staying with me."

"We can talk about that," Womack said.

"Look, I know what you're doing. Quit wasting time. Get me a fully fueled jet and I'll be gone. I want it in 30 minutes."

"Sir, it'll take time to procure one."

"No, I want it here in 30 minutes. We're at an airport. Find me a plane."

201

48

Sergeant Womack said to GQ, "We're working as fast as we can to get you a jet."

Lucy threw her hands up. "Surely they're not going to let him get on another plane with Daisy and take off."

"I'm sure they have a plan," Adrienne said.

Antonio and a uniformed officer zoomed up to the hangar. Adrienne rushed up to him as he got out of the car. "Are y'all really going to get him a plane?"

"Been listening in?" Adrienne grinned. "You know it."

Antonio walked to the mechanic, who had gone back to work on the Learjet. "Your plane?"

The mechanic hesitated for a moment. "No, but I can call the owner."

"Please do. We need a plane that looks like it's ready to fly, but it needs to be disabled so it can't take off."

The mechanic made the call, explained the situation, then handed the phone to Antonio.

He introduced himself, gave a little more background on the situation and asked, "Would you be willing to work with us on this?" He nodded his head while he listened. "Your plane will not leave the airport and we will pay for any repairs." He handed the phone back to the mechanic who clicked off a moment later.

"You have permission to use the jet."

"Thank you," Antonio said. "How quickly can you have it ready?"

"Ten minutes, but once I disable her, she can only go in a straight shot, no turning. We need to line her up to where you want her to end up, before I jam the rudder. The engine will sound great, but she won't take off."

Antonio looked at GQ's jet and assessed the runway. "Let's taxi her up to the beginning of the runway, disable her, and then Officer Warner can taxi in a straight line, right to him. Surendran can think it'll turn and take off the opposite direction."

"Do you need me to taxi out to the runway?" the mechanic asked.

"I can do it," the uniformed officer spoke up. "I've got almost 20 hours toward my pilot's license. We can't risk you being out there."

"Fine with me." He got to work putting the panel back on.

"Will you be able to jam the rudder quickly once we're lined up?" Antonio asked.

"I'll stand on the back of the golf cart and shove a screwdriver between the rudder and the vertical stabilizer. Take 20 seconds."

"Perfect."

Plan in place, Warner zipped an extra pair of mechanic coveralls over his police uniform, then walked up the three stairs. He pulled them up and closed the top hatch, and a moment later was in the cockpit. Antonio walked in front of the plane and relayed an update on his radio. The girls and Al stood to the side of the hangar, out of the way.

The radio crackled in Lucy's hand. "Sir, we'll taxi the jet to you momentarily."

"What are you bringing me?"

"It's a Learjet, fueled up."

"I want all of you to back off. Clear the runway."

"One of us needs to be there to ensure you release the flight attendant. We will leave one car with myself and another officer."

"No, just you. Unarmed. And over by the water, away from the runway."

"I will be unarmed but by your plane to receive the flight attendant. Once I have her, you are free to move to the other jet."

Static.

"Let's keep this peaceful."

More static, then, "Bring the plane."

Lucy moved the radio into her left hand. "What an asshole! I can't believe he thinks he can get away with this!"

Antonio ran over as the negotiator's voice came on the radio. "Whoever that is, please get off this frequency. Do not interfere. This is a police matter."

"Oh shit!" Lucy said as Antonio yanked the radio out of her hand.

"You could have given us away!" He popped the back off the radio and took out the batteries. "Stay out of this!" He stomped off to the plane and signaled to Warner in the cockpit to get moving to the end of the runway.

"Everyone cover your ears," the mechanic yelled and slipped on a pair of orange hearing protectors. He handed Antonio a pair as the engines fired up, then grabbed a large screwdriver and ran to move the blocks around the tires. A few moments later, the plane rolled forward and he and Antonio hopped in the golf cart and followed.

Lucy started searching through the workbench.

"What are you looking for?" Wendy asked.

"Batteries!"

Wendy joined the search while Vivian and Kate watched the plane get into place.

Antonio parked the golf cart under the back of the aircraft and the mechanic stood on the back seat and jammed the screwdriver in place. He sat down and Antonio zoomed away from the plane and headed toward the main terminal.

The police cars began backing away from GQ's plane, some of them turning around and driving to the service road.

Wendy and Lucy joined the group in front of the hangar. Wendy held up a pair of binoculars. "I thought these would come in handy."

Lucy clicked the battery cover on the radio into place. " — front control to Lima niner five niner Tango. Proceed your taxi on the runway."

"Ten-four, tower. Proceeding on the runway."

Sergeant Womack came on the radio. "Sir, your replacement plane is taxiing toward you now. Once in place, the pilot will lower the stairs and move away."

"Good. Only once I'm at the other jet will I release her."

Officer Warner slowly approached GQ's plane and stopped about 30 feet away. He shut off the engines, then opened the top hatch and dropped the stairs. He walked into the grass toward the lake.

"Nothing's happening," Wendy said and passed the binoculars to Kate.

Kate held them up and tried to focus. "I'm going to have to have my eyes checked. I can't see squat."

"Give 'em here!" Vivian said. She took a second to maneuver the focus knob. "All the shades are down, I don't see anyone in the cockpit. The plane's just sitting there."

Womack said over the radio, "Sir, is everything okay? Your plane is ready."

The seven-step staircase on the Gulfstream folded out onto the tarmac. GQ's goon stuck his head out and looked around.

"Who is that?" Lucy asked. "I can't tell."

"The bodyguard," Vivian replied.

The goon grabbed the flight attendant and pushed her in front of him as they started down the stairs, followed by the pilot.

Vivian held her breath as they took each step slowly. "He's using her as a human shield, that pussy."

The goon, flight attendant and pilot hustled to the second plane. The pilot hesitated at the bottom of the stairs. The goon waved a gun at him so he boarded the plane.

"Does he have a gun?" Al asked.

"I'm pretty sure, yeah," Vivian replied.

"Dammit," Adrienne said.

The goon shoved the flight attendant up the stairs before following. He stood at the top step, holding her arm and looking around the plane. The pilot sat in the cockpit and appeared to be looking at the flight controls.

A moment later, GQ appeared in the doorway of the Gulfstream. Daisy, still wearing the burqa, was pinned to his side.

"There they are," Vivian said, binoculars pushed up to her eyes. "And he's got a gun."

49

Daisy's vision blurred as she tried to concentrate on the staircase of the jet. Sonu supported her with his left hand and held a pistol in his right.

"Move it," he said and nudged her with his shoulder.

She grasped the handrail, then took a step down. He moved beside her and she took another step, then another. He followed and she felt a tug on her burqa. His foot was tangled in the fabric and she pulled at it. He slipped and she grasped the railing with both hands as he fell down four steps onto the tarmac. The gun flew out of his hand and skidded to a stop several feet away. He landed hard on his hands and knees, then rolled onto his back.

Daisy's legs felt like Jell-O, but she managed to stay standing as Sonu lay on the ground, stunned.

A man unzipping his coveralls ran toward to the Learjet. He pulled a gun and pointed it at the bodyguard who was standing in the doorway of the other plane. "Drop it! Drop your weapon!"

A different man ran toward Sonu, reaching behind his back. He pulled out a weapon and stopped, standing over Sonu. "Don't move. It's over."

Sonu rolled onto his side and looked at the gun he had dropped.

"Don't even think about it."

Sonu stayed on his side for a moment, then rolled onto his back with his hands up. "I have diplomatic immunity."

"Yeah, yeah, that's what I hear. It's not going to save your ass this time."

Coveralls shouted to the bodyguard again, "Drop your weapon!"

The bodyguard looked at Sonu, then at the runway behind him. Several police cars raced down the tarmac toward them. He laid his gun in the doorway of the plane, held his arms up and walked down the steps.

Daisy's knees buckled and she collapsed onto the step. She pulled the burqa from her face, tucked her head into her knees, wrapped her arms around her legs and started to cry.

Cars screeched and there was more yelling. Daisy never looked up, just stayed in her cocoon, except when she heard the click of handcuffs. Her kidnapper was still on the ground but now on his stomach and handcuffed.

Footsteps sounded on the staircase and a calm voice said, "Daisy?"

Exhaustion prevented her from raising her head.

A soft touch fell on her shoulder. "You're safe now. I'm Antonio Robichaux with the New Orleans Police Department. We have an ambulance on the way."

She looked up at him, his soft brown eyes relaying concern. She nodded and buried into her knees again. She raised her head once more and asked, "Can I borrow your phone?"

***

Vivian lowered the binoculars. "They're loading Daisy in the ambulance!"

The girls, Al and Adrienne cheered. Vivian high-fived Adrienne. "Way to know where he was going!"

Adrienne smacked her hand. "Way to find out who it was!"

"They're probably going to leave soon," Lucy said. "Al, let's follow them. I'm going to go put the radio back." She turned to the hangar.

"They're not going to let us see her," Adrienne said. "No way."

Vivian ran after Lucy and gave her the binoculars, then said, "We can at least see Jason."

Al pulled the keys out of his pocket. "Let's go."

Everyone climbed into the SUV and Al pulled in behind the ambulance as it left the airport.

The lights and sirens helped them zoom through town, and they ended up at the same hospital Simone and the other kidnapper had been taken to. Al dropped the girls and Adrienne at the ambulance bay and left to park the car.

The ambulance backed into the emergency bay and the girls stood just outside the sliding glass door to the emergency room. The driver hopped out of the front, came around and opened the back doors. The two men gently pulled the stretcher out, and the wheels ratcheted down.

As they pushed Daisy by, she was almost unrecognizable with her black hair. Vivian leaned over. "We've been looking for you and are so glad you're okay."

Daisy was covered by a white sheet to her chest, her arms out, still wearing the burqa. She barely lifted her hand and looked dazed. "Thanks."

The girls, Adrienne and Al lingered in the waiting room. Five minutes later, a pair of police officers, one a female, spoke to the receptionist and then went through the secured door. Another five minutes and Jason, his parents and Daisy's parents were at the sliding glass doors.

Jason hustled to the reception desk. "I'm Daisy Easley's husband and these are our parents. She's been brought in by ambulance."

The receptionist clicked on the keyboard. "She's in Signal Five. Only two visitors at a time. I'm fairly certain the police are with her now."

"What is Signal Five?" Jason asked, wide-eyed, panicked.

"It's where we take care of victims of abuse or a crime. The rooms are specialized for collecting evidence that can be used in court."

Jason turned white and leaned on the counter. "Jesus." Vivian thought he might pass out. "We need to see her."

"Let me check with the police and make sure it's allowed. One moment, please."

Vivian approached Jason and touched his arm. "Thank god she's safe. We saw her when they brought her in. She's going to be all right."

His eyes teared up and he gave her a hug. "Thank you so much. Truly." A buzzer sounded and a nurse opened the door, and Jason and Daisy's mom practically raced in.

Vivian made introductions to the family and everyone talked for a few minutes. The waiting room started getting crowded because Jason's band showed up, along with a host of other people.

Vivian gave Jason's mother a big hug. "It was really nice meeting you. I wish it was under different circumstances, but at least Daisy has been found and will be okay."

His mom squeezed her back, then said to the group. "I know all of you played a role in this. We can't thank you enough." Her phone rang. "I'm sorry, family's calling. I need to take this."

Al, Adrienne and the girls left the hospital, and although they were emotionally drained, they had to celebrate. It was the girls' last night in town, Daisy was safe, and Wendy was about to be hitched.

"I know just the place," Kate said as Al valeted at Hotél Versailles. "They have Jell-O shots in great big syringes."

Gary, the doorman, opened Adrienne's door and the back door. His left eye was an ugly reddish purple.

Lucy got out. "You didn't get the day off after getting punched out?"

Gary laughed. "I'm all right. I told them it looks worse than it is."

Al slipped him a business card and a bill. "You ever need a job, call me."

Gary expertly slipped that in his pocket and said, "So what happened to Mr. Surendran?" The girls got him caught up on the events from decoy to Daisy. "I need to buy y'all a drink," Gary said at the end of the tale.

"We'll be at the Funky 544," Kate told him. "You and Lea should join us later."

He smiled. "I may just ask her to do that."

Kate led the way to Bourbon and the Funky 544. A band played downstairs, but she took everyone up the narrow staircase to a lounge and another bar that was pulsing to the sound of "Blurred Lines" by Robin Thicke.

"I love this song!" Vivian said and started dancing, then stopped. "Oh, I almost forgot." She reached into her purse and pulled out Wendy's battered bachelorette sash. "I brought this along, just in case!"

Wendy smiled. "Okay, one last hoorah!" She put it on and did a little shimmy.

The bartender gave everyone two strands of beads, except for Wendy, who got three, and told them that drinks were three-for-one and the giant, plastic syringe Jell-O shots were $2. They commandeered the balcony and Kate bought the first round.

Adrienne, Lucy and Wendy lined up, backs against the railing, heads tilted and mouths open like baby birds as Al, Vivian and Kate played nurse and squirted the red goo into their mouths.* They switched places and everyone got thoroughly medicated.

Vivian scanned the crowd and saw a familiar face walking up Bourbon. She pulled off her beads and chunked them his way. Antonio snatched them from the air and put them around his neck. Then he walked in, downstairs.

Adrienne gave him a big hug when he walked onto the balcony, tired but looking good. His wrinkled, white dress shirt was untucked from his jeans and his cuffs were rolled up.

Everyone congratulated him on the day's events. Al shook his hand and gave him a beer.

Antonio walked up to Vivian. "What can I say?"

"About what?"

"Everything. Y'all are the ones who broke this thing wide open. We couldn't have done it without you."

Her cheeks flushed and she waved him off. "It was a team effort."

He leaned down and kissed her, then held up his beads. "Not sure I did anything to deserve these."

The space between them seemed to heat up.

"There's still plenty of opportunity, you know."

He grinned down at her. "I like new opportunities."

50

The girls, Al, Adrienne and Antonio stood on the balcony of the Funky 544 talking about Daisy's return.

"She's really lucky," Antonio said. "That guy was an absolute narcissistic lunatic, but he didn't sexually assault her. Daisy told us Sonu and a couple of his guys threw her around a few times and she's got some bruises from where Sonu kicked her."

"That asshole!" Vivian said.

"Evidently, Sonu was infatuated with her and became convinced she would grow to love him. He had his guys drug her with Rohypnol and planned on taking her back to Kuwait." Antonio took a long draw of his beer. "Apparently his father is some big-wig politico, but that's not going to save him. You can't kidnap people in America and expect to get away with it. I don't give a shit who your daddy is."

"Is she staying overnight in the hospital?" Kate asked.

"Yeah, because she was drugged. They'll run some labs and stuff and she'll talk to the behavioral health folks. She's been through a traumatic event but should be released tomorrow mid-morning or so if everything checks out okay."

"Thank goodness he didn't rape her," Lucy said. "That's my worst fear."

"That's pretty much all women's worst fear, I think," Wendy said.

They chatted a bit more about Sonu on the stairs of the plane. Antonio explained how he tripped and fell on the burqa Daisy was wearing. Everyone cheersed and had a good laugh at Sonu's clumsiness.

"He fell down before he could be taken down," Lucy said. "I love it!"

Adrienne pointed to Antonio with her vodka and cranberry. "How were y'all going to capture him without hurting the hostages?"

"The plan was to apprehend the bodyguard and intercept Surendran before he got to the other plane. Womack and Warner would have been able to pull it off. They're some of the best."

The group cheersed again to Womack and Warner.

"And one more thing, the undercover you saw everywhere was the problem in investigation. He stole the surveillance video of the club off

Leffall's desk before a copy could be made, and he worked to steer the investigation off-course. If you hadn't alerted me to his random appearances, I may not have picked up on that."

"What are they going to do to that double-crosser?" Al asked.

"Internal affairs is on it, but I think they'll find a large amount of cash in his house."

"How much cash we talkin'?" Wendy asked.

"Twenty grand. And that's just the up-front payment."

Lucy pointed her almost-empty syringe at Antonio. "We knew that guy was up to no good, even if he was cute." Her finger slipped on the plunger and a blob of red goo squirted down the front of Antonio's shirt.

He looked down and groaned. "Great, now I look like a crime scene."

Everyone laughed and Al ducked inside. He emerged a couple of minutes later with two bags of beads. "Let me show you how it's done." He tossed Lucy one of the bags and ripped open the other. He pulled out several strands and leaned over the railing, twirling them on his finger.

Immediately a group began to form under the balcony.

"Ya gotta earn it!" he yelled down, dangling the beads over the balcony.

A woman flipped up her floral top, showing her black, lacy bra.

"I'll let that slide," Al said, grinning, and tossed her a strand.

This spurred a flurry of shirt raising and boob sightings. Al went through his bag quickly, so Lucy ripped open the second one and everyone grabbed a few strands.

"I don't want boobs," Vivian yelled to the crowd. "I want boys!" She smiled at Antonio, then focused on Bourbon. She pointed to three guys walking behind the crowd. "Whatcha got?"

One of the guys lifted his shirt. His belly was more like Silly Putty, but she threw him a strand for the effort.

Antonio came up close behind her. "Wanna know what I got?"

Vivian turned around to face him and ran her hand down his chest. "I think I like what you got." She put the remaining beads in her hand around his neck. "You will definitely need to earn these."

Al bought another round of giant syringes, and the girls took turns snapping pictures leaning over the balcony shooting their "medicine."

Vivian texted Jason a picture of everyone celebrating Daisy's freedom. The Funky 544 sign shined brightly behind them.

He texted back:

More cause to celebr8. We r gettin married 2moro! Workin on plans, will let you know.

Vivian:

Congratulations! We leave tomorrow evening, but we'll try to be there.

Jason:

You HAVE to be there.
Oh, u have a crowd comin ur way. Next round on me!

Vivian smiled and tucked her phone away. "Jason and Daisy are getting married tomorrow!" This got another round of cheers.

"Where?" Adrienne asked.

"He said they're making plans."

"I know just the place. Give me his number."

Vivian did and Adrienne went inside the bar.

The girls danced on the balcony, flirting from afar with men on Bourbon. Al bought another bag of beads, and they got tossed to worthy flashers.

Twenty minutes later, four of the guys who had been in the ER waiting room came onto the balcony. One of them looked at his phone, then walked up to Vivian. He flashed his phone at her and the picture she had sent to Jason, the one of her taking a Jell-O syringe.

"Though your head is back in this picture, I'm fairly sure it's you." He smiled. "I'm Paul. This is Eric, Will and Thomas."

Vivian stuck out her hand. "Nice to meet you. I'm Vivian." She introduced everyone else. "Y'all are in Jason's band, right?"

"We are," Paul said. "I hear you girls are the reason Daisy is safe. Thank you."

Lucy nudged Kate. "This one here's practically a psychic."

Kate smiled. "We just got lucky. Antonio and his team did all the work."

"Whoever did whatever, we're grateful," Thomas said, and he shook Antonio's hand. "I hear Jason owes y'all a round." He held up a credit card. "I think, since the drinks are on him, you deserve two!"

That got the group rowdy again, and they celebrated in true Bourbon fashion. Gary, the doorman, and Lea, the housekeeping manager, showed up, as did Jonathon, which made Lucy extra giddy.

Al and Adrienne called it quits after about an hour. Adrienne grabbed Al's head and pulled it down to her eyes. "Oh my god! Is this *another* gray hair I see?" She kissed the top of his head. "You're gettin' old, old man! Time to put you to bed."

He wrapped his burly arms around her. "I'm not old. I just need some post-excitement excitement."

They said their goodbyes and left the bar, arm in arm.

The girls, Antonio, the band and others danced, drank, sang, laughed and enjoyed the night, knowing tomorrow would be a special day — a new beginning for Daisy and Jason.

Around 3:30 in the morning, Kate turned to Vivian. "I'm about to fall over."

"Too many syringes?"

"Maybe. Or exhaustion. This has been a crazy day."

"Okay, let's hit it."

The girls, Antonio and Jonathon said goodbye to the band, Gary and Lea. "Perhaps we'll see you at the wedding later today," Thomas said.

"Hope so," Vivian responded. "If it works out with our flights, we'll be there."

As they headed out on Bourbon toward their hotel, Antonio wrapped his arm around Vivian's waist.

Holy hellbuckets! I can't believe this! She tried to contain her excitement as they neared Hotel De Lis.

Jonathon held Lucy's hand as they walked. He'd gotten his job back at the pizza place and had worked that night, so he smelled like pepperoni.

When they reached the hotel, Wendy and Kate went on upstairs. Lucy and Jonathon walked to the elevators, but Vivian and Antonio stayed outside.

He pushed a blonde curl out of her face. "I wish I'd had the opportunity to get to know you better."

"It's probably best that you didn't. I live in Fort Worth, which makes you geographically undesirable." She put her finger on his chest and smiled up at him. "Though I do love this city and want to come back soon."

He wrapped his arms around her waist, pulled her in tight and leaned down for a long, passionate kiss. His face was scratchy since it had probably been 24 hours since his last shave, but she didn't care. His lips were soft and he was an incredible kisser. He moved her to the brick wall next to the entrance and kissed her harder, more urgently. His hands roamed up from her waist.

This is tempting.

He pushed himself against her, brushed his hand gently over her breasts and wrapped it around her neck, playing with her hair. He smelled faintly of sweetness, aftershave or cologne, and she moved her hands under his shirt, running her fingernails over his back.

I'm about to give in.

He slowly stopped kissing her and took a deep breath. "I want you to come home with me."

Me, too! Me, too! Me, too!

She pulled her hands out of his shirt and looked down. "I better not. The last one-night stand I had, I thought I was going to get eaten by a bear. I took it as a sign that perhaps I should stop having them."

He laughed out loud. "No bears in New Orleans, unless we go to the Audubon Zoo."

"Yeah, I know, but you know what I mean."

"Actually, I have no idea what you mean, but I understand."

Damn bears!

51

Vivian's phone buzzed on the nightstand. She scrambled around, found it and looked at the display. Nine-fifteen and three messages. The first was Rick asking what time she was picking up the kids, then two from Adrienne wanting to know if Vivian did the naughty with her brother. She responded to Rick first — around 9. Then she smiled as she texted Adrienne that no, she was not that kinda girl. Ha ha ha.

She put the phone back on the nightstand and rolled over. Everyone was still completely out, so she drifted off again, too.

An hour and a half later, hunger drove her to wake up. It was already 10:45. Wendy had a cup of coffee in her hand. Kate was in the shower.

"Sleepyhead snore monster rises," Lucy said, grabbing Vivian's toes that were still covered.

Vivian pulled her foot up. "I don't snore."

"Oh honey, I have hard and fast evidence that, in fact, you do." Lucy pulled out her phone and played a video of Vivian sawing logs like she was building a cabin from scratch.

"Geez, that's pretty bad," Vivian said and threw the covers back.

"Uh, yes. I will be bringing earplugs on our next trip."

Wendy smiled as she folded her alcohol-stained bachelorette sash and put it into her suitcase. "It didn't bother me, Viv."

"You seriously need to go to a sleep study or something." Lucy said.

The water in the shower turned off.

"Why? I slept great!" Vivian stood up and stretched. "Somebody woke up to be a grouchy gus this morning. Didn't have any pepperoni last night?"

Lucy couldn't help but laugh. She folded a shirt to perfection and placed it in her suitcase. "Not the good kind. I came this close to taking a big-ass bite, though." She left about an inch between her thumb and pointer. "This close."

Wendy took a sip of her coffee. "You better hurry, Viv. Checkout's in 10 minutes."

"No problem," Vivian said. "Y'all can go check us out, I'll grab a quick shower, throw my stuff in the suitcase, and shazamm, I'll be ready."

"Isn't that supposed to be shazammapuss?" Kate yelled from the bathroom.

"You're right! Shazammapuss, my ass'll be ready!" Vivian clapped her hands together, then reached for her suitcase. She opened a drawer and started tossing things in. "Kate, move it or lose it! I gotta get in there!" Her phone buzzed. It was a message from Jason.

Wedding, 2:00, Jackson Square in front of fountain. Reception at Flanagan's.

Vivian told the girls. "Yay, we can make it, our flights aren't until 7."

"And we have time to grab lunch!" Wendy clapped. "Let's do this!" She and Lucy went downstairs to check them out of the hotel.

Vivian switched places with Kate in the bathroom and flew through a shower. She double-timed shaving her legs and cut herself right by her ankle. "Ouch!" She jumped out of the shower, stuck a piece of toilet paper on her bleeding leg, ran some mousse through her curls, slapped on some deodorant, rubbed moisturizer on her face and swiped on some mascara and lip gloss. She threw on a sassy, pink, abstract-print maxi dress, slipped on her Shoe-Be-Do shoes and put on her chandelier earrings. "Voila."

Kate nodded, impressed. "Not bad." She wore a snazzy, aubergine purple, silk sheath tank dress and looked at the red toilet paper clinging to Vivian's leg. "Technical difficulties?"

"That's the way it goes, sometimes, but you look simply elegant as usual."

"Thanks." Kate did a room check to make sure they weren't leaving anything behind and brought Vivian her toiletries out of the bathroom. "Don't forget these."

Vivian stuffed them into her suitcase, zipped it up and pulled it off the bed.

There was a knock at the door. "Open up. Police!"

Vivian opened the door to a giggling Lucy and Wendy. Lucy shrugged. "We couldn't help ourselves."

"Wow!" Vivian said. "You girls look fabulous!" Lucy wore a dark gray A-line dress with a plunging neckline and an amazing pair of Jimmy Choos. Wendy wore an off-shoulder, champagne-colored number.

"Love the bag," Kate said to Wendy, referring to her oversized purse. "It's perfect for toting your personal pharmacy."

Wendy patted the coral-colored behemoth. "I thought we might need a thing or two out of here today since we didn't get much sleep last night."

The girls grabbed their bags, got to the lobby and checked them at the bellman's stand.

"Where should we go for lunch?" Wendy asked as he tagged the bags.

"What are you looking for?" the bellman asked. "Something nice? Something casual?"

"It's our last New Orleans meal, so we need something awesome!"

"Then go to Galatoire's. Authentic cuisine. Great service. One of the best." He looked at their outfits. "No shorts allowed, so you should be okay."

Wendy slipped him a $5 and they left the hotel.

It didn't take them long to walk to the Bourbon Street restaurant they had passed at least six times during their visit but not really noticed. How they had missed the white and green trim canopy, Vivian wasn't sure.

They walked in and the delectable scent of garlic and butter made Vivian's mouth water. The décor made her glad they had the Getaway Girlz Trust Fund — chandeliers, dark wood, white bead board and green wallpaper with gold accents and white tablecloths. Waiters in tuxedos hustled about.

"I love it here already," Lucy said, sitting down, smoothing the corner of the tablecloth.

Kate put her white cloth napkin in her lap. "Check out all the mirrors."

The girls enjoyed sharing a delicious lunch of shrimp rémoulade, crabmeat maison, au gratin potatoes, a wedge salad, chicken Creole, lots and lots of water and a side of ibuprofen.

Vivian sucked down the last of her water and the waiter smoothly grabbed the decanter on the table and refilled the glass.

Wendy looked at her watch. "We have 25 minutes. We'd better go."

"Do y'all mind horribly if we cab it?" Vivian asked. "I love my shoes, but I can't fathom walking to Jackson Square right now."

"Fine by me," Lucy said, pushing back her plate. "I'm in my FMPs and I ate too much."

Vivian looked over the bill and used their special account to pay for the pricey but fabulous meal. "Good thing we didn't have any alcohol."

Kate folded her napkin and put it on the table. "Where are we going on our next trip? I need something a little less city-ee. I miss the mountains."

"Do we want to go back to Colorado?" Vivian asked.

"No, there are more mountains in the U.S. than the Rockies," Lucy said. "And since I live there, I'd like to go somewhere else. Branch out. See the world, or at least the U.S."

"What about the Smoky Mountains?" Wendy said. "They border North Carolina, and Jake says Asheville is a cool town."

No one bit at that.

"What about the Adirondacks?" Kate said. "In upstate New York?"

"Oooh, that sounds interesting," Lucy said.

Kate nodded her head. "We can go in the fall, see the leaves changing."

"I would love that," Vivian said, taking the check from the waiter and thanking him. "We don't get fall colors in Texas. They go from green to brown, end of story."

"Okay, I'll start looking at it," Wendy said, getting up. "Upstate New York about six months from now in the fall. Sounds great."

"You sure your new husband won't mind you running off to the wild, burnt-orange yonder?" Vivian asked.

Wendy smiled. "Nah, I don't think he'd care."

"Better run it past him, bride-to-be," Lucy said.

"I wouldn't be marrying him if he was a control freak, but I'll have to get used to that whole checking-with-another-person thing before I make plans."

"I bet he'll be fine with it," Kate said. "Shaun knows I need these trips."

They grabbed a cab right outside the restaurant and took the short ride to Jackson Square. Al and Adrienne were already there, as were Antonio, Detective Leffall, Gary, Lea, all of the 12 Stones, Jason's parents, Daisy's parents, Al's cousin, Gino and wife Michelle and three media trucks. Larry and Sonya from Louie's Flowers were there and had given all the women a single red rose. The moms also had red rose corsages pinned to their dresses. Hairy Harry stood near a light post, away from the crowd. He looked sad, yet maybe a little happy, too.

Antonio walked over to Vivian and gave her a long, tight hug. "How are you?" he asked.

"I wasn't stalked, growled at or eaten by a bear on my way up to my room, so I guess I made the right decision."

He smiled. "Let me know next time you're in town, okay?"

She nodded as Adrienne and Al walked up.

"Did Al do good or what?" Adrienne said.

Vivian looked around. Red rose petals floated in the fountain and were scattered on the ground, but other than that the park looked the same. "What'd you do?"

"Nothin' really," Al replied. "Made a phone call."

Adrienne rubbed his back, obviously proud of him. "Whatever! It's difficult to get a wedding booked here, but my sweetheart has a friend in the Parks and Parkways Department. He made it happen."

"Way to go, Al!" Vivian gave him a high-five. "And it couldn't be a prettier day." A cool breeze blew off the river and big, white, puffy clouds floated across the sky.

Detective Leffall motioned to Antonio, who excused himself. Vivian watched as Leffall showed him something on his phone and Antonio smiled.

Kate moved next to her. "Think that means Sonofabitch is going down?"

Wendy leaned over. "Hell yeah!"

Jason walked to the Square from the cathedral, and cameras started clicking. He had on a modern-cut, black tuxedo, white shirt, silver vest and bowtie. A silver ribbon embraced a gorgeous white rose pinned to his lapel.

The news broadcasters had their lenses focused on him.

He stepped up to the fountain and hugged Daisy's mother tightly for several moments, whispering in her ear. She nodded and kissed him on the cheek. Then he turned to his own mom and hugged her. He shook hands with both dads before taking his place next to his best man, Paul, who wore a sleek, black suit and red tie. Eric, from the band, began playing an acoustic guitar and singing "Unchained Melody."

Daisy appeared in the doorway of the cathedral wearing a floor-length, form-fitting white wedding dress that had skin showing from the lace going down both sides. The bruises on her back weren't visible, and a silver and white beaded belt hugged her tiny waist. Her still-black hair was pulled into a loose up-do. A thin, white ribbon swirled here and there in her hair. Curled wisps gently hung around her face and fell in the back. The last few inches transitioned from black to bright red. She looked fantastic…and happy.

Daisy locked eyes with Jason and never wavered during her walk to the fountain. She carried a gorgeous bouquet of white roses accented with silver metallic swirls of ribbon.

She reached Jason and hugged him. He kissed her on the cheek, wiped a tear from his eye and took her hand.

A female magistrate officiated as they said their vows.

Jason took Daisy's hand. "Daisy, you are my warmth in winter, my cool breeze in summer. I love how you're full of surprises, joy and laughter. You make me want to be a better man. I'm honored you chose me to be by your side and I look forward to our future. I can't imagine my life without you. I love you beyond what I ever thought possible and if you will join me on this path, I promise to always protect you, inspire you and support you."

Daisy was crying. Jason reached into his tuxedo pocket and pulled out two tissues, handing her one and using the other.

She took a moment to compose herself, then gently reached for his hand. She took a deep breath and looked into his eyes. "Jason, the past few days have only strengthened and reinforced the love I feel for you, and only you. You never gave up, and neither will I. I vow that I will be faithful, forgiving, your best friend and, of course, feisty. I love the man you are now and forever."

Their words pounded at the wall of bricks Vivian had piled around her injured heart since her divorce. *This makes me believe in love again.* She looked to her left at Kate, who smiled dreamily. *She's so in love.* Vivian took Kate's hand and squeezed it gently. She turned to her right and looked at Wendy, who had tears running down her face.

219

52

Oh my gosh, Vivian thought. Wendy must be bubbling over at everything that has happened. So not like her to lose it, especially at a wedding.

A few wedding watchers turned and looked at Wendy, who sniffled loudly despite trying to smile through her tears. Her outpour made Vivian start crying, and pretty soon almost everyone was crying. Wendy dug tissues out of her purse and handed one to Vivian, then blew her nose.

Vivian reached over and hugged her. "You okay?"

"They just look so happy," Wendy said and blew her nose again.

Vivian looked to her right and saw the Romanian gypsy woman standing next to a tree. They made eye contact. The lady nodded, gave a small smile, then turned and walked away.

Vivian took a deep breath and accepted the fact that the gypsy had been right — both times.

"By the power vested in me by the state of Louisiana, you are now husband and wife. Jason, you may kiss your beautiful bride."

Jason wrapped his hands around Daisy's face and kissed her.

The crowd erupted, cameras clicked, and the news reporters went live. Eric, on acoustic guitar, started jamming to "Every Little Thing She Does is Magic" by The Police.

The bride and groom kissed again, then they turned to their family and all embraced. The moms were crying and the dads were misty-eyed. Jason and Daisy faced the crowd and everyone clapped again. They made a point to talk to everybody, and there were lots of handshakes, hugs and more tears.

Jason and Daisy walked up to Vivian and the girls. "We're so glad you're okay," Vivian said to Daisy as she squeezed her tight. "And we're super happy for you guys."

"I don't know what to say." Daisy pushed a black and red curl from her face. "Thank you is not enough."

"It is enough," Vivian responded and clasped her hand. "It is."

Daisy smiled at her through teary eyes. After a moment Jason asked, "Are you going to join us for the reception?"

"Wouldn't miss it," Vivian answered.

They led the crowd away from the fountain, into the square where a brass band waited to walk the group, second-line style, to Flanagan's. A band named Crawfish Bones was belting out tunes when they walked in.

"Love it already," Wendy said, nodding toward the small stage. "They sound smooth."

The girls picked a large table strategically placed between the band and the bar.

"Who wants something?" Vivian clapped, then rubbed her hands together.

"Just a glass of celebratory champagne for me," Kate said. Lucy seconded that.

"I don't know what I want," Wendy said, and followed Vivian to the bar.

"Two glasses of champagne, Dos Equis and a..." Vivian turned to Wendy.

"Black and Tan."

"Damn, hitting the hard stuff," Vivian teased.

"Guinness is yummy and it'll help settle my nerves."

"Give her two!" Vivian called to the bartender.

Wendy laughed. "I'm more emotional than usual today. I guess because of the crazy week and the fact that in one short month, I'll be married."

The bartender set Vivian's beer on the bar. She squeezed the lime in and toasted the air. "And it's going to be great." She took a long sip.

Wendy's dark, thick beer was served and she took a sip without flinching. "It was a great bachelorette party despite the kidnappings, but I'm ready to get home."

"Me too, and I'm ready to see my kiddos!"

The glasses of champagne were delivered and they carried them to the table. Al, Adrienne, Antonio and Detective Leffall had joined Kate and Lucy. Vivian sat next to Antonio.

He leaned over to whisper in her ear. The warmth of his breath tingled her neck. "Thought you had a plane to catch."

She leaned back a little to look at him. "I do, but we have an hour or so to kill before we have to get our bags."

He raised his eyebrows. "My place isn't far. I could have you back in an hour." He looked hot in his faded jeans and black polo. The narrow shirt band pulled tight around his biceps and accentuated his tan, muscular arms.

Oh, soooo tempting. Vivian tapped her fingers on the green beer bottle. "If we're gonna do it, I don't want to rush."

He nuzzled her neck. "Desperate times call for…"

She started laughing. "You don't seem the desperate type to me."

He sat back in his chair. "You'd be surprised. I work too much."

She nodded, then grinned. "I'm not going to sexpadite things, sorry."

"Hey, I had to ask. You look fantastic."

She fluffed her curls. "Thanks, the humidity is cooperating today."

Between songs, the lead singer talked about how long he'd known several members of 12 Stones. The rest of the crew — trumpet, trombone, clarinet, bass and drummer — all nodded during the story. "We're honored to be playing at Jason and Daisy's reception, and without any further ado, we'd like to have them come to the dance floor."

Hand in hand, the newlyweds walked out.

"I know this isn't our usual type of tune, but it was one of my parents' favorites and it's still one of mine. I hope you love it."

The trombone started up with a clear, smooth tone and the rest of the band soon joined. They played "It Had to be You," and the couple danced, kissed and laughed their way around the dance floor.

I'm so happy for them, Vivian thought.

After their dance, the music went back to rockin' the place. Everyone danced, including Detective Leffall, which Antonio said was a miracle as he tried to snap a picture but Leffall grabbed his phone.

Al, of course, had bought several bottles of champagne for the table. Everyone partook except for Antonio and Leffall, who had to work later that afternoon. They had details of Daisy's case to sort out and wrap up.

Wendy tapped on her watch and said to the girls, "We gotta hit it. I don't want to miss our flight."

She and Kate were on the same plane headed to Houston. Lucy's left about 20 minutes before them, going to Denver, and Vivian was scheduled a few minutes after, going to Dallas Love Field.

Everyone said their goodbyes, including Jason and Daisy, who were inseparable.

Vivian hugged Jason's neck. "So on to Las Vegas, huh?"

Jason looked at Daisy. "Yeah, she still wants to go. No more stops, though. She's taking a break from everything, for a while at least."

"It'll be a fun honeymoon, and best, best, best of luck!"

The girls grabbed a cab to their hotel for the sake of time, got their bags from the bellman and hopped back into the same cab. They talked about their crazy adventures on the way to the airport. The cabbie was captivated the entire 20-minute drive.

Once at the airport, they said goodbye to Lucy, who had to go to a different terminal.

"It was a wild one," Vivian said and gave her a hug.

"You know, they always are," Lucy said. "But that's okay, I've come to expect it, and I might be bored if they weren't." She hugged Wendy. "I'll see you in a few weeks on your big day."

"Safe travels," Wendy said.

Lucy's phone chimed and she checked it, smiling. "It's Jonathon telling me to have a safe flight home."

"Are you going to keep talking to him?" Vivian asked.

"Nah, he was just a distraction. A really cute, young, energetic distraction, but I've decided enough is enough. I'm going to seriously look into getting a divorce. Things just aren't working."

Kate gave her a squeeze. "We're here for you. Call us any time, day or night. It'll work out one way or another."

Vivian and Wendy dove in for a big, group hug, then Lucy walked away, giving a last wave.

Vivian, Wendy and Kate checked their bags and got gate assignments. They breezed through security and walked to where Kate and Wendy would be flying out since Vivian's flight was a little later.

"I'm going to run to the bathroom," Kate said.

"Buddy system," Vivian chimed.

"I think, surely, we're okay now." Kate laughed and headed off in the direction of the facilities.

Vivian and Wendy found a spot facing the runways and sat down.

Vivian checked her phone for the time. "So I guess I'll be seeing you in one short month for the big day. I can't believe you're getting married!"

"I know. I can hardly believe it myself." Wendy smiled and sat back in her seat, looking out at the planes. "Our engagement has flown by."

Vivian started to ask her about RSVPs but was interrupted by Wendy's phone ringing.

Wendy answered and as she listened, the smile faded from her face and tears formed in her eyes. She slowly lowered the phone and Vivian could hear someone saying, "Hello, hello. Ms. Schreiber," on the other end.

Vivian gently pulled the phone out of Wendy's hand. "This is Wendy's friend, Vivian Taylor. Is everything okay?"

"This is Officer Sue Garrett with the Las Vegas Police Department. I'm afraid there has been an accident."

Appendix

Watch out New Orleans! The Girlz are in town!

Johnell in action with "the whistle."

Blue Ball shots at Tropical Isle – yum!

"Bleeeehhhhhh!" Johnell fake puking on Decatur Street in New Orleans.

Foam Hat guy, he really did exist and he really tried to kiss every girl in sight!

Watch out for those syringe Jell-O shots!

The original Girlz and Joan Rylen's namesake, though we're not in order – Johnell, Angela, Robbyn and Lea.

This pretty much sums us up. Johnell's always doing something crazy and Robbyn's always wondering what it is!

Acknowledgments

We'd like to thank our favorite Getaway Girlz, Lea Bass Rogers (cover design, story input, fellow traveler), whose uncanny ability to make us look fantastic (front and back) continues to keep us in awe. And Angela Wenk (story input and personal stylist!), without whom Lucy would be a bore. You girlz mean the world to us! Now let's go on vacation!

And special thanks to our NOLA crew, Laura Trujillo (Lala Lollipop), Christine Moreno, Ellen Rink and Vikki Shelton (Trikki Vikki). Without y'all we wouldn't have little-dick whistles, Jell-O shot syringes, Blue Balls and oh, sooooo much more! We love ya, girlz!

Thank you to Beth Zimmerman, our forever fan club prez, launch party assistant, Barnes and Noble setter-upper and all-around GREAT friend. We truly appreciate you helping our dreams come true! One day we'll be on that red carpet! Promise!

We couldn't do this without the best editor in the world, John Dycus. We love to throw you off with crazy words like Shazammapuss and make you laugh with commandeered carriages. We'll always try to live up to your eloquently worded image - Bruce Willis with breasts!

Thank you to Janet Neff, PR helper and promoter, beta-reader, pool supplier and friend extraordinaire. You've been an amazing support from day one and we can't thank you enough! Plus, you've got that fantastic Mr. Bill who keeps us fed! Woohoo!

Thanks to Edwin Leffall for being "Eddie" and for showing up Denzel in our book trailer. If that voice could be bottled...just sayin'!

Can't forget our New Orleans-based photographer, Renee Bienevue who trodded with us through the French Quarter to get the perfect shots and video. We succeeded!

Our beta-readers rock! Thank you to Jackie Meeks, who made our story stronger, Janet Neff for the keen eye, Stephanie Surendran for her meticulous moments and Tom Hill for his big brain and detailed eyes.

We have to thank our numerous experts who helped make our story authentic – Brian Simons for his law enforcement input and gun knowledge, Eric MacKenzie for his pilot brain, Justin Tidwell for his vast knowledge of strippers, stripclubs and all things hooker, Blake Borgstede and Dara Browning for their bayou info, Larry and Sonya Buccola for their New

Orleans information and suggestions – dinner was awesome!, Sarah Simons for her drug knowledge (ha ha), Sonny Surendran (Sonofabitch!) for his Middle East input, Steven Hill for the oil and gas info, Louis Begin for his big balls – oh, we mean bowling balls and all things bowling and last, David Foster for suggesting the bowling balls in the first place.

We wouldn't have such great launch parties without our favorite Girlz, Laura Trujillo, Vikki Shelton, Stephanie Surendran, Alicia Jenkins, Christina Judge and April Ciccarello. Y'all wear our GG gear to perfection and make our parties run smoothly and rock!

Our favorite restaurants around Fort Worth continue to hook us up with great happy hours, fantastic service, yummy food, free electricity for our laptops and most of all, friendly faces. Special thanks to Bayou Jacks, Chuy's, Brownstone and Shaw's. Y'all make our hours and hours of writing not only tasty, but fun.

We love music and we love these musicians: Justin Pacy and 12 Stones – Justin, you helped us create a wonderful Jason. Josh Weathers – you keep us wanting more with every song.

We have to thank the New Orleans folks who are helping with the launch – Sue Garrett, press kit deliverer and all-around great gal, Maple Street Book Shop (official launch location!), Forever New Orleans and A Tisket A Tasket, book signing locations and believers in the Getaway Girlz, the Marriott on Canal for the great block of rooms, Harrah's (Johnell just wanted to throw them in because she loves to gamble there), and all the fantastic bars, restaurants and other places we LOVE in New Orleans! You all helped to make *Big Easy X-capade* better and the "research" was fun!

Johnell wants to thank her kids (again) for putting up with the chaotic schedule and always being good Barnes and Noble guests. Just remember...college fund!

Robbyn would like to thank her husband, David. I love you and thanks for supporting me in my dreams! I'm so excited about the next chapter in our lives and glad I'm sharing it with you.

About the Authors

The women behind Joan Rylen are Johnell Kelley and Robbyn Foster, friends since kindergarten. They grew up in Pasa"Get Down"dena, Texas, a suburb southeast of Houston. From Brownies to high school band, these girlz have stuck together through thick and thin…marriages, divorces, births, deaths and of course, destruction.

Their annual girls' trips with two other good friends were the original inspiration for *Getaway Girlz*. Johnell and Robbyn are the authors of three books in the Getaway Girlz series and have plans for many more. They can be seen around Fort Worth, Texas, writing in bars and having an all-around good time.

Johnell and Robbyn hope to inspire women, whether they're 21 or 91, to stay in touch with old friends and take getaways of their own. There's nothing like a good friend who knows all your stories-the ones so crazy you can't make them up, and loves you anyway.

Watch for the next book in the Getaway Girlz series:

Upstate *Uproar*

Available 2014

www.getawaygirlz.com

facebook.com/getawaygirlz

twitter.com/joanrylen

youtube.com/getawaygirlz

www.ingramcontent.com/pod-product-compliance
Lightning Source LLC
Chambersburg PA
CBHW031955240626
47153CB00003B/992